The Ex-suicide

STORY RIVER BOOKS

Pat Conroy, Founding Editor at Large

The Ex-suicide

∼ A MOUNTAIN BROOK NOVEL ∼

KATHERINE CLARK

The University of South Carolina Press

Published by the University of South Carolina Press
Columbia, South Carolina 29208

www.sc.edu/uscpress

Manufactured in the United States of America

26 25 24 23 22 21 20 19 18 17
10 9 8 7 6 5 4 3 2 1

Library of Congress Cataloging-in-Publication Data
can be found at http://catalog.loc.gov/.

ISBN: 978-1-61117-776-3 (cloth)
ISBN: 978-1-61117-777-0 (ebook)

This book was printed on recycled paper with
30 percent postconsumer waste content.

They all think any minute I'm going to commit suicide. What a joke.
The truth of course is the exact opposite: suicide is the only thing that
keeps me alive. Whenever everything else fails, all I have to do is consider
suicide and in two seconds I'm as cheerful as a nitwit. But if I could *not*
commit suicide—ah then, I would. I can do without Nembutal
or murder mysteries but not without suicide.

Walker Percy, *The Moviegoer*

❧

You can elect suicide, but you decide not to. What happens?
All at once, you are dispensed. Why not live, instead of dying? You are
like a prisoner released from the cell of his life. You notice that the
cell door is ajar and that the sun is shining outside. Why not take a
walk down the street? Where you might have been dead, you are alive.
The sun is shining. . . . The ex-suicide opens his front door, sits down
on the steps, and laughs. Since he has the option of being dead,
he has nothing to lose by being alive. It is good to be alive.
He goes to work because he doesn't have to.

Walker Percy, "Thought Experiment: A New Cure
for Depression," *Lost in the Cosmos*

❧

I, now thirty-seven years old in perfect health begin,
Hoping to cease not till death.

Walt Whitman, *Song of Myself*

~ PART ONE ~

Birmingham, Alabama
1997

~ 1 ~

On the drive in to work this morning, he realized he had reached that point when he was going to have to face it; he couldn't continue to postpone the moment of confrontation. The relief he had initially enjoyed from delaying the inevitable had turned into dread of the consequences of delaying the inevitable. So it was time to stop procrastinating and address the situation. This morning his imagination had unexpectedly run riot, and conjured up a horde of nightmare images of what lay in store for him. So he had nothing more to gain from avoiding the actual reality of what lay in store for him. There was always the hope that it wouldn't be as bad as he feared.

But it always was as bad, or even worse. His first quick glance into the main office confirmed this fundamental truth. The narrow slot above his name was positively crammed with papers and ominous yellow manila envelopes.

Realizing that the secretary was watching him, he thought he should risk a small sally.

"Well," he said, as cheerfully as he could, "I can tell that the paper shortage must be over."

This was in reference to the administration's recent announcement that this year's budget had no room for "big ticket items" like paper.

The secretary smiled broadly through two chipped and gapped front teeth. She was a copper colored young woman with hair dyed to match the exotic shade of her skin. "You're wrong, Dr. Whit," she said, obviously prepared to return his pleasantries. "There's still no paper for the faculty. But the administration seems to have all it needs." She glanced in the direction of the mail slots, and then met his eyes, her grin wider than ever.

"It's not a fair fight," he said in as lighthearted a manner as he could muster, while apprehension was overtaking his system like some form of paralysis. "They've got all the weaponry on their side."

"So don't nobody forget," she grinned again. "They the masters; y'all the slaves."

Fortunately her telephone rang at just that moment, so he hastened over to the row of mail slots and began tugging at the pile of papers jammed into his. He hoped the secretary was too absorbed in her phone call, which appeared to be personal in nature, to notice just how hard he had to struggle to dislodge the contents out of his box. As soon as he succeeded, the onslaught began.

"Colleagues," said the first item, a memo from his department chairman. Or chairperson, actually. "Please remember to leave your door at least two (2) to three (3) feet ajar during all of your eight (8) office hours per week. Many students, especially freshpersons, are too intimidated to knock on a closed office door, or even a door left only slightly open. We as faculty must be as welcoming and accessible to our students as we know how to be. After all, they are literally paying for our time. They are our customers, and we are the service providers."

Waves of adrenaline began surging through his body. (He now understood that this unpleasant sensation was what the specialist had meant by "stress," which apparently was partly the cause of his irritable bowel syndrome.) Although he had technically agreed to "reduce stress" in his life, he knew of no means short of his own death through which he could accomplish this worthy goal. He could no more control the surges of adrenaline shooting through his insides than he could control the slings and arrows shooting toward him from the outside. And it was of course this external fusillade which wreaked the internal havoc. "Service provider" was quite possibly the worst thing he'd ever been called in his life. It was downright obscene.

But even worse, he knew immediately that this memo, ostensibly addressed to everyone in the department, was in actuality aimed specifically at him. Of that he had no doubt. During those times in the week when he was actually in his office during his posted office hours, he kept his door just barely open, so as to advertise his presence to the chairman in case she should be checking, but discourage any eager or intrepid students who might be seeking him out. He also needed that barrier against the odor of nail polish and the pungent smell of microwaved buttered popcorn, which could saturate his clothes so thoroughly he'd smell like a movie theater for the rest of the day. All the other faculty members kept their office doors righteously ajar, and they could be easily viewed in a state of equally righteous productivity, busily grading papers or conferring with students or painting their fingernails. Fluorescent light and gospel music poured forth from these faculty offices.

Whereas, if anyone had peered into his, they would have found the office in total darkness, except for the light through the tiny window, where he sat huddled in his chair reading the latest Maigret mystery he had checked out from the library. Simenon had written almost a hundred of these mysteries, but unfortunately they would not be enough to get him through the whole school year.

He supposed he should have known it was only a matter of time before he was busted. The only reason he hadn't been caught before for keeping fewer than the eight (8) office hours he was required to keep was because the chairman didn't keep eight (8) herself. Plus, he had taken the added precaution of scheduling some of his office hours during her class periods. That way she had no way of knowing whether he was in his office or not.

He leafed rapidly through the other material in his hands with more confidence. The worst blow had been struck, he felt, and nothing could be as bad as the chairman's memo. Indeed, the ominous manila envelopes contained only the most innocuous print-outs of the minutes from the last (mandatory) department meeting; the minutes from the last (mandatory) general faculty meeting; and the complete text of the guest speaker's motivational speech at the (mandatory) assembly, all of which he had failed to attend. There was no letter—as he always feared—that his contract would not be renewed for the following year; no summons—as there had been last month—to come talk to the dean about why he had missed the last three (mandatory) departmental meetings.

He said good-bye to the secretary, Ms. Wilson, and flinched as she said in return, "Have a good day, Dr. Whit." It wasn't the persistent formality that bothered him so much as the persistent sensation of being a fraud whenever addressed by his academic title. Having obtained a Ph.D. almost by default, as it were, he did not believe he deserved to be called by the same lofty title as those who removed brain tumors and performed triple bypass surgeries. He wasn't sure, but he strongly believed that even if he *were* a true scholar, even if he *were* a real expert in some subject or field, he still wouldn't think he had earned the right to be called a doctor. Considering that he had embarked on his graduate studies only because he needed something to do when he dropped out of law school, he had a hard time thinking of himself as a professor rather than a law school dropout. "There you go again," he could hear his therapist Lauren admonishing him. "Defining yourself by your failures rather than your successes." But failure is so much more defining than success, he wanted to argue. However, he did not have time to carry on this philosophical debate with himself just now. The matter of the memo was weighing heavily on his mind, and he knew that he could not put off dealing with it right away, as he did with so many other issues.

He made straight for the cluster of "modules," as the administration insisted upon calling the trailers which served as temporary offices, classrooms and even dorms while more than half the buildings on campus underwent extensive renovation. The English Department faculty all had their offices in Module #13, which was clearly marked as such with blue spray paint above the door.

Attempting to be as casual and nonchalant as possible, he popped his head around the chairman's very wide-open office door, but left the rest of his body out of view. "Just wanted to say 'hi,'" he said, with what he hoped was breezy, unconcerned good humor.

The chairman looked up from her desk. "Ah," she said, in that very formal, official manner he had not known her to have until she was made chairman at the end of last year. "Dr. Whit. Come in, come in." She was a tall, statuesque woman of some six feet plus inches when standing, but even sitting at her desk she was an imposing figure who seemed to tower over his five feet five inches. She was dressed, as usual, in her customary African garb, the correct name of which he always forgot. They looked like robes or nightgowns to him. The one she was wearing today was a vivid purple with sunburst splashes of yellow. No doubt he was a prisoner of his unconscious white male bias, but her apparel seemed a direct contradiction of the memo she had sent out at the beginning of the semester, reminding all English Department faculty to wear professional attire in the classroom. This he thought had also been aimed at him, because there had been one day when he'd run out of clean khakis and worn his best pair of blue jeans. If necessary, he had planned to assert that blue jeans were an inextricable part of his cultural tradition.

"I don't want to bother you," he assured the chairman. "I can tell you're busy. But you know . . . I did want to tell you . . . in case you were wondering—you know, about that memo you sent . . ."

"Which one, Dr. Whit? Please do come in and sit down."

"Oh, no," he said. "I've got class in a minute." (He didn't, but was counting on the fact that she didn't keep everyone's schedule in her head.) "I just wanted to let you know that the reason my office door isn't open during office hours is because I've got that first office next to the front door? And whenever anyone goes in or out—of our module, not my office—the opening and closing of the front door creates some sort of suction that pulls my office door shut." (This statement had the benefit of actually being true, although it was not the reason his office door was usually closed.)

6

The chairman nodded her head slowly, as if seriously considering the matter. "I see, I see, Dr. Whit," she said. "These modules are a trial to us all, aren't they?" She paused as if to give him time to reflect on a reply. "One thing you could do," she continued, "is to prop your door open with a chair or some other piece of furniture from your office. Surely there is something that will serve the purpose?"

A stab of panic struck and grabbed hold of his abdomen. He was going to have to improvise immediately. He gulped and plunged on, somewhat blindly, he feared. "Well," he said hesitantly. "You see, there's only one chair in my office—I mean, only one chair other than the one I sit on—when I'm in there—and the other chair—the one I don't sit on—is piled with books and papers and—"

"Oh, Dr. Whit, I'm so sorry," said the chairman in a totally different tone. "I've completely forgotten that you still don't have any furniture, do you?"

He shook his head sheepishly, as if it were his fault. "Just the desk and two chairs."

"Still no filing cabinet? No bookshelves?"

Again he shook his head. The chairman reached for a post-it note. "I'll try to remember to get this taken care of once and for all," she said. "Anything else you're missing? What about your telephone?"

"Well, I can call out," he said, "but apparently, anyone who tries to call me gets the sound of a fax machine." He spoke quietly, as befit the uttering of a terrible truth, but truthfully, this was fine with him. It was wonderful having no ringing telephone, no voice mail, no direct way for students or colleagues or administrators—or his mother, for that matter—to get in touch with him on campus. What would they have been calling for anyway? To ask him to do something he didn't want to do: write a letter of recommendation, provide help with a paper, chair a committee. It was infinitely preferable to have his phone out of order. He had an ironclad excuse for being unreachable.

The chairman was busily scribbling on her post-it note, but as his phone had not been working properly for over a year, he had little fear that service would soon be restored. With half the buildings on campus under renovation and the other half crumbling into ruins, the Physical Plant people and the IT staff clearly had more problems than they could handle.

"I really am so sorry, Dr. Whit. Please don't take these inconveniences personally. We all have to put up with something while the campus is being renovated. You are not being singled out. But do accept my apologies."

"Oh, no problem. No problem," he said, with cheerfulness he didn't even have to fake this time. He now had every reason to be cheerful. He had gone in to the chairman's office on the defensive and left with the upper hand. He had come in to offer excuses for his closed office door, and instead was magnanimously dismissing her apologies for his lack of office furniture. He had turned the tables on her without even trying. There were certainly some advantages to being the token white male at a historically black college populated primarily by black females. Everyone was so concerned that he would take offense where none was intended that they pretty much left him alone, which had lately become his main ambition in life.

A similar experience had occurred last month when he went to see the dean about his absences from the English Department meetings. He had approached his appointment with fear and trembling, prepared once again to be on the defensive. He was even prepared to use his ace in the hole, the card he'd been holding for an emergency situation, and tell the dean about his irritable bowel. (Although this was not the reason he chose not to attend the departmental meetings, he did in fact have an irritable bowel, and he was ready to provide medical documentation if asked.) The real reason he could not attend the meetings was because he also suffered from an intelligence quotient above zero. He invariably found that meetings of any kind held anywhere for any purpose greatly exacerbated this condition. After all, if he had wanted to spend any portion of his life attending meetings, he would have obtained an MBA as his mother had wished. At least this would have guaranteed generous compensation for any portion of his life spent in a group activity he deplored.

But he'd never had to say much of anything to the dean in his defense. The dean had simply gone on at length about how much they valued him on campus, how much they wanted him to feel welcomed, how much they hoped he felt a part of the faculty. Then he had been asked point blank if there was anything or anyone who had made him feel unwelcomed.

"Oh, no," he'd said. "It's just that . . ."

"It's just what, Dr. Whit?"

"It's nothing. Nothing." He smiled.

For fifteen minutes, the dean of humanities—a genial black man with a shiny bald head and clipped mustache—had attempted to coax and prod him into finishing his earlier sentence, convinced that he had been about to disclose some act of prejudice or discrimination from one of the faculty members.

Finally the dean had leaned back in his chair and said, "Well, let's just leave it that you'll come to me right away if ever you're in a situation where you don't feel you're getting fair treatment."

"Oh, of course. Of course," he had said.

As he was leaving the office, the dean had bestowed on him such a look of admiration and gratitude that he'd puzzled over it all day. While he had thought himself little more than a bumbling, mumbling jackass, he had somehow managed to rise exponentially in the dean's estimation. Finally he figured it out. The dean was convinced he was heroically covering for one of his African-American colleagues who must have offended him in some serious way. Then an idea occurred to him. Perhaps if he continued to "keep silent" about this "offense," nothing more would be said about his missing the departmental meetings. He could continue to skip them and suffer no consequences. So far he had been right. He had not attended another meeting, and nothing had been said. He imagined the dean saying something in low, conspiratorial tones to the chairman: "Well, if this is the way he wants to handle the matter . . . who are we to insist that he pursue the official means of redress?" It went without saying that as long as there were no administrative consequences, he suffered no other disadvantage from missing these meetings.

When he was safely behind the firmly closed door of his office, he opened his briefcase and pulled out his latest acquisition from the library: *Maigret and the Killers.*

* * *

Thirty minutes later, in Classroom A of Module #21, he looked out over a sleepy bunch of students who had not yet shaken off the somnolence of a Monday morning. Just last Friday, a mere three days ago, these very same students had been an intelligent and energetic group which had pounced ferociously on the ideas in Emerson's essays. For example: "No law can be sacred except that of my own nature." Hands had shot up in the air. "Who did he think he was?" one student had asked. "God?" Another student had chimed in: "He thought everybody was God. Remember?" Somebody else had asked: "You think he would have felt that way if he'd ever been in the projects, Dr. Whit?" It was fascinating the way his students had zeroed in on what he himself had always considered one of the main weaknesses in Emerson's philosophy. Somehow, he had managed to inspire them to read the material, make some sense out of it, consider it carefully and form their own opinions about it. The discussion had been an enormous success and made him feel just a little bit like God himself. It was not a sensation he was at all used to experiencing, and had certainly not lasted long, but it had boosted him through the weekend, which he had spent in a state of heightened preparation and anticipation for Monday's assignment.

But now that Monday had arrived, it was immediately clear that his students had not spent their weekend in preparation or anticipation of the assignment. Most of them had jobs, he knew. Young as they were, some even had children already. They all had complicated family obligations which frequently intruded on their schooldays. Even during a final exam, one or two cell phones that were supposed to be turned off would ring anyway as if with dire urgency. Today all were avoiding eye contact with him, and no one appeared to have a textbook out. If they were looking at anything in particular, it was either their wristwatch or the clock on the wall. He decided to launch forward anyway and hope for the best. Many years of teaching at a variety of institutions had proved that most students responded as intelligent life forms if treated as such.

"I would like to call your attention to one of the most important statements Thoreau makes in the opening chapter," he began. "'The mass of men lead lives of quiet desperation.' What does he mean by that?"

The classroom remained silent. Unfortunately, it was not the silence of mere mortals overawed by the profound musings of a genius. It was the silence of utterly apathetic students who had not even attempted to read their assignment and aspired only to endure the class period with as little discomfort as possible. He surveyed his pupils with what he hoped was carefully concealed disappointment. His star student—Tameika—the one whose extraordinary intellect he could usually count on to carry the day—was sitting hunched over her desk with her face buried in her elbow. Alice, another of his brightest students, was filing away at the remnant of a press-on fingernail while glancing casually down at her textbook as if it were an outdated magazine in the beauty salon where she awaited her manicure appointment. Vanity was digging through her purse in a frenzied attempt to turn off her cell phone, which had just started ringing in flagrant violation of his "No Cell Phone" policy. Three or four others were doing homework or worksheets for other classes, seemingly unaware, or perhaps unconcerned, that their industriousness could not be interpreted as notetaking for his class, since not one word was being spoken. There was only one member of the classroom even looking at him, and her name eluded him. Indeed, she looked completely unfamiliar, and it was quite possible that she was a new student who had just added the course, although it was approaching midterm. He could feel the bile rising in his gorge. It wasn't the personal rejection that rankled, he tried to tell himself; it was the insult to Thoreau.

"Well, let me provide an example of 'quiet desperation,'" he said, as mildly as he could. Immediately he could feel some of the tension in the room subside, as the students knew they were not about to be called on and could safely remain in passive mode. Paradoxically, this had the benefit of bringing some of his students to life, as they could now afford to pay attention without fear of being put on the spot. Tameika, he saw out of the corner of his eye, had lifted her head out of her elbow.

"Let's suppose you're a professor at a college," he continued. "You entered your profession with high ideals about educating young people and passing on to them your love of say—literature and learning. But what you encountered when you actually began practicing your profession was a series of students who cared nothing for learning and didn't even want to know what literature is. They don't want an education; they want a college degree. And the job they think they're going to get with that degree. Most importantly, they want the money they think they're going to make from that job." He paused as he could feel more and more of the room's attention focused on his words and waiting to hear what would come next. "What these students don't realize," he paused again to draw out the suspense even further, "what these students just don't realize," he repeated, "is that they're not going to get that job." He could hear a sharp intake of breath from more than one desk. "Or these students are not going to succeed in that job or even keep that job." He paused once more as he could feel all eyes now riveted on him. "Because despite their college degree, they don't have a real college education. And this fact will catch up with them sooner or later." There was another collective intake of breath. "So this hypothetical professor is disillusioned and dissatisfied. His job is meaningless and unfulfilling. Yet he keeps performing this job year after year, day after day. This would be an example of the kind of desperation Thoreau is talking about. The desperation is quiet because the person in despair is not protesting or rebelling. He is submitting as if he's resigned himself for life."

He now had their undivided attention. Even Alice had stopped filing her nail. No doubt they were alarmed by his references to students not getting or keeping the jobs they were after, and assumed he was reminding them of his power either to propel them toward the careers they sought or forestall their progress. And of course they assumed he had been describing himself, and were fascinated, possibly even chastened, that a white man could consider himself "desperate" on account of their behavior. But while it was true that his life had always been one of "quiet desperation," his students were not to blame. He'd implied this mainly to goad them out of their Monday morning torpor, which it appeared he had succeeded in doing, as Tameika's hand now shot into the air. She had her finger on a passage in the text.

"Yes, Tameika," he said gratefully.

She looked down to where her finger was pointing on the page. "Is 'quiet desperation' the same thing as being 'the slave-driver of yourself,' which is a line in the paragraph above?"

Inwardly he groaned. Naturally these students were hyper-aware of any reference to slaves or slavery, and resistant to the concept of slavery as a metaphor. Still, this was a beginning. Tameika at least had read the assignment and was now prepared to engage in discussion.

* * *

After what turned out to be a surprisingly productive dialogue between himself and Tameika, he gathered his books as quickly as his students gathered theirs and headed just as eagerly for the exit. *Maigret and the Killers* was proving to be one of the more interesting Simenon mysteries, as the French police chief had to confront violent American criminals unlike what he was used to in France. Two hours stretched ahead of him before he was due to teach his next class. Two delightful, uninterrupted hours of reading Simenon—behind a closed office door—and getting paid for it. He was more glad than ever that he had confronted the chairman right away about the new "Open Door" policy, and essentially received her dispensation for keeping his door unapologetically closed. His therapist, Lauren, would be pleased as well. It was her theory that his tendency to procrastinate, to postpone performing unpleasant tasks—like reading the memos in his faculty mail box—was at least partially the cause of some of his stress, which of course was the main cause of his irritable bowel. If he could learn to stop procrastinating about so many things both large and small, she believed, he would find his "stress level" going down and his symptoms abating.

But his spirits sank as he realized that the unfamiliar face of the new student was approaching him. This was a nuisance. He would be asked to produce an extra syllabus, which he didn't have in his briefcase. So he would have to invite her back to his office to get one. While there, she would no doubt want to know what she needed to do in order to "make up for" over half a semester of work she had missed, as if the burden were on him to prepare some sort of instant soup mix she could simply ingest instead of reading the required material. She might want lecture notes, which didn't exist, or hand-outs, which he didn't hand out. Most tiresome of all, she would probably want to linger in his presence in a chatty and cordial demonstration of good faith, as if one hour in his office could make up for the seven weeks of class discussion she had neither attended nor participated in. It had all been known to happen before. As far as he could tell, there were no rules governing how late in the semester a student could "add" a course; faculty were "encouraged" to welcome all new students, who brought with them tuition dollars, state funding, and the promise of reaching that 2,000 student enrollment mark. He sighed and forced a smile as he turned to greet this unwelcome new face.

"It's Hamilton Whit, isn't it?" she said. "Or should I say, Dr. Whit?"

He was thrown. Obviously she wasn't a student, although this was what she looked like: young and petite, in a tee shirt and blue jeans. His colleagues on the faculty, except for the chairman, were all older women of generous proportions, gaily be-decked every day as if for church, in dresses with vibrant colors or bold patterns. They tottered heroically through the mud-holed campus on precarious high-heels while sporting careful and complicated hair arrangements which changed daily. This young woman in front of him wore close-cropped hair, no makeup or jewelry, and running shoes. What or who could she be? Was it possible this was some new administrator who had just evaluated his class? Vaguely he recalled one of the memos warning of surprise visits to faculty classrooms by administrators in the humanities. He felt his insides tighten in that vise-grip he had come to know so well.

"I'm sorry," she said, extending her hand. "I should have introduced myself first. I'm Ivy Greer. The new hire in the English Department this year." She clasped his hand. "You *are* Hamilton Whit?"

"Ham," he said, smiling hugely in relief that she was only a new colleague, and not a new administrator.

"Ham?" she repeated, clearly baffled.

"Short for Hamilton," he explained. "I'm afraid my mother was as grandiose in choosing my name as she is in everything else she does. But I can assure you that no one else who's ever taken one look at me has ever called me Hamilton."

She gave a deep, full-throated laugh. "I hear you on that," she said. "Would you believe my birth certificate has me down as Ivory?" She grasped the flimsy railing attached only tenuously to Module #21.

Until then, he hadn't realized how stock-still he had been standing, frozen in that moment of fear when he suspected she was an administrator. He followed her down the rickety metal staircase just in time to avoid the horde of students who clattered up toward Classroom A.

"Are you headed back?" she gestured in the direction of the module housing their offices.

He nodded tentatively, not sure what else was expected of him and hoping it wasn't much. He figured he'd lost ten minutes already of his precious

Maigret time. Not only did he not want to lose any more of that time, but even more importantly, he did not want to be pulled into too much interaction with the world outside himself, or he would have a much harder time blocking it out so he could read with the total concentration he normally enjoyed.

For a few moments they walked together in silence. Then she turned toward him, squinting against a surprisingly strong November sun. "I really admired what you said to those students in there," she said.

"What did I say? I've already forgotten."

Again she laughed in frank, open enjoyment, as she had earlier, as if he were some witty and clever interlocutor whose company gave her deep pleasure. He found himself warming to this encounter in spite of himself.

She cupped a hand over her brows to shield her eyes from the glare. "What you said about them not getting a real college education. Not being able to get jobs. I didn't think you'd been to that meeting. And I didn't think anybody on this faculty would have the guts to tell those students what you did. But obviously, it needs to be said. I just hope you don't get in trouble."

"Wait a minute," he said, as those guts of his cramped in pain. He found himself at a standstill again, not only frozen in fear, but dizzy and lightheaded as if on the verge of a full-blown panic attack. "What meeting? What could I possibly have said that could get me in trouble?"

She looked around as if to check for eavesdroppers. "Why don't we talk in my office?" she suggested.

Reluctantly he agreed. He didn't see that he had any choice. If he wanted to be able to clear his mind and enjoy his detective novel, he had to find out what she was referring to before he could consign it to the trash heap of oblivion. He began to trudge forward.

Then she was the one to seize up and stop in her tracks, laying a hand on his arm. "On second thought," she said, "I don't know about the office. The walls are too thin. Let's go sit in the coop. Or do you have office hours?"

Of course he had office hours. Every daylight hour that wasn't spent in the classroom, it seemed, was supposed to be an "office hour." He shrugged.

"Me too," she chuckled, apparently reading his mind and seconding his thoughts.

* * *

They sat in silence for several minutes on one of the new teak benches facing Carver Hall. Ham did not think it was his responsibility to initiate conversation. There was nothing he wanted to say. He just wanted to get it all over with and go back to his office by way of the nearest bathroom. But she appeared in no particular hurry to state her business. Instead, she seemed to be enjoying the sun and gazing thoughtfully at the spectacle in front of her.

The generous expanse of lawn in front of the main administrative building had been nicknamed "the coop" because usually the campus's bedraggled peacocks were there pecking dispiritedly at the grass. The purpose of these peacocks was to complement the effect intended by Carver Hall, an imposing edifice of white limestone, fronted by fat white columns, all of which resembled nothing so much as a plantation manor from the Old South. It was affectionately called "the Big House" by every student, faculty member and administrator Ham had met so far at Cahaba College. He himself was the only one he knew who referred to it as Carver Hall, or Carver, and most people didn't know what he was talking about. But he simply could not bring himself to invoke such a visceral symbol of human slavery in the American South as "the Big House." To his ongoing astonishment, the black population on campus could not have been more proud of the building they happily called "the Big House," as if they were now owners of their own plantation. To them, "the Big House" seemed to symbolize the possibility that they could be masters in the society that had once enslaved them.

No doubt this was the fantasy it was supposed to conjure when constructed 100 years ago on the land grant dedicated by an Alabama State Legislature which was probably less interested in truly emancipating former slaves than it was in devising an educational system that was definitely separate and undoubtedly unequal. At any rate, the campus's embrace of "the Big House" suggested to Ham that many important lessons had never been taught or learned on this campus. First of all, black slavery in America was not over: Abolition and emancipation had never been thoroughly accomplished. It seemed to Ham that descendants of slaves should be striving to achieve this state of grace, and until abolition and emancipation had been fully established, they should only beware of the world that had imposed slavery on them and failed to completely eradicate it or atone for it. Because in striving to become masters in a society that had once enslaved them, these descendants of slaves had mainly been taught how to enslave themselves. Indeed, a few years back, the black population of Alabama had helped to elect the world's most notorious segregationist when he courted their favor for a fourth term as governor.

Ham suddenly felt the weight of the world thud into his bowels with the threat of imminent explosion. It was never safe for him to dwell too heavily on the implications of where he was and what he was doing at any given place or time. Unfortunately, one of the inescapable legacies of his former days as

15

a philosophy student was his ingrained habit of thinking everything through to its logical and inevitable conclusion. Instead of helping him achieve success or happiness, however, this habit caused him only distress and despair. The ability to take the long view and see his whole life before him gave him only the vision of his own coffin being lowered into the grave. Nothing he could do would avert this particular endgame. So what was he to do with those few decades between this moment and that? In his thirty-seven years, he had arrived only at the conclusion that he would be neither a master nor a slave. He wasn't sure what this left him with, since the ultimate implication of doing anything within his abilities, in terms of its consequences for either himself or others, meant it would be far better just to sit alone in a room, like Pascal, and do nothing at all. In fact, there were several dark periods in his life when he had done just that, and the consequences for himself had been so dire that he had been forced to seek out practitioners of the mental health profession, who in turn had urged him to "get out of [him]self," "re-join the world," and "do something with [his] life," in an uncanny echo of his mother's exact words.

So in lieu of going crazy, committing suicide or taking Prozac for the rest of his life, he was obliged to inflict himself upon the world, and had tried to do so in as inoffensive a way possible without involving the abuse or exploitation of his fellows. If he had to *do* something with himself and his time on earth—as everyone from his own mother to a celebrated psychoanalyst had agreed—then he could only do something which caused no harm to anyone else and brought more meaning into his life than he could derive from sitting alone in his own room and reading a good book. Otherwise, what was the point? How could he believe in his own self-worth, or the worthiness of what he was doing, if he was engaged in an occupation which caused harm, posed a threat, or added to the burden of absurd, pointless activity which harassed the universe?

Thanks to his grandmother, he didn't need the money. So as far as he could see, it was no less than his moral duty to make absolutely certain that whatever master he served in the form of a corporation, institution, government, profession, trade or craft was using him for a greater good that he believed in and agreed with. Up to now, he had succeeded mainly in figuring out what he did *not* want to do with his life, and unfortunately, this list comprised just about all known occupations. However, the world of education struck him as one of the few masters worth serving. Since he could not, like a doctor of medicine, help heal the body, he would offer what small assistance he could in helping others tend to the needs of the mind. He didn't kid himself that he was any huge success at what he did. But at least he could believe in what he was trying to do and find meaning in it as well; at least he wasn't hurting anyone or destroying anything in the process. In choosing to become a teacher, he believed he had adopted one of the few "pure" professions, which benefited other individuals and society as a whole while providing him with a small paycheck and some small measure of satisfaction without causing any harm in return. Although he knew it was possible that even the noble vocation of teaching could be twisted to serve despicable purposes, it's not as if he was an instructor for a fascist regime or a religious cult. As a professor of literature at an obscure college in the Deep South, he was fairly certain that he was not a mindless pawn in some overarching scheme of evil intent. As for being a do-gooder—as some on campus believed him to be—performing some form of charitable mission work by teaching at a black college, the simple truth was: it was the only place that would have him.

Today this place appeared utterly benign, and in no way deserving of the dark and sinister thoughts which had boiled up in him unexpectedly moments ago. Carver Hall was simply a beautiful building. A few years ago it had undergone a total renovation, its first in the 100 years since it was built. The limestone, which was indigenous to Alabama and had been dug from a nearby quarry, had been carefully and chemically scrubbed to gleaming white perfection. The inside had been gutted and transformed into thoroughly modern administrative offices, complete with the latest computer and telephone technology and lavishly furnished in the style of the corporate boardroom. The campus was justly proud of its architectural jewel. It was a welcome contrast to the other buildings on campus, which were empty inside and obscured by scaffolding and construction equipment outside. This morning the beleaguered peacocks were nowhere to be seen, the lawn was full and freshly mown, and "the Big House" positively dazzled in the sunshine. It was, in fact, a gorgeous fall day. Still, Ham wished he were inside his enclosed 10 x 6 foot space in Module #13 reading *Maigret and the Killers*.

He coughed and cleared his throat, but his colleague remained lost in her reverie. Perhaps, after all, it was incumbent upon him to speak; indeed, he reflected, he probably should apologize for not knowing who she was at this point in the semester. He had of course skipped the "Meet New Faculty" gathering earlier in the year. Just as he was managing to produce the garbled beginning of an explanation, she turned to him and said, "Were you at that meeting last week?"

He cleared his throat again. "Which one?"

"That special joint meeting," she said. "With the English Department faculty and the Education faculty."

"Oh, that one," he said, though he had no memory of such a meeting being scheduled. "No, I wasn't at that one," he added, as if he might have been at any other one.

"I didn't think I'd seen you there."

"Well, I would have stood out pretty clearly," he joked.

This time she failed to laugh and he silently chided himself for attempting such a stupid and obvious joke. It never paid for him to forget that he could only generate humor when he wasn't trying to be funny and saw no humor himself in whatever he was saying or doing. In other words, he himself was the joke.

"Then how did you know?" she asked quietly. "Who did you talk to? They said there weren't going to be any minutes from the meeting."

"How did I know what?"

She waited as a lone student passed on the walkway in front of them while casting a furtive look in their direction.

"The administration is in an uproar," she said, stretching her legs out in front of her.

Instinctively he looked around him as if he could verify the accuracy of her statement with one quick glance then and there. All he saw, of course, was the peaceful beauty of a graceful old building rising up from lush green grass. Ordinarily this pastoral serenity irritated him, as it was such a contrast to the drab, dreary and defunct industrial community where it was located in Fairfield, containing what little was left of U.S. Steel, just west of Birmingham. Every morning when he turned off the main road and passed through the gates of the campus, he felt as if he were entering an alternate universe of fantasy and make-believe whose purpose was only to escape, or perhaps deny, the brutal truth of the real world outside the gates. In no way was that real world being confronted, challenged or overcome by those within the gates. He had grown up uneasily in a similar kind of alternate universe in an all-white suburb of Birmingham known as Mountain Brook, where most of the residences strived for the same "Big House" effect as Carver Hall. After spending most of his conscious life endeavoring to get away and then stay away, it was normally deeply troubling to feel that he had liberated himself from the artificial world of his youth only to become part of another artificial world as an adult. But after what his colleague had just told him, the calm gentility of his surroundings was reassuring. Nothing was in uproar around him; no one was running around in frenzy. Apart from the two of them sitting on the bench, no one else was even in sight at the moment. He waited for her to continue, though he didn't particularly want her to. He found himself gripping the edge of the bench and bracing his stomach against an onslaught.

"To put it bluntly," she said, "our school here just got an F."

"Huh?" He'd been expecting a bombshell, but didn't know what to make of this.

She looked over at him with amusement playing at the corners of her mouth. "You don't know what I'm talking about, do you?" she challenged.

Sheepishly he shook his head. "I'm sorry," he said.

"Well you *do* know how we're a teacher's college? Right?"

A teacher's college? What was that? He frowned slightly as if in concentration.

"That was our mission from the get-go, as a historically black college," she explained. "Like Tuskegee was an agricultural college. For black males. This place was a teacher's college. For the females. To produce teachers who could educate black children. That's basically what we're still doing today. Most of our students are girls, most are education majors, most get their teaching certificates, and most become teachers in the Birmingham public school system. You with me?"

He nodded bashfully, aware that she had explicated basic facts he should have known. And come to think of it, he did know all this—especially the fact that most of his students were girls—it's just he'd never thought about it or put it all together.

"Well," she went on. "You know how all public school teachers get evaluated every year? Before they get tenure?"

"Uh, yeah." He supposed he knew that, but was failing to understand why any of this was so compelling as to take over his free time. At least it was proving less stressful than he'd feared. He felt his grip loosening on the bench.

"Last spring the state board of education began tabulating the results of these evaluations," she said. "The board wants to implement accountability standards for all teacher education programs in the state of Alabama. Each program is going to be rated based on the evaluation scores achieved by its graduates."

She paused to allow for his response, but the situation was becoming hopeless. She had lost him at "implement accountability standards," which sounded like a foreign language he had not been required to take in order to earn his doctorate in American literature. He stared miserably at his lap, afraid to meet her eyes. Fortunately she was able to resume without his input.

"They're trying to trace problem teachers back to their source. Find out what colleges graduated the failing teachers in the first place. Figure out if there are problem colleges as well as problem teachers."

"Sounds reasonable," he offered, resisting the temptation to shrug. He didn't see how any of this had anything to do with him.

"Yeah. Well, apparently a very high percentage of teachers in the Birmingham public schools who fail their annual evaluations are graduates of this college." She looked at him pointedly. "*That's* what we learned at the meeting."

"I can't say I'm too surprised," he piped up quickly, glad he could finally play a part in the conversation.

"No," she agreed grimly. "You were quite right that the students here are not receiving a real college education. And now that has serious ramifications for everyone on this campus."

He felt his jaw go slack. Of course he had made that statement about an hour earlier, but he had not intended it to be taken so seriously—or literally. She glanced around the coop where a few students were beginning to trickle onto the walkways toward their next class.

"It gets worse," she said, lowering her voice.

"How?"

"You know the main reason our graduates fail their teacher evaluations?"

He shook his head.

"They fail the written portion of their evaluation exam."

"Meaning . . . ?"

"Meaning," she glared at him as if it were his fault. "They can't write a simple paragraph with basic proficiency. Stands to reason they can't teach anybody else how to read and write, because they can't read and write all that well themselves."

For a second time he felt his jaw go slack, although it was not news to him that most of his students couldn't read or write very well. Since becoming a teacher at Cahaba College last year, Ham had trained himself to overlook this point, because his basic survival instincts had told him the administration wouldn't like it if ninety percent of his students received failing grades.

"I've wondered," he ventured tentatively. "How do our students even get their teaching certificates in the first place? Isn't there a—what did you call it?"

"Writing proficiency evaluation."

"Don't they have to do that to become a teacher in the first place?"

"Yeah. They have to do it." She smirked.

"Well?"

"They don't need to pass it."

"What?"

"If they fail, they can get their certificate anyway, *if* their college GPA is high enough."

"And somehow, our students' GPA is always high enough," he murmured, almost to himself.

"Yeah, it's a racket," she concurred. "You know what happens to the teachers who fail their evaluation?"

He shook his head.

"They get tenured."

He shut his eyes tightly and wanted to put his hands over his ears. He sincerely hoped she was not going to tell him how failing teachers ended up with tenure. He didn't want to know. She had already assaulted him with enough troubling information that he hadn't had time to process. He literally couldn't take any more.

"Things could be about to change, though," she smiled at him ruefully. "The Board of Education has already changed some of the rules. Come this spring, whoever doesn't pass the certification test doesn't get certified. Period. Your GPA can't bail you out. So you can see what this means for the college."

Students were now beginning to fill the walkways surrounding the coop. Standing up, she smoothed out her pants' legs and slung the strap of a battered leather carry-all across her shoulder. He stood up alongside her and was just about to make his farewells when she turned to him abruptly and said, "It's not as if the headlines in today's paper help either. You know?"

Ham didn't know. He read Shakespeare when he got up in the morning, and didn't see the point in subscribing to the local paper.

"About the mayor?" she prodded.

He nodded slowly. The news on his car radio had mentioned something. . . . "You mean the indictment?" he said, hoping he'd heard right: something about the mayor of Birmingham being indicted by a federal grand jury for. . . . what? That part he couldn't remember.

"Embarrassing, isn't it?" she said.

"I'm sorry," he said, confused. "I don't see—I'm not sure . . ." He waited for her to supply the connection. When he realized she wasn't going to, he said "What does the mayor's indictment have to do with . . . ?" With what? What had they been talking about? He was already blocking it out. This conversation had lasted way too long already—one whole class period, apparently. Not only had he lost a precious hour of his reading time, it remained to be seen if he would be able to make use of his second hour. The protective cocoon he needed around himself in order to block out the outside world and focus on his reading had been pierced and unraveled as he sat there with her on the bench. Now he just wanted to hurry over to his office and at least build his defenses back up before his next class. With dismay he saw she was looking at him with something like despair. She was also leaning over toward him confidentially, so that none of the passing students could overhear what she said.

"The mayor is a graduate of this college," she whispered.

He was flabbergasted. Of course, he knew the city of Birmingham now had black mayors, but . . .

"Our graduates can't do shit!" she muttered bitterly. "The ones who become teachers can't teach because they can't even read and write. And the ones who become mayors?" She shook her head in disgust. "This guy thinks being mayor means taking kickbacks, spending the money in gambling halls that aren't supposed to exist in the state of Alabama, and then failing to report his '*winnings*' to the IRS!"

Ham had really reached his capacity for hearing tragic news. He looked at his watch. "Listen," he said.

"I know. I've got class in a few minutes, too," she said, squinting against the sun. "But I'd like to discuss this further. I think you and I must be the only ones on campus who really *know.*"

"Know what?" He couldn't have been more surprised. He didn't know anything.

"Don't give me that," she smiled at him. "I know you know. Otherwise, you wouldn't have told those students what you did this morning. Can I drop by your office sometime?"

His insides rose up in rebellion. No, really, he thought. He'd had quite enough for one day. First the chairman; now this.

"Why don't I give you a call?" she offered. "If you're not busy, we can go grab a coffee or something."

"The phone in my office doesn't really work," he said apologetically. "But my home number is in the faculty directory. Why don't you call me at home and we'll set something up?"

"Great," she said. "I've got to dash. My class is at the other end of campus. But I really do need to talk to you. I'll call."

"Okay," he said to himself mostly, though it was to be hoped that the natural reluctance of most decent people to invade the privacy of a near total stranger's home would prevail and prevent her from actually making the call. Still, he was haunted by that "I really do need to talk to you" bit. What could that mean, exactly? If she had thought he was the type to get involved in things like accountability systems and state boards of education, surely his lackluster contributions to their discussion had demonstrated otherwise. She couldn't pick a worse person for an ally: he could barely manage the picayune affairs of his own insignificant existence. Tackling anything outside himself, especially if it involved a bureaucracy and bureaucratese, would be utterly beyond him. Surely when she'd had time to reflect on the content of their discussion, she would realize how woefully lacking he had been and conclude that his effort wasn't worth enlisting in whatever cause she had decided to undertake.

* * *

When he reached Module #13, looking very much forward to resuming his reading of the Simenon novel, he was greatly chagrined to find Tameika waiting outside his office door.

Misinterpreting his look of consternation, she said cheerfully, "Don't worry, Dr. Whit. I haven't been waiting long."

"Good, good, Tameika. What can I do for you?" He hoped he could dispense with this matter in the narrow hallway without having to invite her in to his office.

"Don't you want to go in your office?" she said, checking her watch. "I can stand to miss a few more minutes of the class I'm supposed to be in right now."

"Are you sure? I wouldn't want to keep you," he said doubtfully. "Why don't we make an appointment for another time?"

"Oh, no," she protested energetically. "I got to see you now. I need your signature for this 'Change Major' form which is due by noon *today*." She put tremendous emphasis on the last word.

"Well, if that's all," he sighed in relief, opening the door and flipping the light switch which flooded the small space with so much fluorescent light it felt like an operating room. To his dismay, she looked around for a place to sit, and he was forced to remove the stack of books meant to discourage visitors from sitting in his only chair for visitors.

For the next fifteen minutes he listened politely as Tameika launched into a high-spirited declaration of how much she had enjoyed his classes since he started teaching last year; how much she had gained from reading the literature; how greatly she valued him as a teacher and considered him the best instructor whose courses she had taken in her three years at the college. Indeed, her entire experience under his tutelage had caused her to re-evaluate her career goals and her vision of the future. She had been forced to re-think her whole life, and in the process had come to the realization that she did not, after all, want to be a public elementary school teacher. She wanted to be a college professor like he was. Instead of getting her teaching certificate at the end of this, her senior year, and begin earning money the following year as her parents wished, she wanted instead to "go for" her Ph.D. Her parents were neither supportive nor encouraging of this decision, and she knew Mrs. Cooke, her advisor in the education department, was going to balk. Accordingly, she had been struggling with herself for the past month and had tried to reconcile herself to sticking with her original decisions and plans. But her reading of Thoreau over the weekend and this morning's discussion in class had opened her eyes once and for all. In fact, that's why during class she had actually closed her eyes and put her head on the desk. She was resolving to fight her parents and Mrs. Cooke right now rather than fighting quiet desperation for the rest of her life. She just needed his signature on the form so she could change her major from English education to plain English. Since she had taken so many literature courses already, she would still graduate in time with the rest of her senior class. But she might need his help getting into graduate school.

"Oh," he said, trying to snap out of it. "Yeah. Right. Sure. Of course." He knew that more was required of him in response to her effusive and copious flow of words, many of them quite complimentary to himself. "So do you have that form for me to sign?"

As soon as she had gone he pulled the Maigret out of his briefcase without bothering to look at his watch and learn just how little time he had left to enjoy it before his next class.

* * *

When he got home late that afternoon, the red light was flashing ominously like a warning signal on his answering machine. The only person who ever called and left messages for him was his mother, and the red alert was an entirely appropriate precursor to any and every communication with her. Unfortunately, ever since his father's bypass surgery a few years ago, he could not afford to ignore his mother's calls. And usually, she never stated on any of her messages the reason for her call, although it was invariably "an emergency situation." So he never knew whether his father had just suffered another heart attack, or UPS had just delivered a package she wanted him to come carry into the house. A reasonable person might think he could assume that if there really were "an emergency situation," his mother would surely not fail to let him know what it was on her voice message, and he could safely ignore any others as false alarms intended to manipulate and control him. But the reasonable person standard could not be used with his mother, who was so far from being a reasonable person herself that norms of behavior simply couldn't be applied. Her sense of entitlement was so extreme that she expected others to read her mind, to know what she needed or wanted without her having to actually communicate it. If his father had just had another heart attack, she expected him to know it without being told; likewise if the UPS truck had just deposited a large box outside her front door. Nor did he think his mother was capable of even understanding what constituted a true emergency as reasonable people would define it. To her, anything that caused her the slightest inconvenience or annoyance was an emergency that had to be dealt with right away: like a hose the yardman had left uncoiled on the patio. In any case, whenever she called she was simply delivering his official summons, and she expected him to obey immediately. No doubt she was waiting for him even now and wondering why he wasn't there already. Through considerable experience he had learned that it was less aggravating in the long run simply to head over to his parents' house and perform the task his mother indicated. If he tried to refuse, postpone or even negotiate the time frame for completing the required chore, he succeeded only in provoking his mother's contemptuous wrath and prolonging the inevitable ordeal.

But this evening he was more exhausted than usual on the Mondays, Wednesdays, and Fridays he taught class at Cahaba College. Events had conspired to deny him almost any down time between his four classes, primarily because of the deadline in his two freshman composition courses. Less than half the students had shown up at the allotted class time to hand in their papers; most of the others had shown up at various other times in his office to explain, apologize, beg, plead or otherwise appeal to his mercy in all sorts of creative ways.

Then at a quarter till four, when he thought the onslaught was over and he had fifteen precious minutes before his last class, the telephone had unexpectedly started ringing. Every so often toward the end of the day, a caller might actually be able to get through on his telephone. He hoped his theory was correct: that the decrease in phone traffic in the later hours relieved some of the stress on an overburdened system, which enabled a call placed to his office number to make it through. It was terrible even to entertain the alternative: that the chairman's complaints—which he was hoping had never actually been lodged—had indeed reached the attention of the IT personnel, who had finally fixed his phone.

But when he picked up the receiver, the static and crackle at the other end of the line had been immediately reassuring. Eventually he gathered that his caller was a Mrs. Cooke from the Education Department. She appeared to be upset about their mutual student, Tameika Young, and her change of major. As their connection flickered on and off, he could make out only random words and phrases, such as "not fair," "sorry," and "irresponsible decision." He assumed Mrs. Cooke was apologizing for the imposition Tameika's change of major would be on him—and come to think of it—there *would* be an imposition. Tameika herself had said something about needing help getting into graduate school, he now recalled, and furthermore, he realized she would probably become his advisee instead of Mrs. Cooke's. Still, Tameika was his brightest student, which meant she did her work, showed up for class, turned in tests and papers which required little marking, and therefore, she never needed to come to his office to manufacture excuses, requests or distractions regarding bad grades or poor performance. How much advice could this advisee need other than to keep up her good work? Accordingly, he had assured Mrs. Cooke that he was very glad Tameika had changed her major and quite happy to take her on. To his astonishment, Mrs. Cooke had exploded with anger and furiously questioned whether he had heard one word of what she'd been saying. At that point, he'd had to admit he'd heard very little of what she said, as there seemed to be something wrong with their telephone connection. Then the worst had happened, and she'd demanded to meet with him as soon as possible. His four o'clock class prevented "soon" from being right away, but he would have preferred this to the alternative, which turned out to be tomorrow—a Tuesday—when he taught no classes and usually didn't go in to campus at all, although technically, faculty office hours were supposed to be "dispersed over five days of the week regardless of teaching schedule."

So instead of heading over to his parents', he picked up the phone and called his mother.

"Where are you?" she said. "I called over an hour ago. I expected you'd be here by now."

"I just got home, Mother. It's been a long day."

"Well, the sooner you get on over here, the sooner you can get this over with. Your father and I will need to eat our dinner soon, you know."

It never occurred to her to wonder what he would do about *his* dinner while he was attending to his mother's needs, and she never invited him to join in their own meals. That experience was reserved only for well-established, long advertised and heavily promoted family gatherings, which usually took place when there was a football game he wanted to watch. Heaving a deliberate sigh, he asked what the trouble was.

"Didn't you listen to my message? There's a tornado watch until ten-fifteen tonight. I need you to move all the bromeliads and hibiscus from around the patio."

He looked at his watch. 5:30. "Harry's already left?"

"What does that have to do with anything?" she demanded impatiently, though Harry was her yardman, handyman, and even her cook, who worked for her six days a week. "The last time Harry moved the hibiscus, all the buds were knocked off and they didn't bloom again for two weeks. I want my patio to look nice for tomorrow's party. Anyway, Harry's busy with something else right now."

Probably preparing her dinner. He tried his best to conjure up a vision of his therapist and command the words Lauren had uttered to come from his own mouth.

"I'm afraid I can't come tonight, Mother," he mumbled.

"What? When did you say you were coming? Speak up! I can't hear you."

"I've got plans tonight, Mother," he lied. "I'm already late as it is."

She sighed heavily. "I'll just have to go get your father. You know I hate to disturb him, and he really shouldn't exert himself in this fashion. But it *is* your sister's birthday tomorrow, and if you won't help me out, I don't see that I have any choice. I just hope he doesn't suffer any consequences."

Briefly he considered pointing out to his mother the difference between a tornado watch and a tornado warning, along with the low probability that tonight's winds would be high enough to knock over any of her patio plants, all of which were well rooted in big pots that cost at least $500 and seemed to weigh at least that much in pounds. But the last time he had tried something to this effect, she had retorted that she didn't need him to be the weatherman; she needed him to help her prevent his father from having another heart attack. It was only Harry who could play weatherman, and say emphatically: "Oh, no'm. No need for dat. Wind ain't g'on get dat bad *tonight*." She appeared to believe that Harry's African ancestry had imbued him with some supernatural access to the workings of the weather system, and she treated his pronouncements on what the weather was or was not going to do as if God himself had spoken.

"I'll tell you what, Mother," he said. "You ask Harry before he leaves if he thinks those plants need moving. If he does, then I'll come over—later on tonight—and do it."

Grumbling something unintelligible, she hung up the phone. With relief he poured himself half a glass of Scotch and sat down on the sofa beside his cat Tink, with the Maigret mystery open on his lap. As he took those first few transportive sips of his drink, he reflected that all the interruptions and irritants he had endured during the day had at least prepared the way for him to take particular pleasure in his quiet evening and as yet unread book. He was jarred out of this pleasant reverie by the shrill sound of the telephone, which normally didn't ring at his home any more than it did in his office, as his mother preferred to reach his answering machine when she knew he wasn't there, the better to issue marching orders without interference from the sound of his voice. He stopped himself from picking up just in time, in case it *was* his mother, expecting to reach that machine, since he had told her he was going out. But the voice being recorded on the message tape was that of his colleague Ivy Greer, wondering if there were any time he could meet with her tomorrow, on campus if necessary, but preferably off. He took another sip of his drink and stared into space.

~ 2 ~

Upon arriving at his parents' house for a Family Gathering—in this case the celebration of his sister's forty-third birthday—the safest course of action was to head straight for the room where the boys were kept entertained by television and plied with their favorite foods in hopes of keeping them properly penned up as his mother believed boys should be. It was unthinkable that they join the grownups in the living room, and out of the question for them to play on either the spacious front lawn or equally spacious backyard. They would tear up the grass, trample the flowers, perhaps break a window or flower pot with their ball play. They would cause immense disruption when they barreled indoors, hot, sweaty, hungry and thirsty; full of rambunctious excitement and tales to tell of outdoor exploits; clamoring for their needs to be met. They would also track in dirt, mud and grass, and ruin the floors and the furniture as they had already ruined their clothes. His mother would not have it.

The room where his nephews were to be found was his old bedroom, now converted more or less into a den, with comfortable, overstuffed sofas and a large television. Long before the grandsons were even born, his mother had complained about not having a den and at one point proposed converting the library for this purpose, until Norman Laney—her friend and his former teacher—had talked her out of it. "Under no circumstances can you do that," he had told her. "That was LeRoy Percy's library, and if you alter it in any way, history will never forgive you." His mother was not fully aware who the Percy family was: there were no longer any Percys in Birmingham that she needed to know, impress, or entertain. And she felt no responsibility either to history or the literature that one of the Percy sons had written, which she had no intentions of reading. But she depended heavily on Norman Laney's guidance and followed it without question, though not always without grumbling. So the library had been spared and his bedroom was transformed by an expensive interior decorator. He didn't much mind, though he would have liked to know the precise mental calculus by which his mother had selected the site of his childhood to be obliterated rather than his sister's, which adjoined the hall bathroom and would have made the more obvious choice. He put no stock in his mother's contention that his sister's old room made the better guest quarters, as his parents never had guests who stayed the night, not even their own grandchildren.

This evening the boys had a different sitter who nevertheless looked quite familiar to him. Of course his nephews—ages seven and nine—did not in any way need a sitter for these occasions, but as his sister had pointed out: if their mother was actually willing to part with cash to pay for services rendered by another person, why stop her? And if it gave their mother the peace of mind to be more agreeable—or less disagreeable—for the duration of the Family Gathering, then it was all the more worthwhile.

Normally, Ham spent the entire cocktail hour with his nephews, laughing happily along with them at whatever movie had been supplied, and snacking from the bowls of popcorn and pretzels placed on the coffee table. It was usually the most enjoyable part of any Family Gathering for him, and one less hour of ammunition for his mother, who invariably called him the next day to deliver her critique of his clothes, his conversation, his manners, his personal grooming choices and general demeanor. Lapses in any of these areas were treated as serious moral failings. But tonight his sister unexpectedly appeared in the doorway ten minutes after he had arrived. He rose dutifully to greet her and wish her a happy birthday.

"I'm here to summon you," she said, withdrawing from his embrace. The swift scrutiny of the medical professional she gave him was in some ways more uncomfortable than what he endured from his mother. "She wants you in the living room."

No need to ask who "she" referred to.

"Sure," he said, smoothing his pants. "What's up? Nothing wrong, I hope?"

"Someone she wants you to meet."

That would explain it. "Someone of the female persuasion, I take it?"

"You're to be polite to her, attentive to her, sit next to her at dinner and converse with her. Then after a suitable interval, propose to her, marry her, and have children."

"Well, if that's all," he said, trying his best to be cheerful. Inwardly he frowned. His mother had done this to him before, of course, but always he had advance warning in the form of a phone call telling him what to wear, what to talk about, what not to talk about, what the girl's father did for a living, and what sort of people the girl's mother came from.

"Everything all right here, Patrice?" said his sister, turning to leave.

Patrice. Quickly he looked over and caught her eye before she lowered her gaze bashfully as she had done when he first entered. "Patrice?" he said.

She met his eyes again and grinned this time.

"Patrice is a freshman in my composition class," he explained to his sister.

"Yes, I know," said his sister a bit impatiently.

"You know?"

"She's also Harry's granddaughter, if you'll recall. We better get in there before Mother comes in here on a rampage."

This point was too compelling to argue, and he didn't have time to say anything further to Patrice or wonder how he was supposed to recall something he'd never been told before.

In the living room along with his parents and brother-in-law was a young woman he already knew but hadn't seen in such a long time that his image of her was that of the gangly kid she'd been when he last saw her. He'd liked her then, and was so relieved by his mother's choice he was able to greet her with all the natural enthusiasm his mother would have wished him to simulate otherwise. No doubt it was just his imagination, but he believed he could even feel his mother's rarely given approval wash over him as he turned back to his "date" after greeting the other family members.

Erica Cooley was not quite ten—perhaps seven or eight—years younger than he was, and he knew her primarily because her father, who owned a construction and development company, had been involved in many business ventures with his father. There was an older sister closer to his own age, but he had never liked her and used to avoid her whenever he found himself around her. Ginger was a carbon copy of her mother, both in looks and in personality, which seemed deliberately designed for the sole purpose of prevailing at cocktail parties. With either Ginger or her mother, there was no such thing as even a simple hello or good-bye. Once they entered a room, everything they said or did possessed a kind of madcap theatricality calculated to draw every eye and command a large audience. Both the mother and the older daughter had the natural advantage of being about six feet tall and lean-limbed like exotic zoo creatures. Most people thought they were beautiful; perhaps he would have thought so too if not for the personality that accompanied their looks. They combined the graceful, slender elegance of the giraffe with the chattering antics of a gibbon monkey. Mrs. Cooley had always been the one in his parents' circle he most detested, the living proof that those who talk the most have the least to say. He could remember wondering as a boy whether she ever turned herself "off."

Erica was altogether different, as if in self-conscious opposition or reaction to her mother and older sister. He'd always been intrigued by the way she declined to go along with the whirlwind of their public personas. She was quiet, shy, diffident and self-effacing. Yet there had always been much more sense in whatever she'd had to say, as far as he could remember. As a teenager she'd shown signs of becoming as tall as Ginger and her mother, but this height had apparently not materialized. However, she was every bit as stick-legged as they were, though on her much shorter frame, the effect was of an awkward, spindly colt with knobby, trembling knees likely to buckle at any moment. Where they were domineering and utterly commanding, she seemed frail and wispy, as if too delicate to engage in the kind of aggressive social interaction that made Mrs. Cooley and Ginger so popular with everyone but himself, it seemed.

Ginger had bamboozled her way into the Ivy League, with Mr. Laney's help, of course, but Erica had refused even to apply to Mr. Laney's choice of Mount Holyoke for her. Instead she'd ended up in some obscure small college in Boulder whose name he couldn't remember if he'd ever known it in the first place. Colorado had apparently agreed with her and she had remained there after getting her degree, which is one reason he'd rarely seen her since she left for college. Just then it came back to him from his mother's recent natterings, which he was in the habit of barely listening to, that Erica had lately come back home, had suffered a nervous breakdown or the break-up of some long-term relationship or some kind of devastating blow. But then again, she'd always had the look of someone who'd just suffered a devastating blow: dazed, shaky, nervous, hesitant and apologetic. She reminded him of someone else he knew, though at the moment he couldn't remember who.

Tonight his heart went out to her, because even he—with his total lack of clothes sense—could tell that she was badly dressed, which was one of the cardinal sins in his mother's lengthy catalog. Without even registering what exactly it was she was wearing, he was struck by the general impression of a thousand wrinkles in a skirt which also had a badly frayed hem, accompanied by a half un-tucked blouse missing several buttons. Her mother and sister, he remembered, were always clad in the most chic garments. Their hair was similarly sleek, jet-black and absolutely straight, cropped razor sharp at the jaw-line and in bangs above the brows which of course perfectly emphasized the angles of their faces and the aristocratic projection of their aquiline noses. Although Erica had the same basic hairstyle and bangs, her muddy-brown hair fell in loose, indifferent tendrils around an almost child-like face and snub nose sprinkled with freckles. Compared to them, she looked like a hopeless waif.

"Pitiful, isn't she?" muttered his mother in his ear as she passed by on her way to the kitchen to check on the progress of dinner.

So this was the reason his mother hadn't warned him of the set-up: this was not a set-up. This was one of those goodwill invitations that his mother sometimes extended as a favor to any of her friends who had a stray on their hands. Out of the corner of his eye, he could see his mother pause on the threshold of the door leading to the kitchen. Early in life, she had obviously realized that no one would ever call her beautiful. So instead she had opted for the look of "intellectual," which she accomplished by having a pair of reading glasses on a thick black cord always around her neck in lieu of any piece of jewelry, even on supposedly festive occasions like this evening. Ham had never known her to read much of anything, except *Southern Living Magazine,* and very occasionally, the society page in the local newspaper, which otherwise did not interest her or pertain to her existence. This publication was The Birmingham *News,* and she lived in Mountain Brook, so she failed to perceive its relevance to her.

In honor of tonight's occasion, she'd had her hair done that afternoon, which meant her face now appeared to be encased in a piece of heavy-duty military equipment, polished by her subordinates to a shiny brass. There was something equally military in her bearing and demeanor, suggesting a sharp look-out for the least infraction, and a total readiness to go to war over the slightest misstep. The permanent frown lines chiseled down the sides of her chin indicated her deep displeasure with the state of affairs over which she presided as commanding general: of course her inferiors were either actively disobeying her orders, failing to perform their duties, or for the moment, getting away with something she'd have to call them to account for as soon as she discovered what it was. Although she'd turned seventy last summer, she showed no signs of laying down her arms or negotiating a cease-fire. The stoutness increasing around her middle somehow only added to the forcefulness of her posture. At the moment she was conducting rigorous surveillance of the unfortunate Erica Cooley, and would have a full report to issue to the girl's mother in the morning.

As he took a seat beside her on the sofa facing the boxwood rimmed backyard where no boy had ever played while his mother was in charge, Erica plucked nervously at a loose thread dangling from the hem of her rumpled skirt. What should he say to her? Gratefully he accepted the glass of Scotch

33

his father handed him with a wink. He knew he should avoid any subject which might pertain to whatever trauma she had just undergone, but didn't know what that left him with. Noticing she had no drink, he said, "Can I get you something?"

"Oh, no," she said, looking over at him and smiling. "I'm fine, thanks."

He took a large sip of his own drink and set the glass down on the coffee table. Her voice still had that same flutey, high-pitched, little-girl quality he remembered from years ago. And yet there was a startling degree of determination in her tone, as if she were no little girl at all, but a force to be reckoned with. How old would she be now? he wondered. About thirty, he calculated, though she looked about twenty-one and sounded about twelve, except for that hint of steel at the bottom of her voice.

"So you're back from Colorado?" he ventured, rubbing sweaty palms down his pants' legs before remembering not to.

She nodded and resumed plucking at the loose thread of her skirt.

"For good?" he asked uneasily, hoping he wasn't treading on tender territory. For once he actually wished that his mother *had* called to tell him what to talk about and what not to talk about.

"For a trial period," she said, looking back up.

"What does that mean?" He reached for his drink.

"To see if I can stand it," she said.

He laughed appreciatively at her candor and took a swallow from his glass. "I'm sorry," he said tentatively. "I've forgotten what you were doing in Colorado after you graduated."

"Not much," she said matter-of-factly. "I wrote for the alternative newspaper in Boulder."

"That doesn't sound like 'not much' to me," he said kindly.

"It was only a weekly. I wrote four articles a month. Big deal. It didn't even pay my rent. Basically, I was living off what my father gave me."

Although again he admired her frankness, he wasn't sure how to respond to this.

"Until I turned thirty, I was able to justify this arrangement to myself," she said. "You know: figuring out my life, finding myself, et cetera. But at thirty, I had to face up to the fact that I hadn't figured out much if I was still living off my father."

A chuckle escaped and he looked over quickly to see if he had offended her. The smile playing about her own lips appeared to indicate that he had not.

"So you're back . . . " he prodded lamely.

"So I'm back because Mr. Laney offered me a job at Brook-Haven," she said.

What a coincidence, he almost said, since Mr. Laney had also offered him a job at Brook-Haven not too long ago. It appeared to be Mr. Laney's way of bailing out favored alumni who found themselves at loose ends or, in his case, a dead end. He might have accepted it too, if it hadn't been for the close alliance between Mr. Laney and his mother. The last thing he needed was an informant passing inside information to his mother; she was good enough at gathering clandestine intelligence about his supposed life on her own.

Erica's gaze was now appraising the contents of the living room. "I'd forgotten how much I loved this house," she said. "It's been years since I was here, but I don't think it's changed at all, has it?"

He didn't think so either. Occasionally his mother swapped one antique table or secretary for another antique table or secretary, probably at the behest of the decorator who earned handsome commissions by procuring these items for her at the antique stores in Atlanta where they all came from. These changes never made much difference as far as he could tell: all the pieces looked basically the same and created the same effect, though his mother fretted endlessly over every minor detail: every drawer handle, every door hinge. What made the room really stand out, however, were the pieces studded here and there on the walls and tables from his grandmother's art collection. Most of this was modern, comprised of weird nudes and abstractions that his mother did not appreciate, understand or admire in the least. If left to her own devices, she would have allowed her brother-in-law to claim the whole collection, but Mr. Laney had saved the art just as he'd saved the library, and insisted that his mother display it prominently "in the tradition established by the family matriarch." Mr. Laney knew just the words to get his mother to do what he wanted. She had grudgingly acceded to his wishes and then told him he better come arrange the "stuff" himself. Since this "stuff" included a Matisse and a Brancusi, among other works by masters of 20th century art, Mr. Laney had been only too glad to comply, and now his mother was so wedded to Mr. Laney's vision that she wouldn't allow even a small piece of sculpture to be moved a quarter of an inch without Mr. Laney's blessing. The living room had been photographed once for *Southern Living Magazine,* and appeared in a panoramic two page spread under the heading: "Delightful Juxtaposition of the Old and the New in Historic Mountain Brook Home." Now the room had to remain frozen just the way it had been captured in the photograph for the magazine. His mother appeared to believe this was the debt she owed to posterity.

Suddenly his gaze was interrupted by a large silver tray thrust before him by Lois, who urged him to help himself by continuing to nudge the tray forward until it was almost upon him. Reluctantly he picked up a mushroom cap filled presumably with crabmeat. He really hated eating finger food in front of anyone because he was such a klutz he inevitably ended up embarrassing himself and staining his clothes. Erica had no such scruples, and reached eagerly with both hands for a mushroom cap and an escargot on a slice of French bread.

"Lois!" his mother called sharply from the doorway of the kitchen. "Come get Miss Erica an hors d'oeuvre plate."

"Yes'm," said Lois, in a subdued voice belied by the big grin she gave Erica, wide enough to show the two gold framed teeth at either end of her smile.

"I'm a put the tray here," she said, setting it down on the coffee table. "And go get *every*body a plate. I told your mother this food too messy to eat from a tray, but she don't pay *no* attention to what *nobody* try to tell her. She got to think of it herself." Shaking her head and still grinning, Lois returned to the kitchen, where his mother had also disappeared for the second time.

Meanwhile Erica had consumed her first two bites and was reaching unapologetically for another. Clearly her skeletal thinness owed nothing to anorexia. He'd always wondered about this with Ginger and Mrs. Cooley, whom he never saw eating. Mrs. Cooley was always the one wildly waving a drink around as she vividly illustrated some anecdote that was supposed to be hilarious. At the dinner table, she would pick at her food and make a show of eating without consuming much of anything at all, as if bored by food and annoyed when it became the focus of attention once a meal was announced. At a party, she'd be the last to find her seat or join the buffet line. The cocktail hour was her favorite time slot, the best stage for her performances, the perfect showcase for her talents. Only reluctantly would she give way and often only when forced to. Many a time Ham had seen Mr. Cooley go drag his wife to her chair so the other stragglers still in thrall to whatever act she was putting on could go get their food and come to the table. And once there, Mrs. Cooley still didn't stop waving her drink around and telling her story while largely ignoring the meal in front of her. Again Erica was the reverse, with no drink and a hearty appetite.

"So this job at Brook-Haven," he began, trying to resume the thread of their former conversation.

"Teaching French," she said, covering her mouth, which was full of food, with the back of her hand.

He frowned in concentration, trying to remember who the current French teacher would be.

"Madame Boyer," she said, swallowing, "is retiring after this year."

Now he remembered. "But she can't be old enough—"

"No," she agreed. "But she's pregnant. After being married fifteen years, she finally got pregnant. The baby's due in June. So she told Mr. Laney she was going to quit teaching after this year and raise her child."

He absentmindedly accepted the plate Lois handed him.

"You eat on up," Lois told Erica as she handed her a plate. "Girl got to get some meat on them bones. Look like a plucked chicken."

Lois deposited the rest of the plates next to the tray on the coffee table and went back to the kitchen. If his mother had been there to observe, this would have duly been entered in the ongoing log of Lois's "lazy, good-for-nothing" behavior. She had not passed either the tray or the plates around the room as she'd no doubt been instructed. But what she did do was infinitely more practical and less disruptive. His father and brother-in-law abandoned the armchairs where they'd been re-hashing last week's Alabama game to fill their own plates.

His brother-in-law Mark, who taught English at Brook-Haven, remained standing near them and asked Erica if she'd decided whether or not to take the job teaching French.

She shook her head. "Mr. Laney has given me till the end of this school year to make a decision," she said. "So I'm taking some French classes at UAB and trying to figure out if I want to live here again."

Mark and Erica continued to discuss Mr. Laney, the Brook-Haven School, the responsibilities involved in Michelle Boyer's job, and whether Erica's various qualifications would enable her to fulfill them. He was grateful that she refrained from mentioning the summers she and her sister used to spend studying French at the Sorbonne. He'd heard enough about France years ago from her sister Ginger, and hoped he had never so irritated anybody about the time he had spent in Germany. He reached again for his drink and reflected that Erica's situation was not sounding quite so much like the nervous breakdown he'd heard about. She had evaluated her existence, found it lacking, and decided to do something about it. Obviously this would be stressful and painful. But that didn't mean she'd had a nervous breakdown. Of course, Mrs. Cooley's histrionics combined with his mother's hyperbole could make a nervous breakdown candidate out of anyone who lacked the Mountain Brook look of smug complacency. As he himself well knew. No one leading an examined life and grappling with its consequences compared favorably with those blithely leading their unexamined lives. On the other hand, he had to admit, his mother might have provided a detailed and accurate account of Erica Cooley's return to Birmingham, to which he had failed to pay close enough attention.

"The last I heard about you," said Erica, turning to him as Mark left, "you had just quit Harvard Law School."

He could feel his neck suddenly get hot and leaned over to put his drink back on the table. The exertion caused a full flush to suffuse his face.

"I almost wrote you when I heard," she said softly. "My mother said you just couldn't stand it anymore, and I was so impressed. She told me you were in the last semester of your third year."

He nodded miserably. The pleasant buzz of enjoyment from the single malt Scotch had become the sour aftertaste of too much alcohol on an empty stomach. And his initial enjoyment at seeing Erica again after so many years had instantly evaporated. Now he just wanted to eat dinner and go back to his apartment, where *Maigret and the Bum* awaited him. The "bum" in the story was a former physician who found himself unable to function in society as a productive individual and preferred instead to live the life of a hobo. Ham was fascinated by this character, who was not unlike himself. "That was a long time ago," he mumbled to Erica, hoping she would get the hint and change the subject.

"I know, but it made such a deep impression on me. My mother said you could easily have finished your degree, you just didn't want to."

"What's impressive about that?" He tried to laugh, as if it were all a joke.

She picked at the hem of her skirt. "It just seemed like such a heroic thing to do."

"Heroic? I don't think I've done anything remotely heroic in my entire life. With the possible exception of the home run I hit when I played baseball in the fifth grade."

She fiddled now with a button on her blouse, and he understood why several were currently missing. "It's just—" she blurted, and then stopped abruptly. He waited and watched as she twisted the button around and around with her fingers. Before the evening was over, this button would be missing as well. "Every time I turn around, it seems like someone is trying to wave their Ivy League degree in my face. When I heard you dropped out, it seemed like an act of courage. I thought it was noble."

"That's not what they called it when I was admitted into McLean Hospital," he said. "Would you excuse me for a minute?" He rose suddenly from the sofa, but realizing he'd been rude, turned back around. "Can I get you anything?"

She was pushing her bangs out of her eyes and chewing her lip. She shook her head.

Instead of visiting what his mother called "the powder room," he returned to the private wing of the house where the boys were watching the end of their movie. They clambered happily around him as he sat between them on the couch and stared into the space occupied by the television set. Nothing made him more uncomfortable than when his dropping out of law school was misconstrued as some "courageous" statement of protest or rebellion, or some "noble" crisis of conscience. He was not noble or brave. He was a pitiful coward and a weakling. No doubt his mother's euphemisms were precisely designed to put a positive spin on his failings as a human being and gloss over these unpleasant facts she didn't want anyone, even her "close friends," to know. But the p. r. propaganda only brought those failings more powerfully home to him, and put him on a dishonest footing with everyone else.

The sad truth was: he had not dropped out of law school because he couldn't stand it. He had actually enjoyed law school as an intellectual exercise in reason, logic and analysis. If he could have remained a law school student—or any kind of student—for the rest of his life, he would have. But as he approached the end of his last year of law school, he realized he had no idea what he was going to do after he graduated. The next thing he knew, he was unable to get out of bed in the morning. He began missing classes and couldn't finish the article he'd been writing for the Law Review. After waking he would lie in bed for hours, unable even to get up so he could go to the bathroom. And it was only the pain of a fuller and fuller bladder that would finally force him out of bed, hours after first waking. Getting out of bed would be his only accomplishment of the day, and he could never bring himself to leave the apartment. When his adviser came to investigate, she found him practically catatonic on the sofa, in clothes soiled by his own waste, unshaven, unwashed, and dehydrated. She had taken him to McClean Hospital. They called it severe clinical depression. There was nothing brave, noble or heroic about it.

He had missed the rest of the semester, and had seen no point in making up the work so he could obtain his degree, because he'd never once entertained the possibility of practicing law. The only reason he had even applied to Harvard Law School in the first place was to placate his mother, who was pressing for him to come home and "learn the family business" after his two years on a Rotary Scholarship at the University of Heidelberg. He was simply trying to buy a little time with his application, and never dreamed he'd actually be accepted at Harvard Law School, because he'd been completely honest on his application essay about never intending to enter a law firm or practice the legal profession. Later, one of his philosophy professors at Heidelberg told him that was probably the very reason he was actually accepted.

He wasn't sure he believed that, and still couldn't believe in his acceptance. At first, he'd had no more intention of going to law school than he had of practicing law. But then he realized how completely propitiated his mother was by his Harvard acceptance, like it was the ultimate offering he could lay before her altar. And although he knew it was not the permanent solution to the problem of his existence, it was soon obvious how quickly society's questions about that existence could be answered with that one magic word of "Harvard." His mother so enjoyed going around town and using that word in conjunction with the phrase "my son," that she even stopped mentioning "the family business." The Ivy League school he'd attended for college had not had this same effect, because no one in Birmingham really knew of Williams. It just sounded like an ordinary last name. It became clear that three years in Cambridge, Massachusetts would not be a bad fate and would surely give him enough time to work out the real answer to his existence before the issue came up again with his mother.

At one point during his law school days he believed he'd arrived at such an answer, and had discovered a way to do as a lawyer what his sister did as a doctor. There were plenty of government agencies, political organizations, social services and non-profit or charitable institutions that needed attorneys willing to perform more socially useful work for a lot less pay than was to be found in most law firms. But after investigating and interviewing at several such places, he found himself unable to ally himself with their causes as fully as necessary in order to be the advocate they required. Apparently the years he had spent as a student of philosophy had trained him to be anything but a zealot. And after barely completing a disastrous internship at one such place, he realized that even this work involved a certain amount of conflict and confrontation with opposing forces that he couldn't handle. The many years spent under the same roof as his mother had turned him into what his therapist called "a conflict avoider." He literally had no stomach for confrontation of any kind. Except for when he'd played sports as a boy, he had no aggressive drive to compete, to win, to prove himself or demonstrate his prowess in the real world of adults as opposed to the playing fields of youth. So it was one thing for him to study law; it would be quite another for him to practice it, and he knew instinctively he was unsuited to do so in any form whatsoever. By the time graduation loomed in his final semester of law school, he had come up empty-handed with no further peace offerings to place before his mother.

When his two squirming nephews suddenly became still, he realized it was because Erica Cooley's face was peering anxiously into the room. A wisp of her hair was stuck in the corner of her mouth, and she seemed to be sucking on it. He rose with the alacrity of the malingering schoolboy, hoping to obscure his unexcused absence along with his failure to complete the assignments. Inside he had that hangdog feeling of guilt and defeat which had become his sense of himself. He was sure these sensations were also etched into his face and physical appearance, so that he looked every bit the loser he felt like he was. It was small comfort that Erica looked no better, nervously chewing on her hair and pushing at her bangs. He had probably reduced her to a new low with his ignominious retreat from the living room battlefield, where she'd only been trying to administer a little salve to his war wounds.

"I—ah—I," she stammered, looking up and down the corridor. "Is the bathroom near here?"

He pointed across the hall. "Just over there."

At that moment his sister entered the hallway carrying two melamine plates covered with cartoon characters and the boys' dinner. Patrice followed behind her with two plastic cups and a stack of paper napkins. It was clear he needed to vacate the den and make room for the process of setting up a spill-proof meal for the two caged animals. He found himself abruptly face to face with Erica, who appeared to have no real pressing need to enter the bathroom. She brushed the hair out of her mouth.

"I'm always saying something stupid," she said, low enough to avoid being overheard. "I didn't mean to offend you."

"Oh, I wasn't offended," he assured her, laughing in order to prove the truth of this assertion. "Just appalled that my mother's propaganda machine paints such a false picture of me."

She showed no inclination to laugh and forget about it all, as he'd hoped. Instead she stood there searching his face with serious intent, while trying to gather the nerve to express some deeply felt emotion. He had come to loathe and fear serious discussions full of deeply felt emotions, but could not bring himself to bolt on her a second time. Fortunately his sister saved the day by informing them that dinner was about to be served, and they followed her silently to the dining room on the other side of the house. As his sister had forewarned, the place cards had them seated next to each other, but conversation at his mother's dinner table never allowed for either intimacy or meaningful subject matter. For once he was grateful for that.

Tonight's meal also demanded everyone's full attention, as it was picnic food meant to be eaten outdoors, with bare hands that could wipe themselves on rolls of paper towels after every messy mouthful. It was actually one of his favorites—Harry's barbecued chicken—prepared that afternoon on the large black barrel grill Harry transported from his own home on the back of his truck for these occasions. Harry had tried but failed to convince Mrs. Whitmire to let him keep the grill permanently on their patio. Of course his mother had scoffed at the idea of having something that looked "like it belonged on the front porch of a place in the projects," on her patio, while Harry had scoffed at the shiny, expensive and much smaller Weber grill that served mainly as a decorative piece of patio furniture. "This here grill was made by black mens down in Atmore," explained Harry, proudly referring to the black barrel grill made by convicts in the state prison. "They know how to *make* a *grill.*" The Weber was just an expensive child's toy, useless to a grown man who wanted to do real cooking. So Harry had to tote his own grill to and fro whenever he needed it, which worked well enough except that his mother always complained about the truck being in her driveway "for the whole world to see when they drove by." Trucks were tacky, and she did not want them associated in anyone's mind with her premises. This was one reason she always gave Harry her old Cadillac whenever she got a new one. He was glad enough to use it too, except on days when he needed his grill.

Whenever Ham had been asked by anyone he went to school with in the Northeast what "the South" was like where he had grown up, an image of the meal before him tonight usually came to mind. Barbecued chicken, smoked to perfection by a black man on a black barrel grill made by black convicts in the Alabama state correctional system, served on his grandmother's fine china, eaten with his grandmother's sterling silver, and managed with heavily starched, fiercely ironed white linen napkins embroidered with a curlicued monogram soon obscured by the thick, dark barbecue sauce made by Harry's wife. That was "the South" as he knew it. Unsure how to convey this image effectively, he usually just shrugged whenever asked to describe "his culture." In fact, this particular shrug had become his response to all Northeastern questions about "the South," especially the ones about growing up in Birmingham during the Civil Rights Movement. Although born in Birmingham in 1960, he had been so unaware of any Civil Rights Movement that it might as well never have happened. "But weren't your parents discussing it?" his Ivy League classmates had wanted to know. "Wasn't everybody talking about it? Wasn't the town caught up in it all?" 'No' was obviously not the answer they expected to hear. But in fact, the Nobel Peace Prize laureate and his historic revolution, fomented apparently in Ham's own native city and state, had registered so dimly on the consciousness of anyone he knew that it might have all taken place in another realm. Mountain Brook was its own private club, in which the 1960s, or any of its various revolutions, had never gained admittance. His teacher Norman Laney used to say it was even as if the *1860s* had never happened, and Mountain Brook was that mythic Garden of Eden known as the Old South, where every house was a mansion, every woman was a belle, and all the darkies were happy to work there. The fact that Birmingham was a postwar city only added to the perfection of its exalted enclave for the white and wealthy: this New South city got the Old South right when it produced Mountain Brook. As there were no flaws or problems in this paradise world, there was no need of any revolutions. The only thing Ham could ever remember anyone in his hometown discussing with any intensity or urgency was the viability of Alabama's football team.

"So, Ham, tell me," said Erica. "How did you come to be a professor at a black college in Birmingham?"

Her voice, squeaky and high-pitched as it was, nevertheless managed to penetrate the clatter of silverware and the undercurrent of compliments flowing to the hostess about the magnificence of the food. In fact, her question created a stunned silence, as it had violated almost every unwritten taboo of his mother's dinner table. First of all, Erica had used his nickname, which his mother detested and forbade anyone to utter. Those who couldn't call him by his full name, which was everyone but his mother, avoided calling him anything at all in her presence. Next, Erica had brought up a serious topic which asked for a thoughtful response. Although his mother had spent many days preparing for this party, countless hours arranging the table, and hundreds of dollars on the floral centerpiece, she was offended if anyone used the occasion to engage in a substantive exchange with another guest. Only the most routine and desultory small talk was encouraged, so as not to take the focus away from the food, the flowers, the silver, the linen and the china, which seemed to be the main point of the occasion. Finally, Erica had used the word "black," which was another forbidden word as well as topic in his mother's household. Regarding her servants, his mother thought it her duty as a white person to demand too much, pay too little, and refrain from mentioning the unfortunate circumstances of their particular human condition. It was as if Erica had uttered a dirty word and raised an ugly issue. And his mother had gone to so much trouble to put on a lovely dinner party.

He could see the frown deepen on his mother's face, but Erica couldn't, as she was turned toward him awaiting his reply as to why he was teaching at a black college. Wiping his mouth, he said, "It was the only place I could get a job."

Erica refused to accept this bit of banter as the definitive response he hoped it could be, at least for now, under his mother's frowning gaze. His sister was attempting to deflect their mother's attention by continuing to praise the barbecued chicken, with its perfectly crisp outside and perfectly moist, tender inside. Naturally their mother took full credit for this marvel, though Harry had done every bit of the work, even purchasing the chicken himself at the grocery store he favored near where he lived.

"Don't get me wrong," said Erica. "I have the highest admiration for what you're doing. You and your sister. I think it's great. Both of you are such an inspiration. I'm just curious how you arrived at it. I know with a Ph.D. from Harvard, you had job offers from lots of places."

"It was time for Hamilton to come home," interposed his mother, in the tone of a final pronouncement ending any further discussion.

Erica missed that signal. "So you only applied to schools in Birmingham?" she said. "How come?"

In an inadvertent reply to this last question, his eyes darted towards his father, whose allegedly precarious health had finally forced him to accept what he had somehow always known would be his fate, and come back to Alabama. It could have been that his mother had always presumed and then insisted upon his return; or that his mentor Norman Laney had always spoken of the debt everyone owed their origins, *especially* if you had transcended those origins. (You've got to help others grow up; you've got to help your *home town* grow up, Mr. Laney would say.) For whatever reason, he had always known he would return home one day, though he had struggled and fought against this fate until his father's illness thrust it upon him for once and for all.

Fortunately Erica appeared to observe his tacit reference to his father, and didn't press the Birmingham issue. "But there are several other schools here," she said. "UAB, Birmingham-Southern. . . . It's so good of you, to choose the place that needs you the most."

"I would have loved Birmingham-Southern," he told her bluntly, hoping to destroy any illusions of his "goodness." He could not have her reverting to this idea that there was anything the least bit noble or heroic about him or the choices he had made in life. Taking a job at a black college in Birmingham was no more heroic than dropping out of Harvard Law School had been for him. These were deeds born of necessity, not nobility. "Birmingham-Southern didn't offer me a job," he explained.

"It's just as well Hamilton didn't take a position there," said his mother emphatically, sweeping completely past the fact that he had not been offered such a position. "Hamilton did not come back here to be a schoolteacher," she said.

His sister and brother-in-law exchanged glances of amusement, as Mark himself was a "schoolteacher," and not even at a college, black or otherwise. Erica remained intent upon him.

"They didn't offer you a job?" she was incredulous. "Why not?"

He shrugged. "There weren't any openings in the English Department," he explained.

"Ridiculous," said his mother. "But just as well."

"Academia is not like corporate America," said Mark. "Or any other important profession, for that matter. It doesn't seek out a constant flow of fresh talent. If there should happen to be a vacancy in the academic world, the position might even be eliminated instead of filled because of budget constraints. Otherwise, the job goes to one candidate and the door is shut to the hundreds of other equally qualified candidates who applied for that position."

"Yes, of course. I knew that," said Erica apologetically, chastened by the bitterness creeping into Mark's voice. No doubt she was now remembering that his own presence in Birmingham stemmed from his inability years ago to obtain a teaching position at a university or college, despite an MFA from Columbia.

"So there weren't any openings anywhere but Cahaba College?" she turned back to him.

"I even tried at the University of Alabama," he said. "It's not so far away. Just forty-five minutes, really. But they weren't hiring either—except for part-time adjunct instructors. Which would hardly have been worth the trouble—of living in Tuscaloosa, or driving over there."

"Absolutely out of the question," said his mother, pushing away her plate. "Hamilton did not leave Harvard in order to live in Tuscaloosa or teach school anywhere. He came back here because it is his duty to take over the reins of his family's business and take the burden off his father. And after this school year, that's exactly what he's going to do."

This was as much news to Hamilton as it was to Erica. "Oh," she said. "I had no idea. I see: you're just teaching for a few years before your father retires?"

He didn't know what to say now, not wanting to lie, tell the truth, commit himself to his mother's plans, continue this discussion or even remain at the dinner table any longer. Sensing his distress, Mark caused a diversion by asking Harry, who was offering seconds from a platter, if he could have another glass of wine.

"Oh, here," said his father-in-law, reaching for the bottle. "Please let me.

We're still hopelessly behind the times, Adelaide. I keep forgetting that the younger generation prefers wine."

He poured Mark a generous second glass, much more than the token, almost purely decorative amount that had been poured initially and still remained in his and his wife's crystal wineglasses. They preferred the bourbon and water in the tumblers in front of them, and did indeed tend to forget that others might want something besides the cocktails favored by their generation.

"Anyone else?" called the host, looking around the table. He winked when he caught his son's eye. It was a friendly, conspiratorial wink such as Wilmer Whitmire had been giving his son since he was a little boy. This particular wink said: "Don't worry. We'll find a way around your mother. If you really don't want to/can't do it/hate the whole idea/would rather die this instant, I'm not going to force it on you. We just need to bide our time and figure out the right way to handle this." His father had communicated with him forever this way, rarely expressing himself through words but through a wink of the eye, a twinkle in the eye, or a pat on the back. In this case his father was telling him that if he really did not want to assume any role in "the family business," and he definitely did not—he would rather do what Walker Percy's father had done with a shotgun in the attic of this very house—then his father would see to it that he didn't have to. He could leave it to his father to square it with his mother. But they both knew that this would be the most difficult and delicate counteraction his father had ever undertaken, and it would need to be accomplished in such a way that it could never be reversed, even after—God forbid—his father's eventual demise, which he hoped was a long way off. He also hoped his father was equal to this task.

"You know something funny?" asked Erica of the table at large. "I know our two families have been involved in business for years, but I've never really known exactly what your family's business is."

This unfortunate declaration was such a total breach of all unwritten rules of polite conversation that it was instantly ignored as the babbling of an idiot girl. Erica had now so clearly shown herself to be someone who should not—indeed, better not—be taken seriously as an intelligent adult, that no one even bothered to offer a reply or register the shock caused by her remark. Mrs. Whitmire instructed Harry to begin clearing the table, though several guests had just received second helpings, and told her daughter to go prepare the boys for the arrival of the cake. The only time during the evening the boys were allowed into the dining room was when the candles were lit, "Happy Birthday" was sung and the cake was sliced. They would be given their pieces on melamine dishware sporting cartoon characters they'd stopped watching years ago, and the sitter would shepherd them back to the den, where they could actually eat the cake. Erica's untoward utterance was banished from the room by all the bustle, which served as the only response she was going to get to her perfectly legitimate but thoroughly gauche observation. Valerie rose from the table, Lois was brought in from the kitchen to help Harry clear the dishes, and Ham and Mark proceeded to plow through their second helpings of barbecued chicken without the silverware or the table manners normally expected.

Poor Erica could never have guessed that the reason her question was so rude was because most of those she had asked didn't know the answer. She had assumed that the family knew what its own family business was, when in fact, Ham himself had only the vaguest idea what the family business was, and had always had the impression that this so-called family business was itself only a vague and amorphous concept involving "real estate holdings." As far as Ham had been able to determine, his father simply managed commercial properties that had been bequeathed to him by his own father. Once when he was twelve or thirteen, his parents had taken him downtown to dinner at John's Restaurant. On the way there, his mother had pointed out a large red-brick building and the sign **Whitmire Realty** affixed to one side. This was an apartment building owned by the family, she explained. Ever since, this boring, ordinary building had become the image associated in his mind with what his mother liked to call "the family business." As for what his father actually did, Ham really had no idea, despite having taken the usual tours of his dad's office when he was a boy. His father's actual responsibilities seemed to consist primarily of simply being there at the office, where there were several employees who performed any actual work. Apparently, his father made a lot of money not because of any work he did there, but because Ham's grandfather had bought several strategic parcels of land in downtown Birmingham during the Depression. At any rate, this was the explanation Ham's father had given him, and it was reinforced by his mother, who tended to regard her husband's office as the place where he went to avoid doing the things she needed him to do at home. All during Ham's boyhood and indeed up until his health troubles began, his father was in the habit of going to his office on Saturdays, which his mother thought was absolutely, outrageously irresponsible of him; and he often didn't get home on weekday evenings until seven, which she regarded as a deliberate slap in the face. Although Ham knew early on he never wanted to spend his life in an office like his dad's, as a boy he often wished he, too, had a place where he could go and get away from his mother.

As Ham reluctantly relinquished his dinner plate to Harry and accepted a dessert plate in its stead, he chanced a glimpse at Erica, fidgeting beside him in her chair. Her right hand twisted her wineglass around and around on the table as she had earlier twisted one of the buttons on her blouse. Her gaze appeared to be occupied by a small blob of barbecue sauce on the white table-cloth. She showed no inclination to exchange glances with him or exchange words with anyone for the rest of the evening, as if she knew she had failed and had resolved not to risk further failure which would no doubt be communicated to her mother, at least through the absence of favorable commentary on her presence or any future invitations, if not from an outright account of her shortcomings, which his mother was fully capable of delivering. He felt sorry for her, and stole another glance, hoping she would turn her head in his direction.

It was rare for him to feel that someone else had been more awkward than he at his mother's table. Of course, there was nothing objectively wrong with anything Erica had said or done. But where they were had nothing to do with objective reality; they were in Mountain Brook, which had been deliberately designed from its very inception in the 1920s to be a refuge from reality, or certain harsh realities of life in Birmingham, like steel mills and the black people who worked in them. In order to preserve this carefully constructed alternate universe, there were all sorts of codes and rules which were unwritten and seldom articulated. You were expected to know them and follow them even as they varied from one household or situation to another. He himself had never been very good at this, and the many years he'd lived away from home had made him even worse. But one strategy for survival he'd learned early was quite simple and easy to follow: Never say what's really on your mind or what you really think, and never express how you really feel. In fact, say as little as possible. The less said, the less the risk of making a faux pas. How she had survived in Mountain Brook without learning these lessons, he did not know. Perhaps she thought she needed to emulate her mother and sister, who did nothing but run their mouths; however, she did not possess their talent for transforming gossip and idle chatter into a Broadway show. Nor did she have the fallback that even he enjoyed, of discussing sports with other men, like his father and brother-in-law had done earlier in the evening. In sports there were plenty of simple definites and absolutes, and it was easy to participate in the exchange of received ideas: a 56-yard field goal attempt was ridiculous; an 80 yard touchdown run was a thing of beauty.

After the cake, the coffee, and the departure of his sister's family, he offered to walk Erica out to her car, not only because he still felt sorry for her, but because it would enable him to make his own getaway and avoid his mother's brutal postmortem of the occasion, which would spare no one but herself. Erica had remained subdued for the rest of the evening and seemed only too glad to seize this chance of escape. He was equally eager to leave, though he did have a nagging feeling that he ought to say something more to Patrice out of deference to the fact that she was both his student and Harry's granddaughter. But what should he say? He couldn't think of anything that wasn't hopelessly lame or possibly inappropriate. This was actually the same trouble he had with everyone in any situation, including the current moment, when he emerged alone with Erica on the walkway leading from the front door of his house.

Erica was the one to break the silence. "I don't think your mother likes me very much," she said.

"That's okay," he assured her. "I don't think she likes me very much either."

The laugh she gave was like the release of all the oral energy she had suppressed during the latter half of the evening. Emboldened, he added, "I don't think there's anybody my mother likes very much." Though she did not repeat her laugh, she was clearly amused and encouraged by what he said. When they reached her car parked at the curb, she turned to him. There was obviously something on her mind she was determined to say, but as soon as she faced him, her courage began to drain out of her face. She stammered something he couldn't make out and began pushing at her bangs.

"I-I'd really like to get together with you," she managed finally. "I know you've recently come back, and I-I'd like to compare notes. If-if you ever have any free time. If you're not too busy."

"Sure," he said. "Any time." The idea had not occurred to him, but he had no objection to it. He had always liked Erica Cooley, and if he could help her arrive at the sense of future direction that had so far eluded his own life, he was happy to try, though he didn't know how he could be of much assistance. She stood there waiting as if something more needed to be said and fumbled behind her for the door handle. Was he supposed to open the door for her? He was always forgetting his manners. Across the way, laughter erupted from the porte cochere of the country club, where some big event had evidently just concluded.

"I guess," she faltered. "Should I call you sometime? Is your number in the phone book?"

"Oh," he said, suddenly realizing his duties. "I'll call you. Sometime next week, maybe?"

She nodded, a bit unhappily he thought, probably because she doubted his ability to procure her telephone number and actually place the call. As if to prove himself, he reached beyond her to open the door of her car. It was locked, which was obviously why it hadn't opened earlier during her own attempts at it. Apologetically, she rummaged through her purse at length, finally producing her keys, and then, as if to make up for all this wasted time, quickly opened the door for herself, got in the front seat and drove off with a brief wave of her hand. He could only hope, as always after an encounter with another member of the human race, that he had not made too much of an ass out of himself.

Instead of going immediately to his own car, he remained for several minutes at the curb of Country Club Road, gazing across at the Birmingham Country Club, where laughter still rang out from the crowd of well-dressed guests waiting for the valets to bring their cars from the parking spaces only a few feet away from where they all stood. (But, as his sister had once remarked, the tips given to the valets were one of the few ways people in Mountain Brook redistributed some of their wealth to those less fortunate.) The club had always evoked longing in him, especially as a boy, when he used to pester his mother endlessly about why he couldn't go there. It was right across the street, and held out the promise of good times such as he had never known as a child.

"We don't belong there," she had told him.

"Why not?"

"We belong to the Mountain Brook Club."

"Why can't we belong to this one? It's right across from our house. I could go there by myself. Please."

"The Whitmire family will never be members of the Birmingham Country Club."

"But why not?"

"They let anybody and everybody into that club," she had explained. "Be thankful that your family belongs to the Mountain Brook Club." Often she would use this opportunity to remind him of another important difference between the two institutions: One place was called the Birmingham Country Club, whereas the other was the Mountain Brook Club. "Never call it the Mountain Brook Country Club," she admonished him, as if that mistake would call into question his status as an elite insider, the crème de la crème.

But as a kid, he had other concerns on his mind. Going to the Mountain Brook Club entailed a ten minute car ride, which his mother could rarely be prevailed upon to provide, especially because she would never agree to leave him there alone like some "hooligan" child. Plus, the swimming pool was much smaller and the French fries were not nearly as good as those at the Birmingham Club. As for anybody and everybody belonging to the Birmingham Country Club—that was another of the reasons he preferred it. The parents of most of his classmates were members there, and whenever he went as their guest, he always encountered many more from his school splashing happily in the huge pool. At the Mountain Brook, the pool was usually only half-full with much younger children, and during the day, the most frequent new arrivals were old ladies coming to play bridge. The only thing the Mountain Brook Club had more of was its own exclusiveness. Obviously this meant a lot to his mother, but he would have opted for the better French fries and the bigger pool containing more of his classmates.

Even as he grew older, he still didn't understand why anyone wouldn't want to belong to the club with better French fries, and remained baffled by the distinction his mother drew between the two clubs. As for letting "anybody and everybody" join, the Birmingham Country Club had a seven year waiting list for prospective members, who could not be black, Jewish, or even Catholic, though a few exceptions were sometimes made in the latter category, as long as the last name did not end with an active vowel. Newly accepted members had to pay tens of thousands of dollars for the privilege. The Percy family, which had built the house now occupied by his own family, had been members of the Birmingham Country Club. Walker Percy's father had even been president of this club. There was a photograph of him in the portrait gallery of past presidents lining the corridor leading to the main dining room. Wasn't that good enough for his mother?

Eventually he had appealed to his grandmother, who was one of about two people with any influence over his mother's opinion. From her he learned that the original difference in the two clubs had nothing to do with membership but with architecture. When the Birmingham Country Club was being built in the 1920s, a majority of its members wanted a stone clubhouse in the style of an English country manor. The minority who preferred a white columned colonial in the style of an Old South plantation mansion had left to form their own club, which became the Mountain Brook Club. This struck him as powerful ammunition. An Old South plantation mansion was no more authentic or proper a representation of Birmingham's heritage than an English country manor. Therefore, members of the Mountain Brook Club had no right to claim superiority of any kind. He had passionately argued his case, but to no avail.

Back then he had been possessed by the belief that if he could just join that club, he could join the group, the human race that everybody else belonged to. But it was to remain forever out of the reach of his daily grasp, accessible only on special occasions when his mother consented to the invitation from another parent, usually for a birthday party. It never ceased to be a symbol, a potent reminder like it was tonight, that somewhere close by, though out of his league, other people were laughing and having a good time. Other people were enjoying themselves, each other, and their lives. This did not happen in his own household; this was not to be his fate. But happiness and joy were possible for some people, and perhaps could be for himself as well, if only he could come up with the key to this realm, to a destiny different from the one marked out for him.

As he drove off, this old hope flared within him like it always had whenever the murmur of laughter and good times drifted across from the club. He didn't really believe or trust in this hope anymore: he had long since begun to think the hope was as false as no doubt the laughter was, generated by artificial personalities like Mrs. Cooley, who herself was fueled by nothing but ego and alcohol. Still, he couldn't stop this hope from shooting through his limbs like waves of desire for a contentment he had never known and of which he had no proof.

~ 3 ~

On Thursday afternoon, Ham waited for Ivy Greer in a nondescript coffee shop downtown near the medical center that catered to busy residents and physicians who needed to grab a quick jolt of caffeine and head back to the hospital. The place had neither atmosphere nor very good coffee. There were a few obligatory tables and chairs, but no one ever sat and lingered over a book, a newspaper, or a conversation. Unlike the charming and idiosyncratic cafés in the college town where he had gone to school, this was not the kind of place where an eclectic mix of people brought their laptops, parked themselves for half a day and created an informal little intellectual salon. This place was strictly business: get your goods and go. The tables served mainly as places to cream and sugar your coffee before you headed out the door. Over the course of the day, these tables became littered with empty pink Sweet-n-Low packets and miniature cartons of half-and-half, along with soiled plastic spoons and napkins which were rarely cleared. The glaring overhead lights were like those in the exam rooms the doctors were going back to with their coffee, and the constant stream of customers coming in and going right back out the noisy front door was not conducive to a quiet or lengthy tête-à-tête. But these were all virtues in Ham's perverse perspective. The main virtue was the unlikelihood of running into anyone he knew. Also, the shop was located near his therapist's office, where he would be going to his weekly Thursday appointment after his meeting with Ivy Greer. And as for that meeting, he hoped the fluorescent non-atmosphere of the place would keep it as brief as possible.

As he waited, he could feel adrenaline shooting in fits and starts through his system. Resentment began to surge with it, because normally on Tuesdays and Thursdays, when he taught no classes and didn't even go to the campus, he could remain free of this kind of stress. He had not wanted to agree to this meeting, but that "I really do need to talk to you" business had continued to worry him, especially when he remembered the contents of one of the memos he'd retrieved from his mail slot on Monday. Apparently a plan was in the works to have all faculty members evaluated not just in surprise visits by administrators, but also by departmental colleagues, who were supposed to produce at least half a dozen "constructive criticisms," along with an equal number of "affirmations." It occurred to him that Ivy had never explained what she was doing in his classroom in the first place on Monday morning. Could it be that she'd been there to evaluate him after all, just like he'd feared?

Although he was watching the door for her arrival with some anxiety, he must have become lost in thought, because all of a sudden she was at his table with a cup of coffee in hand.

"Aren't you going to get anything?" she asked.

He stared down at his empty place. Typically, he had forgotten to supply himself with the necessary prop. "Just wanted to save us a seat," he said with a tight smile, painfully aware that every other table except the one where he was sitting was unoccupied. She smiled as if at a good joke, which proved he could only be funny when he wasn't trying to be. When he returned with his own mug, he was dismayed to see her settling in at the table, arranging a large 3-ring binder in front of her and stowing her leather bag underneath the chair. The scenario had the definite look of "evaluation" about it. His mouth suddenly flooded with the taste of metal, and unfortunately, he had left his Tums in the car.

"Uh, hey," he said gracelessly, forgetting in his nervousness both his vocabulary as well as his cup, which sloshed coffee when he sat down at the table. "I—ah—forgot to ask what brought you into my classroom the other day. I understand we're all supposed to start evaluating each other, and . . ." his voice trailed off, afraid of going any further with these uncomfortable thoughts.

"Yes, I do want to talk to you about that," she said briskly, crumpling the napkin she'd used to wipe up his spilled coffee. "I don't know what your opinion is, but I was appalled." She started flipping through her binder.

His worst fears were being realized, and his throat constricted to the point where speech was impossible.

"So what *did* you think about it?" She looked up at him.

"About . . . about . . ." was all he could manage.

"About the plan for us to evaluate each other," she said impatiently, as if he were the cretin he felt like. When his eyes followed the tapping of her pen, he saw it was beating down rather fiercely at the very memo which had announced this evaluation plan. It took a moment for him to realize that her disgust was directed at the idea of evaluating her colleagues rather than at any evaluation she had made of him. It took a moment more for his muscles to relax and allow the flow of speech.

"I had greater hopes for our so-called paper shortage," he said. "I'd hoped it would curb some of these administrative enthusiasms."

"I haven't yet decided how I'm going to handle it," she mused, tapping her pen now against her chin. "Whether I'm simply going to refuse to participate, or actually protest the whole idea. What are you going to do?" She looked piercingly at him while taking a tentative sip of her coffee.

"Perhaps there's a way to do both while appearing to comply," he said boldly, hoping to impress her. She looked at him expectantly and took another sip of coffee. "We could make all the visits and hand in the evaluations, but do so in such a way that none of our colleagues are the worse for wear and the administration is none the wiser."

This would be, of course, the instinctive strategy of everyone else in the department, including himself. Most of his colleagues were easygoing black women of a certain age who enjoyed each other's company and wouldn't dream of causing discomfort to the others any more than they wanted such discomfort for themselves. He had grown quite fond of these women, who treated him like a little pet with warm, motherly familiarity. In this way, Cahaba College was a stark—and welcome—contrast to the academic world he had come from. He was never asked what he was "working on," but when he was going to get married. Just the other day, one of his colleagues had said to him: "Did you know—you are just the cutest thing? When are you going to get married and make some lucky girl happy? You remind me of that white guy in the movie just came out. You know which one I'm talking about? You know that short guy?" In many ways he felt fortunate to be where he was: he could never have made it in one of those places where everyone was competing to get published and get tenured. It was one thing to be a student seeking knowledge at a place like that; quite another matter to be a professor seeking tenure at a place like that. He wanted no part of that struggle. Here there was nothing to fear from being "evaluated" by his current colleagues. "Constructive criticism" would amount to helpful suggestions about trying assigned seating arrangements and pre-printed attendance rosters. The evaluation forms they handed in would contain smiley faces, stray popcorn kernels, and accidental dabs of Red Lacquer nail polish.

Ivy Greer replaced her mug with an angry bang on the table. "Yes," she said bitterly. "The slaves' resistance."

"I'm sorry?" he said, taken aback at her reaction. (It never paid to forget that he could no more impress other people when he was trying to than he could make them laugh when he was trying to.)

"Slaves didn't have a choice about whether or not to follow a master's orders," she explained in a sarcastic third-grade teacher's voice. "But they could choose to perform their work slowly and poorly. This has remained one of the black responses to authority and power."

Suddenly an image popped into his head of his family's maid, Lois, who had not been given a raise in fifteen years, if his mother could be believed. But during the course of an eight hour day at his parents' house, Lois performed about three desultory hours of work, ate three full meals, and regularly took home leftovers, cast-off clothing, worn-out appliances and discarded electronics. In return, his mother derived the satisfaction of maintaining her sense of racial superiority and complaining witheringly about the quality of her "worthless" help. And then, of course, she had Harry, who actually did most of the work.

"It may be okay for you as a white male at a black institution," she said fiercely. "And it may be okay for the *church ladies,*" she said with disdain.

"Who?"

"Our *colleagues,*" she said, with even more contempt.

She opened her binder and began flipping through it. Although it appeared she had not been evaluating his class on Monday, he could not stop his heart from racing at the sight of this heavy-duty administrative equipment. As she continued to turn the pages, he realized with dawning amazement that it contained what must have been every single memo and the minutes from every single meeting so far this semester. To him these pieces of paper were like cancerous cells which he avoided until they had formed a tumor in his mail slot which he had to surgically remove, as he had done Monday morning. And as promptly as he could, he disposed of it like medical waste which belonged only in the nearest incinerator. She, on the other hand, had saved every scrap, punched holes in every scrap, and had arranged these scraps in what was no doubt chronological order in her 3-ring binder. It was also no doubt a damning record of administrative inanity, a small masterpiece in and of itself depicting the horrors of bureaucratic administrations. He was unable to confront it, let alone have it in his house or carry it around with him as she appeared to do.

"Two of our colleagues are retired high school teachers," she said, looking up at him from the page which was giving her this information. "One is a speech therapist. Another used to be a social worker. And yet another," she narrowed her eyes, "was a *receptionist* at an advertising agency." She paused to let this register. "None of them even has a master's degree."

"What about the chairman? The—ah—chair*person,* I mean."

"All right," Ivy conceded unwillingly. "I'll grant you—she *does* have a master's degree. But it's in *elementary education!* She makes the perfect pawn for the administration."

She looked at him, obviously expecting something; he wasn't sure what.

"Well?" she demanded.

"Well what?" he said nervously.

She closed the binder back with a bang.

"Well I'll be damned if I'm going to behave in such a retrograde, passive-aggressive fashion!" she declared. "As to *evaluate* my colleagues as you suggest! And I'm not going to participate in something I don't believe in!"

He could only nod, afraid to open his mouth and reveal more of the cowardice that prevented him from standing up for his own principles, one of which she had just articulated: about not participating in something you couldn't believe in. Unfortunately for him, he had a hard time believing in anything at all, including the world around him and life itself. So his participation in both was extremely minimal.

"Look," she said, staring at him accusingly and thumping her middle finger against the handle of her coffee cup. "There's a lot of shit about to come down the pipe. The school's going to have to get its act together; changes are going to have to be made. But this is not the way to do it. Incompetent, unqualified teachers don't need to be *evaluated by each other.* They need to be *fired.*" She shook her head.

Speaking of shit coming down the pipe, he could feel that very thing happening to him at the moment. How could he have been so careless as to forget what coffee would do to him and actually take a sip from his cup? He loved coffee and couldn't do without it, but for the past few years had been forced to rise no later than five so he could both enjoy his coffee and deal with the ensuing side effects before heading to work. He shifted uneasily in his seat.

"It's no secret the school has been struggling for years," she continued, either oblivious to his squirms or choosing to ignore them. "Even before this bad news about the teachers we graduate, there's been talk of merging Cahaba College with that four-year degree program up there in Cullman." Her chest heaved once to emit a sardonic hiss of something like laughter. "You know as well as I do, that if Cahaba College is '*merged*' with that school up there in that all-white county, it's just a way for the white boys in Montgomery to shut us down."

"Would you excuse me?" he said desperately, rising abruptly from the table and bee-lining toward the rear of the building, where he assumed the restrooms were located. In the course of his mad dash, Ivy Greer's wasn't the only startled face he noticed. Another familiar face leaped out at him from the blur of faces waiting in line as he passed by. When he arrived gratefully at the empty stall in the equally empty men's room, he realized it was the face of his sister. So much for not running into anyone he knew: he was always underestimating how small this town was.

* * *

Given the length of time he had to remain in the bathroom, he hoped that if his sister had likewise recognized him, she would have departed the shop by the time he returned to the table. The white lab coat she was still wearing suggested she had stepped out for a quick cup of coffee between patient visits and needed to get back immediately. And for all he knew, Ivy Greer might have left as well. It had been a particularly brutal episode in the bathroom. Of course, all the ones occurring in public places rather than the privacy of his apartment seemed that way. According to his doctor, some people with an irritable bowel had to quit their jobs and couldn't even maintain a social life. He could at least be thankful that his case wasn't so bad—yet. Thankful? his therapist had quizzed him. Or would you prefer to have a disabling condition which gave you license to remain more or less confined to your apartment? She had caught him off guard, because he couldn't deny that he had always sort of envied the writer Walker Percy's "luck" in contracting the tuberculosis which de-railed his medical career while launching him into another career as a reader of philosophy and literature and a writer of some very fine novels, a few of them even set in their mutual hometown of Birmingham, Alabama. On the other hand, if he himself had been capable of pursing a medical career—if he had possessed the ability to perform any sort of heroic deeds or labor—perhaps he wouldn't have needed an out.

"I'd prefer a more pleasant disabling condition," he had quipped in Lauren's office, but she hadn't even cracked a smile. Although she had not gone so far as to suggest that his condition was psychosomatic, she did point out the "metaphorical implications" of having a physical problem which dovetailed so conveniently with his emotional proclivities. However, much as he admired her ability to spot a metaphor, there was nothing metaphorical about what had just happened in the bathroom.

When he finally emerged, his stomach lurched in a different way as he saw that his sister was not only still in the coffee shop, but engrossed in conversation with his colleague Ivy Greer. She was standing with her Styrofoam cup of coffee facing the rear of the building where she could not fail to see him as soon as he reappeared. Though his first instinct was to duck back into the bathroom and wait for his sister to hurry off to her next appointment, he knew he was stuck when she raised her eyes briefly to meet his, precisely in order to forestall his avoidant behavior. He had no choice but to join the two women, who had moved far beyond introducing themselves to one another and appeared to be exchanging their life stories in that amazing way that two total strangers could do if they were both female. No doubt they knew more about each other now than he could hope to learn in his lifetime. He sat down laughing gently at his own joke, while his sister looked over at him as if he needed to be on medication, which was indeed her professional opinion.

Fortunately, she was good about keeping her own counsel, and he could trust that she would neither pry into his nonexistent affairs nor relay to their mother any tidbits of information which would inevitably be misconstrued. Still, he felt put on the spot in some way, although his sister showed no inclination to greet him beyond that quick exchange of glances as he sat back down. Instead, she was busy learning that his colleague Ivy Greer had grown up in the community of Fairfield where Cahaba College was located; had attended Spelman College in Atlanta on scholarship; had earned her doctorate at the University of Alabama in Tuscaloosa; and had accepted a position at Cahaba College because her father, a retired factory hand from Fairfield Works of U.S. Steel, was dying of cancer. Her mother, it appeared, was a teacher and administrator at Ramsay, which he believed was in the inner city of Birmingham.

Unfortunately, he knew little about the city beyond the enclave where he had grown up, which was as far away from black Birmingham as white city planners and developers could make it. As a post-Civil War industrial city, Birmingham was a product of the Jim Crow South; its white and black people inhabited completely different worlds, which were far apart geographically as well as culturally, and never came in contact. Black people entered the white world of Birmingham only as maids, yardmen and waiters at the country club. White people like himself never entered the black world of Birmingham. The fact that he had done so was a sheer accidental by-product of his need to be shielded from his mother's beck and call now that he was back in Birmingham. The location of his job allowed him to insist on living downtown, which was close enough to the campus in Fairfield and far beyond the usual path his mother traversed in Mountain Brook. The daily demands of this job conferred a certain amount of immunity against the daily demands of his mother. And basically, the precarious state of his mental health required a daily structure or routine that got him "out of the house" and "out of himself."

Only in departure did his sister turn to him. "We'll see you at practice this afternoon?" she asked, referring to his nephews' soccer teams that he assisted his brother-in-law with coaching. That and the Little League baseball season in the spring were the highlights of his current existence, such as it was.

He watched his sister exit the shop and turned back around to find Ivy Greer's head cocked at him. "So your sister works at the health department, and you teach at a black college?" There was a gleam of amusement in her eyes.

He shrugged in embarrassment, hoping he wasn't about to be mistaken again for devoting his life to charitable mission work. He didn't know which was worse: being taken for a racist, or being taken for a liberal do-gooder. At least if Ivy wrote him off as a racist, then nothing would be expected of him.

"But you grew up in Birmingham?"

He nodded.

"Let me guess," she said. "Your parents are not from around here. They're both physicians—or at least, one of them is—and came here to take a job at UAB. You grew up in Forest Park."

Ham coughed, cleared his throat, and hoped this could pass for a response.

"What was that?" she persisted. "Where did you say you grew up?"

Coughing again, he tried to obscure the words "Mountain Brook."

"Mountain Brook?" she stared at him dumbfounded. "You're telling me you're a Brookie?"

A Jewish person could hardly have invested more disgust into the word "Nazi."

Gritting his teeth, he inclined his head once, very briefly.

"You're serious?"

He nodded again ever so slightly and glanced beyond her at nothing.

"Well, that's cool," she said, lifting her palms from the table as if offering a gesture of peace. "So what is this for you, then: teaching at a black college? White guilt?"

He shook his head.

"Come on," she leaned across the table toward him. "You can't tell me it's just a job for you."

That's what it was. It was just a job.

"And it can't be just by accident that a white man—a Brookie, of all things—ends up at a struggling black teacher's college."

That's what it was—an accident.

"I heard you went to Harvard," she said. To his enormous relief, she leaned back in her chair. "Is that right?"

He nodded.

"So you must have come back here to help lift up your hometown. Isn't that what Harvard's all about? Isn't that their mission—to educate people who are going to go out and make the world a better place for everybody else?"

He had to think about that one. Did Harvard even have a mission? Besides the mission of any institution to perpetuate and aggrandize itself? Ideally, he supposed, if Harvard had a purpose beyond itself, it should have been to challenge its students to fulfill a purpose beyond *themselves*—to use their supposedly world-class education for the world's betterment. But in the decade he'd spent at Harvard, most students he'd encountered—even in the English Department—had mainly been preoccupied with their own advancement. That's how they'd gotten into Harvard in the first place. From an early age, their own personal mission had been to advance themselves, and Harvard was not their ultimate destination, but only a plateau they must reach first before climbing to other heights. And if they'd come from some backward hometown like he had, they didn't dream of going back there. Going back to a backward place was not their definition of advancement. Their definition involved making life a better experience for themselves, not making the world a better place for others. Who cared about the rest of the world?

"Well?" she raised her eyebrows.

He shrugged, hoping this reply would suffice like it often did for him.

"Are you being modest?"

"No," he said quickly, happy to be able to answer honestly while also uttering a word.

Out of the corner of his eye, he could see the server behind the counter make his way into the open seating area, which was now empty except for their table. The mid-afternoon crush was over, and no one was waiting in line for coffee at the moment. With noisy speed the clerk began seizing handfuls of debris cluttering the empty tables and piling it on a tray. When he glanced surreptitiously at Ham and Ivy, he caught Ham's eye.

"You're good; you're good. Don't worry," he grinned. "Take your time."

Ham's cheeks began to burn. He wondered if the café server suspected he was witnessing a romantic encounter. Did Ham look like such a loser that he'd pick this place to have one?

"Look," said Ivy, leaning across the table again and lowering her voice for an urgent, intimate communication. "I'm not going to be offended if you tell me you're here to help lift up Birmingham's black people or help save the college. That's what you *better* be here for. That's what I *need* you to be here for. I'm counting on it. You're the only other person in the department who even has a doctorate. When I heard it came from Harvard, and then heard your lecture the other day. . . . I knew I'd found the person who was going to help me. Even if you *are* a Brookie."

Panic squeezed his chest. This was worse than his mother declaring that he was going to take over the family business. At least with her, he had his father to help get him out of it. Now it was up to him alone to set Ivy straight. He had to do so immediately, before she placed any more demands on him. He couldn't take it. He literally could not handle it.

"I don't think I'm the person you want," he told her.

"You're exactly the person I want!" she insisted emphatically.

Behind her back, the server winked at Ham and gave him a thumbs-up gesture over a tray piled high with coffee shop clutter.

"A Brookie with a Harvard degree," she went on. "The more I think about it, the more I see how perfect it is. You don't need to save yourself. You're already saved. You can start saving the world, a little bit at a time. Cahaba College is a good place to start."

"You don't understand," he said.

"If anybody in this town can *afford* to care about something other than their own survival, it's someone from Mountain Brook."

On the contrary, his own survival took up all his time, and even then, he didn't do a very good job of it. How could he convince her? He decided to shift tactics.

"What exactly are you proposing?" he glanced at his watch, which wasn't there. He hoped the gesture might help bring this meeting to a conclusion anyway. "What is it you think we can do? I wouldn't even know where to start."

"I think we have to start at the beginning," she said. "We have to face facts and accept the unpleasant truth that the ground we thought we were walking on is simply not there. What we've got to do first of all is to lay that groundwork."

"What does this mean?"

"We have to start teaching some folks how to read and write," she said. "For real."

~ 4 ~

Ham hurried through the two blocks from the coffee shop to the building where his therapist had her office, not only because he was late for the appointment, but because he was desperate to talk to her after his encounter with Ivy Greer. Ever since meeting his new colleague on Monday, his anxiety level had noticeably spiked. Monday's memo, the confrontation with the chairman, and the dinner party at his parents' hadn't helped either. He hadn't exactly had trouble getting out of bed in the morning, but when his alarm rang at 5:30, he went back to sleep until seven instead of drinking coffee and reading Shakespeare for an hour and a half. At seven he showered, drank a cup of herbal tea and prepared to leave for work. He had not yet been late. But on Tuesday and today, when he had not taught any classes, he had slept till eight. Did this new pattern constitute one of the warning signs he'd been told to look for? Perhaps it wouldn't be long before he couldn't get out of bed at all. Was the crash that he and many others had feared after he left Massachusetts, where he'd lived for over a decade, about to occur? If so, he could not get to his therapist's office fast enough, and did not want to waste a minute of his appointment time.

But as soon as he was seated before his therapist in the cool quiet of her office, he suddenly lost all inclination to talk and didn't know what to say. Lauren wasn't about to help him get started, either, as she waited calmly for him to begin without even commenting on his breathlessness or obvious agitation. True to traditional therapy practice, Lauren expected him to arrive charged with a purposeful agenda, and to eagerly initiate each session's discussion. It took him hours of careful planning and preparation to execute this approach, which was utterly out of keeping with his personality and psychological temperament, which she was supposedly treating. Nonetheless, she still insisted on it. After his meeting with Ivy, however, he had forgotten his planned opening monologue, and simply wanted to unburden himself. But spontaneity was not one of his strengths or even part of his personality.

He cleared his throat. "I think I'm in trouble," was all he could manage before he felt his throat closing up on him.

Fortunately, this was enough to activate his therapist, who began to pull it all out of him, question after question.

"I might as well quit my job now," he concluded.

"Well, why don't you?" she said calmly.

He was taken aback. No doubt he had expressed himself badly and given such a garbled narrative that he'd made it impossible for her to offer the sympathy he had expected. Still, her bald suggestion indicated a callous disregard for all their previous sessions, in which they had examined in minute detail all the reasons he had ended up where he was today. Asking him to upend all that and change course so abruptly demonstrated that either she didn't really care about his fate or didn't really comprehend his troubles. And instead of making things better, she was making them worse.

"If you think the work you're being asked to do is not worthy of your time or abilities," she continued, "I don't see that you have much choice." She paused to give him a chance to respond. All he could do was spread his hands in a gesture of helplessness.

"As I understand it," she went on, "your whole adult life has been haunted by the need to find positive meaning in everything you do. This is why you've never wanted to step into your father's shoes. He just manages an office for a business that runs itself and collects rent from the properties he owns. Early on you decided this work wasn't capable of generating the meaning you require from your life. You didn't think the practice of law would be any better, so you didn't see the point of finishing your law degree. Now in your academic career, you're being asked to do something 'absurd,' as you put it. Is there any alternative but for you to stop what you're doing and go back to your original search for an occupation that provides the meaning you desire?"

He felt challenged on too many fronts all at once and didn't know how to respond adequately. In fact, he was overwhelmed. "Did I say 'absurd'?"

She referred to the notebook on her lap and ran a pencil down the lines on the page. "Absurd," she affirmed, nodding her head and tapping with her pencil, presumably on the line where the word was written. "'It's absurd for her to expect me to teach these students grammar and spelling,'" she quoted to him.

He winced as if she'd struck a blow. "I don't mean that it's absurd for these students to be taught grammar and spelling," he assured her.

She inclined her head sympathetically. "You just don't want to be the one expected to do it," she said.

Was she ridiculing or reproaching him? He couldn't tell. Her voice had been absolutely inflectionless.

"It's like all menial work," she added. "We believe it ought to be done, but by someone other than ourselves."

Again he found himself at a loss for a reply, oddly unprepared and even unwilling to enter into a philosophical discussion of the topic she'd raised. Afraid that his allotted hour was approaching its end, he wanted to achieve some concrete resolution for himself, not wander off into theoretical discussions of abstract issues.

"Let me get this right," she said, shifting in her seat and re-crossing her legs. "From what you've told me, it sounds as if the college where you're teaching is not much more than a diploma mill, granting degrees which will enable unqualified individuals to obtain jobs in the public school system, where they will not be teaching their students what they need to know. Instead, they will be perpetuating the problems of their own people."

He started to object—he had certainly never used the phrase "diploma mill," nor had he ever thought of the school in such brutal terms. But she raised her palms as if to stem the flow of any objections.

"Now don't get me wrong," she said. "I don't mean to be disrespectful of what you call your search for meaning or your insistence that any job you undertake have a certain purity or nobility of purpose. But how does what you're doing pass your own smell test? How is it any better than working for a corporation that makes junk food, or a law firm that defends insurance companies trying to dodge their obligations? Just to use your own examples from previous sessions."

He stared at her. She was right, of course. It was all absurd and hopeless, starting with his own miserable existence. He put his head in his hands and stared glumly at the floor.

"What can I do?" he moaned. Thinking he was speaking to himself, and raising a rhetorical, existential question for which there was no reply, he was astonished when Lauren had an answer ready.

"Why don't you at least try doing what your colleague has suggested?" she said.

"What are you talking about?" he said.

"What were *you* talking about?" she retorted with impatience. "Saving the college. Saving the students there."

All he could do was stare at her.

"What's wrong with that?" she challenged him defiantly. "Surely there's meaning in that."

"Sure there is. But that's a job for a superhero. I'm just a pathetic human. I wouldn't know how to undertake a mission like that. I wouldn't know how to begin."

"Well," she said, suppressing a smile. "Since none of us are superheroes, and we're all just pathetically human, you're as qualified as anyone else for the job. What is a hero after all but someone who steps in and does what needs to be done? And it's like your colleague said: You do it one step at a time. Maybe even one student at a time. Like that student you went to bat for yesterday."

He hoped he had not spoken of going "to bat for" anyone, especially as it hardly characterized his encounter with Mrs. Cooke about Tameika, which still puzzled him. Why Mrs. Cooke had so adamantly opposed Tameika's switch from the Education to the English curriculum, he had no idea. Coward that he was, he had assured the irate Mrs. Cooke, ranting on and on about Tameika being the best Education student of her class, that he had never suggested or even really wanted Tameika to change her major. Mrs. Cooke had calmed down a bit and seemed somewhat mollified. Then he had simply inquired whether faculty members or a student's advisor had the authority to dictate or deny a student's change of major. This was a sincere and simple request for information. But somehow it had served to infuriate Mrs. Cooke all over again. On the verge of another angry outburst, she had suddenly clammed up and seethed with barely restrained fury. What had he done and why was she so mad at him?

"Is there something I don't know?" he'd asked her. "Is it against school policy for a student to change her major in her senior year?"

Instead of responding, Mrs. Cooke had stormed out of his office, saying only, "Okay. You win." The next day, Tameika had showered him with gratitude, as if he'd fought and won some major battle on her behalf. If he had done so, it had been purely accidental. He had been trying to avoid any conflict with Mrs. Cooke, not win it. He still didn't understand what had happened or the exact role he'd played in it. The whole episode was inscrutable to him.

"I don't know that I went 'to bat' for anybody," he told his therapist.

"Well you stood up to the chairman of the Education Department," she informed him proudly.

"I did?" He was astounded. He hadn't had the slightest intention of standing up to Mrs. Cooke, or the slightest awareness that he'd actually done so.

"Clearly the head of Education did not want to lose her star pupil at a time when the department is being forced to prove itself and send competent graduates into the public school system."

Obviously Lauren understood a lot more than he did. He'd simply been gratified that a student in his class wanted to go further with her education, and naïvely assumed that any other faculty member would encourage a student's higher aspirations. Wasn't that the goal of higher education? He'd been oblivious to the politics of the situation. If he had been more aware, he no doubt would have behaved in his usual craven and cowardly fashion, and failed to "go to bat for" Tameika Young.

Lauren looked at her watch and rose quickly up out of her chair.

"I'm sorry," she said. "I'm afraid we're five minutes over time and I've got another appointment right after you. But there's just one other thought I'd like to leave you with. Let me put this as a question." She paused to formulate it. "Do you think it's possible you could be going about your search—this search for meaning—in the wrong way?"

"I must be," he said. "Seeing as how I keep arriving at one dead end after another."

She ignored his sarcasm and seized on his admission of failure. "Yes," she said. "I think you may be attempting to find meaning in the wrong way."

"How else do you try to do something meaningful other than by trying to do something meaningful?"

Again she seemed not to hear the bitterness in his voice. "Perhaps you're trying to derive, or define—or is it determine?—meaning by what you get out of something," she mused, as she walked him toward the door. "But perhaps meaning doesn't come that way. Perhaps meaning comes from doing something others can get meaning out of," she said. "Maybe if you stop worrying about saving yourself, and try to save something else, you'll find that you've saved yourself in the process. At least think about it." She opened the door into her waiting room. "I'll see you next week."

* * *

When he reached his apartment, he was so unsettled by his session with Lauren that he didn't even have the will to avail himself of his latest murder mystery. As usual, he'd been a stupid fool, deluding himself with convoluted rationalizations and justifications to the point where he couldn't see the obvious truths or his own abject despair. Although he supposed he should be grateful to Lauren for removing the veil from his eyes, he wasn't sure what to do or where to turn now that his vision was supposedly clear. What had Lauren told him to do? "Think about it," she had said. How was he to "think about it"? Well, the stack of freshman compositions he'd collected on Monday was sitting untouched on the coffee table in front of him. The assignment was a comparison/contrast essay on the differences between high school and college. He plucked the first one from the stack and began reading.

"The comparison/contrast of high school and college is okay," it began. "Mostly high school was easier in comparison/contrast to college. In high school you usualy make A as long as you turn your work on time. My english teacher never put no marks on my paper or finding nothing wrong with it. Where as in college, my prof. Dr. Whit put alots of marks on my pages.

"But in comparison/contrast, Dr. Whit seem like he care. My english teacher (Mrs. Simms in high school) usualy be on her cell phone when we in class. Sometime she leave to take care her personal busness. Then we don't get substitute, just assignment on the board and we best keep quiet. We get the substitute when she gone all day. The substitute don't tell us what to do, she just sit there. Some times I am bored. But I always make good grades.

"College is hard in comparison/contrast. It is hard to make A. Now I get C though I turn my work on time. But don't get me wrong I like Dr. Whit. He come every day and stay the whole time. He never talk on a cell phone and don't even have a cell phone. So he say. He a good teacher I just need to work harder and hopefuly one day make A."

There was a smiley face drawn in purple ink at the end of the last sentence. The paper itself had come from a computer printer, probably one in the lab on campus, since not one of his students had a computer at home. No doubt they spent more time reserving a computer in the lab, laboriously typing their work into it and triumphantly printing it out than they did actually writing these essays. The one he'd just read probably didn't even fulfill the required 500 word minimum. He sighed and dropped the paper back on the stack lying in front of him on the table. How was he supposed to comment on it or correct it in a way that would actually teach this student how to write grammatically? How could he convey that this composition lacked sufficient content, or give this student the wherewithal to produce more substance?

If he had known how to do so, he would gladly do it. But he himself did not possess the necessary skills to teach this student, and all the others like her, the skills they needed. Indeed, he possessed no "skills" at all. What little ability he did possess involved merely a love of literature that was mostly useless to the rest of humanity. The college, his students, his colleagues and even his therapist required him to do something he couldn't do. He was just a poor lost soul who had only his love for a few literary texts to offer the world. That love was not even enough to save himself. How had the thought it would help anyone else?

He was in a terribly false position, where his professional activity would generate the very absurdity and futility he had scrupulously sought to avoid in whatever he did. Even worse, as his therapist had pointed out, he was a cog in a very bad machine which was supplying unqualified teachers to a public school system that couldn't help but produce poorly educated students. In just the short while since he'd entered the working world, he had quickly become exactly what he had never wanted to be, *without even knowing what was happening to him*. And he should have known. There was no excuse for his ignorance. Ralph Ellison had spelled it out years ago, when his invisible man narrator was given a scholarship from the white business community to attend a historically black college, modeled on Tuskegee. A dream reveals to the narrator the purpose of the gift, and possibly the black college itself: "Keep This Nigger-Boy Running."

As usual, Ham had been blind and stupid. So what was he to do now?

This, of course, was the eternal question that had plagued him since the age of seven, and to avoid having to confront it yet again, he peered over on the table to see who would have the nerve to put a smiley face in purple ink at the end of her paper. Patrice Pearson. He pulled back sharply as if the shock he'd received was a physical one. Patrice: the granddaughter of Harry, his mother's handyman. The granddaughter of Ella, Harry's wife, who'd been their maid and cook and who'd looked after him until she'd developed rheumatoid arthritis and could no longer work. He had only a fuzzy memory of Tilly, their daughter, though he knew she'd never attended college. She had a minimum-wage job of some sort—at a Dollar General, he thought—near where she lived. He had no idea where that was—North Birmingham or Fairfield—or where Patrice would have gone to school. But his nine year-old nephew, who was in fourth grade and still ate dinner on plates with cartoon characters, (at least at his grandmother's house), could produce a composition with more substance and fewer—if any—grammatical errors. He knew this for a fact because he was often shown his nephews' work by their father, Mark, an English teacher himself and the published author of a "well-received" collection of short stories.

Just a few days ago, he recalled, Patrice had been babysitting for two little boys whose education and prospects already far surpassed hers, though she was a college student ten years older. She would never obtain the education or the opportunities his nephews already possessed. It was too late; and there was nothing he himself could do about it. The problem was way beyond him and began, no doubt, over a hundred years ago when her ancestors came on a slave ship from Africa to America. The country had never redeemed itself or its victims from that original sin. What attempts had been made had not succeeded. The very college where he taught, founded right after the Civil War for the express purpose of training black teachers to instruct black children, had clearly and completely failed in its mission from the very beginning up until the present moment. He did not begin to know what he could do to make it right even for one individual whose family was closely connected to his own. He was equipped neither by temperament nor training to help her acquire the "skills" she needed. It was becoming increasingly clear that he wasn't really equipped to do much of anything at all that would help him redeem even his own existence, let alone anyone else's. It was all a hopeless mess.

~ 5 ~

The afternoon's soccer practice was at four o'clock at John Bynum Field, where Ham had played football, soccer and baseball when he himself was a boy. The happiest moments of his existence had been spent on this playing field, which had given him his fondest memories. As a boy, he had not been the shortest male in any group, as he usually was now, and had possessed speed, excellent hand-eye coordination, and a wiry, agile body which enabled him to excel at any sport he played. Those were his glory days. Now with his nephews, Ham enjoyed the weekday practices and the Saturday games because they took him back to a simpler time in his own life, when it was possible to feel good about himself, when the biggest threat looming on the horizon was the upcoming game against a formidable team.

But today, he was unable to throw himself into the occasion like he normally did. In fact, he wasn't even sure how he'd come to be at the field. He didn't remember getting in the car or driving over. And once he was there, he found himself at a loss, as if he weren't sure what to do with himself, although he'd been helping his brother-in-law Mark with the boys' various practices for over a year. He felt almost as if he were inhabiting a strange and different body possessing a foreign pair of eyes which forced him to view the world around him through a new and distorted lens.

For example: John Bynum Field. He'd never paid particular attention to this place before, either as a boy or now as an adult. It had merely been a fixture in his youth, part of the background he took for granted and didn't really notice. But today it leapt to the forefront of his vision, as if binoculars had been jammed up against his face to provide a frightening and shocking perspective on what was right before him.

But what was so shocking? John Bynum and the lower field, Roger Scott, were part of a community facility run by the Mountain Brook Youth League. Both fields were beautifully manicured and maintained. Even when it rained, there were no weeds, no puddles, and fresh chalk lines on practice and game days. The scoreboard, the announcer's booth, and the lighting system were state-of-the-art. During the games, motorists driving by could see the score, hear the names being announced, and view the action on the field at night. Bathrooms were air-conditioned and immaculate. The concession stand from his childhood had been replaced by something that looked more like a Cracker Barrel Restaurant. In his youth, this place had provided his greatest pleasures. But today, the scene before him rose up and crowded his vision in a menacing way that made him feel faint and slightly dizzy. He actually stumbled on his way to the practice field and just managed to catch himself on the bleachers.

Nothing was wrong with John Bynum Field. It was perfect. But its very perfection was an indictment of what was so wrong with a world in which a playing field for white children was state-of-the-art, while a college campus for black children was filled with crumbling ruins.

And something was wrong with him. His sister had warned him last night to get a flu shot. Was it last night? At any rate, it was too late now: he already felt sick. Looking at his watch, he saw it was a few minutes till four. Mark was already on the field with Andrew, but none of the others had arrived yet. He groped his way onto the bleachers. He needed to sit down and catch his breath before going onto the field.

But as soon as he sat down, a series of expensive automobiles—BMWs, Mercedes, Lexuses and enormous SUVs—crunched onto the gravel parking lot of John Bynum Field in quick succession. Little boys spilled out the doors of the cars and ran eagerly to the playing field. On the way, there was a bit of horseplay and tag, but as soon as they passed through the gate, the boys quickly formed into their pre-arranged lines to start the drills which began each practice.

If only his students could come to class this way, he thought ruefully, as the mothers began invading the bleacher seats around him. But on any given day, at least half a dozen students in each class might not show up at all. Others trickled in five, ten, fifteen minutes late. Even if half of his class was promptly seated at their desks by the time he entered the room, the absence of some and the intermittent late arrivals of others prevented the whole enterprise from feeling charged with important intent. Those who were there seemed proud of themselves just for being there. Many came to class without the necessary materials, including textbooks and assignments. Some had never even purchased a textbook, and had no intention or money to do so. During class time itself, many of his students simply slouched in their chairs, chewed gum and stared at the ceiling, as if their mere presence in the room were all that was required. The campus as a whole generated something of the same attitude, which treated four years of boredom in classrooms as the penance that must be paid in order to enter the promised land of professionalism. Most of his students were the first in their families ever to attend college; the parents he had met were excited and proud. Yet neither the parents nor their children seemed to possess the faintest inkling of how to achieve true success in college or beyond, and the concept of excellence seemed not to occur to anyone. They all appeared to believe that success was indeed primarily a matter of showing up, and after they'd shown up enough times for the required number of years, they would be issued a permanent pass into some magic kingdom.

And yet they had enormous difficulties simply showing up, since most lived at home rather than on campus in the rows of "modular" buildings that had served as temporary dorms for the out of town students after the dry rot, mold infestations and crumbling asbestos tiled roofs on the old dormitories had caused them to be condemned by the city. The students who had cars to get to campus had jobs to pay for them, and these jobs meant they were often late for class or missed it altogether. If the parents had cars, they needed these to get to their own jobs, and chauffeuring their children like he'd been chauffeured as a boy to school and extracurricular activities was not a possibility or even an idea that crossed their minds.

Patrice's mother Tilly had often been given a car whenever his mother replaced her Cadillac. Harry got the latest cast-off and passed the previous one on to his daughter. Over the years, she had wrecked one, had one impounded for failure to pay parking and traffic violations, and had lent another to a boyfriend who painted it pink. Later he was arrested when a kilo of cocaine was found in the trunk of this car, after the police received a tip on the hot line about a pink Cadillac. The car had still been registered in Harry's name, and Ham's father had been put to a great deal of trouble to extricate Harry from the legal and criminal implications. Afterwards Harry had been made to promise he would never give any of these vehicles to his daughter again.

Patrice took the bus to get to campus. Some had to take one bus to get to another bus to get to campus. Although he had never once ridden on a bus in his native city, he was well aware that the bus service was unapologetically and irremediably slow, erratic and unreliable, as if second-rate service sufficed for those deemed second-class citizens by their society. Buses could be as much as an hour late for a scheduled stop, or miss it altogether. Routes could be temporarily changed or suspended without any prior notice whatsoever. Ella's arrival at his parents' house each morning was naturally as tardy and unpredictable as the bus service she depended on. His mother had complained incessantly, though Ella always patiently explained what the bus had done that morning, and never left before completing all her work to his mother's satisfaction. But his mother would never be satisfied unless she could count on Ella to be there by nine each morning. The bus ride from Ella's part of town took an hour, but it hardly ever left at eight from Ella's stop like it was supposed to. This was the main reason his parents had begun giving their old cars to Ella and her husband Harry. So it was little wonder that for his students, simply showing up felt like a major accomplishment. Anything that took a major effort was going to feel like a major achievement, and getting anywhere on time on a Birmingham bus took a major effort.

He closed his eyes tightly as if he could in this way close his mind off to this disturbing train of thought. He tried to remind himself that he was at a simple boys' soccer practice which contained no larger and certainly no sinister implications. "Take a deep breath," he told himself, echoing the words of a pamphlet he had stashed somewhere in a drawer at his apartment. "Exhale slowly. Take another deep breath. Exhale slowly."

"Are you all right?" his brother-in-law was asking.

He hadn't realized that the drills were over and the boys were gathered around the bench drinking from their water bottles. He had remained rooted to his seat on the bleachers, lost in thought.

"Yeah, sure," he said. "I'm fine." He followed Mark over to the bench on the field where the boys would be divided into teams for the scrimmage.

But in truth, he felt like he was going under. This was another warning sign he knew to look out for: the loss of interest in the surface reality; the inability to pay attention to it, as if it did not even exist; the immersion in his own thoughts to the point that the outside world—the external reality—disappeared from his consciousness. To some extent, this was simply his personality and had been since late adolescence. Yet normally this tendency to become "lost in thought" was not so extreme that he lost all cognizance of what was going on around him, especially if he actually enjoyed what was going on around him, as he did with the boys' soccer. Coaching had even proved to be that rare activity capable of "taking him out of himself," which so many mental health professionals seemed to view as a desirable state of being. Apparently it was better for him to be far outside himself than deep inside himself. Although philosophically he had never agreed with this premise, he couldn't deny the pleasure and happiness coaching gave him. When he gave himself to the coaching, it gave back to him a joy in the actual moment he normally never knew. It was like he became the uncomplicated boy he used to be, as if his adult personality was transformed, and instead of getting lost in his thoughts, he became lost in physical exertion, and lost all sense of himself or his thoughts.

But today this transformation had not occurred; indeed, he felt himself drifting so far below the surface he feared he might not be able to come back up for air in time. Years ago at McLean Hospital, he had described this exact sensation when the doctors asked him to relate the psychological events leading up to his plunge into severe depression. This particular event became one of the warning signs he'd been asked to write down for himself after opting to discontinue medication when his condition had "stabilized."

This afternoon, as always, Andrew was assigned to his team; Mark thought it preferable to have someone else coaching his son. Andrew tugged at his uncle's shirt so he could whisper in his ear the names of the teammates he wanted for the scrimmage. Naturally these were his best friends and the best players, and normally, Ham dismissed the suggestions with a knowing laugh. But today he found himself strangely lacking in volition, unable to assert any authority or command of the situation. In fact, he was losing his grasp so entirely that even the boys' names were eluding him, and he had no choice but to go along with his nephew's wishes.

Once the teams were in place, he approached his brother-in-law on the sidelines at mid-field.

"I think I *am* coming down with something," he said.

Mark removed the whistle from his mouth just before blowing to signal the start of the scrimmage. "I thought you looked off your game back there," he said. "If you need to leave, I can take it from here. Just a minute, boys!" he called out.

"I think I'll go sit on the bench. Maybe I won't be totally useless."

Mark nodded and blew the whistle. The game began and a chorus of cheerleading immediately erupted from the bleacher section where the mothers were sitting. The mothers cheered with the same intensity as on the Saturday mornings when the official games were played. It had been the same when he was a child. Even his own mother had sat on the bleachers with the ramrod posture of a woman well aware of performing her duty and proud of it. She cared nothing for sports and knew even less, but since it was something boys were supposed to do, and do well, she was determined her son would not only do it but excel at it. She could not be content that he was the best shortstop, lead-off hitter or base-stealer in the league. She wanted him to be the best player period, and recognized as such. She demanded nothing less than total perfection and utter triumph.

Of course this had nothing to do with wanting him to win athletic scholarships or become a professional athlete. Either of these would have been a preposterous notion to his mother. What she wanted was to get a glimpse of the man he would one day be through the boy he now was. She wanted to envisage his future success and stature as a man through his athletic supremacy as a boy. And it was as if she thought the one might ensure the other. If her son was the ultimate winner on the playing field, then he was destined for greatness as a man. All the other mothers appeared to feel the same way, back then as well as now.

Perhaps it was this above all, he thought, that his own students were lacking. This sense of their world cheering for them and urging them on toward their goal, while standing by ever ready, completely prepared and utterly committed to helping them achieve it. It wasn't that the parents of his students didn't care. The ones he had met so far all cared. But as much as the individual parents might care, there didn't seem to be a society engineered for the success of its youngsters. In his world, an occasional failure such as himself occurred despite his society; in their world, it was the occasional success that occurred despite the society.

He winced in pain as if from the physical malady he'd fabricated earlier. His world was set up for success; theirs was set up for failure. It was as simple and terrible as that. He couldn't bear to contemplate the numerous causes of this disparity—the public schools, the public transportation, the criminals and drug dealers like Tilly's former boyfriend; not to mention all the other never-ending legacies of racism, segregation and slavery. He raised his arm to shield himself from the thoughts that assailed him like bullets. He had no armor, no way to deflect the rifle balls aimed directly at him. He was completely exposed and vulnerable, largely because he did not believe in his own innocence, his right to protect himself or seek cover, or even his right to live. He deserved to die.

When he was a boy, his mother had refused to let Ella leave work to go take care of her daughter Tilly, who had come home sick from school. His mother had a meeting at the museum, where she was a member of the board. She needed Ella to take care of him, her son, who at age five was only in kindergarten half a day and needed looking after in the afternoons. She had insisted Ella make other arrangements, or she, Mrs. Whitmire, would need to find other help. "Other arrangements" had apparently been made for Tilly. Just as "other arrangements" had been made for black people as a whole in his city. These "arrangements" had not been anywhere close to adequate. What could he do about it? Even in the field of education, which perhaps provided the best means of redress, he was incapable of offering what was most needed despite his own advanced degree in that very field. If large amounts of money could magically solve the problem, he would gladly have signed away the contents of his own personal trust fund. But in a world that was far from magical, that would have amounted to little more than a symbolic and useless gesture, and might even have turned into another pink Cadillac. In any event, the trust fund his grandmother had set up for him had been structured in such a complicated and careful way as to prevent him from "blowing it" or withdrawing suspicious amounts for purposes deemed "dubious" by the trustees and executors, one of whom was his mother. And unfortunately, he had every reason to fear that he might one day need to rely entirely on the proceeds of his trust fund to support his own hopeless existence as he drifted in and out of mental institutions. He shut his eyes. "Inhale deeply," he told himself. "Exhale slowly."

"We won! We won!" Andrew clambered on the bench and pummeled his uncle's shoulders.

"Of course you won, you rascal. How could you not win with a team like that behind you?"

"I scored three goals! Did you see? Did you see the one that hit the post and went in?"

The mother dispensing snacks held out a 100% juice juice-box to him. He smiled and shook his head. "No thanks," he said.

"You look a little under the weather," she said.

"Yes," he admitted. "I think I am."

She picked up a plate of cookies from the bench. They looked like oatmeal raisin, home-made. He took one from the top just seconds before a crowd of dirty hands descended on the cookies. The mother turned around to scold them for rudeness and poor hygiene. Admonishing them not to touch a single cookie before washing their hands, she retrieved a bottle of hand sanitizer from her purse, and the boys dutifully held out their hands for the liquid goo she squirted onto each and every palm.

She turned back to him. "I hope you didn't catch anything from one of the boys. There's always something going around."

"It's okay," he assured her. "I feel like I spend my life being sick. I have good days and bad days, but no completely healthy days. I don't even remember what it feels like to be healthy."

She nodded. "That's what it's like being around kids," she said. "Especially when they're young. As soon as you get over one thing, you come down with another. We sure do appreciate what you and Mark are doing for the boys. It is so important. What they're learning goes far beyond soccer."

Just then his brother-in-law came up, carrying the equipment bag and bending over to collect the extra balls. "Did you see that goal Andrew scored?"

"The one that hit the pole and bounced in?"

"Wasn't that incredible?"

He concurred enthusiastically, although he had not seen that goal nor any of the game despite having watched the entire scrimmage. Here was another sign: the inability to engage in his normal activities or derive any enjoyment from them. Or was this a different sign: the inability to focus or concentrate such as he'd experienced this afternoon, when he couldn't even get started on his new Maigret mystery? Last year at this time he had read *The Man Without Qualities* in its entirety, in the original German. Now he found himself unable to read any philosophy or serious literature, and couldn't even crack open the Simenon which never let him down. Shakespeare he could still do, but that wasn't reading. That was like reciting the litany of his own personal faith, as others might recite from their catechism or the Book of Common Prayer.

Suddenly the realization exploded like a bomb in his face that of course he was on the brink of another severe clinical depression. He felt himself collapsing and gasped for breath in short, ragged gulps. His heart was racing uncontrollably as if in a frantic, desperate attempt to keep him alive despite the crushing odds which pressed like a dead weight on his chest and made it impossible for him to breathe. He knew he was dying or would soon be dead. Already he was in that transitional state where the soul was departing its physical trappings, because he was losing all sense of his body or its boundaries. He could feel the earthly matter of his being fall away as the particles of his soul seemed to merge and become one with the universe represented by the darkening sky of the dying day staring down at him and coming to claim him.

The next thing he knew, his sister was squatting down beside him on the ground where he'd fallen off the bench. She had her hand on his forehead. "I think you may have fainted," she said. "You're sweating like you've got a fever." She accepted a water bottle from the snack mother and helped to lift his head so he could take a sip. "I'm afraid it's probably the flu. It's early this year. I must have seen half a dozen cases today."

Even doctors like his sister didn't realize how physical a thing mental illness could be. It wasn't the flu; it was a panic attack, brought on by the terrifying prospect of imminent clinical depression and the nightmarish memories of his stint in the psychiatric ward of a mental hospital. Should he tell her? He knew he needed to do something. But as ever, he just didn't know what.

~ 6 ~

At nine o'clock the next day, he went into the main office to inform the secretary that he wasn't feeling well. She confirmed his worst fears by telling him he didn't look at all well, either. The emphatic voicing of this opinion and the naked concern on her face suggested he appeared to be suffering from a terminal condition, which, in a way, he was. "Go home," she ordered, offering to take care of cancelling his classes for the remainder of the day. It was all too easy to do, and yet the reprieve only released him to the widening abyss of his existence. He had forced himself to teach his eight o'clock class instead of simply calling in sick, largely to ensure he didn't sleep too late and miss the appointment he'd made for noon. But what would happen tomorrow and the next day, over the weekend? Would he find himself unable to get out of bed? The prospect made his heart start to pound, his throat go dry, and his abdomen clench. Suspending his routine wasn't good for him, but on the other hand, his routine hadn't exactly safeguarded him either. No matter what he did, he always came up against the need to find a reason for living. He wished he could be one of the many people who just did things without always having to ask why he did them.

He didn't expect his twelve o'clock appointment to supply that reason, but he hoped he might gain something to carry him through the blankness of the weekend. Ten minutes early, he sat down in the foyer of the high school he had once attended, on a leather sofa behind the Lin Emery sculpture that had once belonged to his grandmother. His palms began to sweat so profusely they left damp streaks where he rubbed them on the legs of his khaki pants. At noon the receptionist came out to tell him that Mr. Laney would be with him soon. Another ten minutes passed before he was summoned into the headmaster's office. No sooner had the 450 pounds of the post-bypass Mr. Laney risen to greet him than the phone rang. Ever the lover of gossip, invitations and the ongoing spectacle of human behavior, Mr. Laney could never ignore a ringing telephone. He snatched up the receiver.

"Oh, hey, darlin,'" he said, sinking back into his chair.

As Ham had just been abandoned by the receptionist but had not yet been greeted, welcomed or offered a seat by Mr. Laney, he remained awkwardly on the threshold of the door, staring at Mr. Laney's girth as it settled in the chair and seeped out the sides under the arms. He had not expected to be so shocked by the colossus of Mr. Laney's supposedly reduced body. Ham had been a student for many years at the school, before Mr. Laney underwent the gastric bypass that eliminated 150 pounds from his hulk. Expecting rather to be surprised at how much smaller Mr. Laney had become, he was caught off guard to encounter a man even larger than he remembered. Mr. Laney motioned him in and pointed to a chair opposite his desk.

"Now listen," he said into the telephone. "It's been way too long. But I've got a former student in my office who's been back in town a year and a half and only now has come to see me. So, I need to run. Call me next week."

He hung up the phone without farewells and pulled himself up to the desk. Then came a knock at the door followed by the entrance of a student carrying two large grease-stained paper bags from Gus's Hot Dogs. The smell of hot dogs and French fries took over the room.

"Thank you, darlin,'" said Mr. Laney, reaching out for the bags. "What do I owe you?"

The student dug a receipt out of her purse while Mr. Laney opened a drawer with one hand and plucked a hot dog out of the bag with the other.

"Eight fifty-six," said the student, offering the crumpled piece of paper to her headmaster, who ignored it. Instead he plopped his wallet on top of the desk and began peeling back the thin paper holding the hot dog together. A riot of chili, cheese, relish and mustard instantly erupted and was almost as instantly captured by Mr. Laney's mouth.

"Take a ten out of my wallet," he told the girl, his mouth impossibly full. "Keep the change."

"I think I've got a dollar," she said, starting to dig again in her purse.

Mr. Laney took another bite of the hot dog and waved her off. "That's for your gas and your time, darling. And thank you, hear? You've saved me from starvation and allowed me to have this delightful visit during lunch with an old student. Ham Whitmire, meet Rebecca Crenshawe."

Ham rose politely to shake the student's hand. Mr. Laney concentrated on the last two bites of his hot dog, leaving his guests at a loss. Ham didn't know if he should sit back down, and the student didn't know if she should leave the room. Neither knew what to say to the other.

"You know the second Mrs. Keller, don't you?" said Mr. Laney to Ham, balling up the hot dog wrapper and throwing it in his waste can. "Beverly Crenshawe, before she married Frank Keller, after he divorced his first wife." Mr. Laney peered into both bags before deciding to retrieve the second hot dog.

"I think so," said Ham dubiously. He now realized it had been a mistake to come here. There was nothing to be gained. His reluctance to visit Mr. Laney until now had not been unfounded. The pungent smell of freshly chopped purple onions from the second hot dog was making him nauseous. At the same time his own empty stomach turned on itself against the odor of onions, his mood flipped somewhat as well, though not for the better. When he had first arrived at the school, he had been possessed by a sense of the urgency and importance of his problems. But now it seemed stupid to take either his problems or life itself so seriously when such things as chili cheese dogs existed in the world to be devoured by preposterously obese individuals. Nevertheless, as ridiculous as his problems might be, they still remained. And Mr. Laney could do nothing to help him solve them.

Yet he knew he was in the presence of a great man. Mr. Laney was not only a great man, he was also a happy man. Though normally Ham was the kind of person who failed to see the obvious, the irony of this situation was not lost on him. Anybody looking at the vital statistics of his own privileged background—his upbringing in an affluent suburb; his Ivy League degrees; his family's wealth and his own personal trust fund; the opportunity to enter a family business or the luxury of doing nothing at all—would have assumed that he had it made. As an abstraction, he would be a target for envy, hatred, ridicule or contempt. But those who actually knew him could only pity him. On the other hand, Mr. Laney's blue-collar background, grotesque obesity, limited income, small apartment and life with mother would seem to designate him as one of life's losers. Yet he was a winner if ever there was one, a happy man doing important work that Ham himself had benefited from first hand. If there was a secret to Mr. Laney's ability to carve an unlikely success out of the most improbable of materials, Ham hoped he would share it.

"Well, anyway," Mr. Laney was saying. "This is Beverly's granddaughter. She's applying to Bowdoin and Middlebury. Ham is one of our most distinguished alumni," he told Rebecca. "He's just come back to town after spending a decade pursuing graduate work at Harvard. Strange," he said, examining his hot dog. "They put onions on this one and relish on the other."

"Oh, I'm sorry, Mr. Laney," said Rebecca. "I told them two super dogs, both all the way." She scrutinized the receipt for confirmation of her diligence.

"Doesn't matter," said Mr. Laney, swallowing. "As long as they don't put the rat poison or the roach powder on it. There's not much more I ask of Gus's Hot Dogs. Now you go on and get busy with those application essays if you've got nothing better to do. You're bringing them to me next week?"

She nodded.

"Good. I'll see you then. Close the door on your way out."

"What brings you here?" said Mr. Laney, contemplating the remaining half of his second hot dog. "Have you reconsidered the position I offered you? It's still available. I know you don't want to teach lower level students, but maybe after seeing what it's like out there, you've changed your mind. I distinctly told that child two super dogs all the way, hold the onions. I hate purple onions."

Ham tried to make a murmur of sympathy.

"Teaching English to fifth and sixth grade students at the Brook-Haven School would probably be more satisfying than teaching the college students at—what is the name of that place again?"

"Cahaba." Ham had to clear his throat. "Cahaba College."

"I believe our fifth and sixth grade students are probably more advanced than your college students at Cahaba."

Did he know how right he was? Or was it the usual hyperbole all his students came to know so well? Mr. Laney stuffed the final bite into his mouth and wiped his lips.

"I understand that place is not long for this world, anyway."

"What do you mean?" Ham felt himself moving nervously to the edge of his seat.

"Why don't you talk to your uncle about it? He's on the committee that deals with the state budget for higher education. I give the place two or three more years at best. You don't have a future there because I don't believe that particular institution has a future itself. Here you have the chance of moving up. Gayle Naughton has got to retire some time, and she does the tenth grade English plus the A.P. classes. I know your brother-in-law expects to get those A.P. courses, but he doesn't have a Ph.D. in English from Harvard like you do. I can promise you those classes when Gayle retires. But I have to fill the lower level position *this year.* Right now I've got an art teacher, a music teacher and a soccer coach covering for me. Either they or the parents or both will have my head if I don't get somebody in for next year." He sucked at his teeth to extract the loose bits of chili, relish and onions lodged in the crevices.

Ham did not know what to say, having foolishly expected to present his own problems rather than addressing Mr. Laney's. Perhaps he should simply cut his losses and leave. Mr. Laney continued to suck at his teeth while dislodging the stray bits with his tongue. He searched through one of the paper sacks and extracted a soggy container of limp French fries. Before Ham could think of a way to excuse himself, the phone rang again. Mr. Laney picked up the receiver, and after greeting his caller, swiveled around in his chair so that his back faced his hapless visitor, who briefly considered sneaking out. Whatever the news being imparted to Mr. Laney on the other end of the line, it was obviously extremely absorbing. It was quite possible that by the time Mr. Laney turned back around, he wouldn't notice Ham's absence and would have forgotten he'd ever been there to begin with.

Yes, coming here had been a mistake. There had been a time when Mr. Laney was the most important person in his life, as a teacher, as a guiding spirit, and as a college counselor who came up with the idea of Williams when Ham's mother had wanted him to attend the University of Virginia and then its Darden School of Business. Mr. Laney had not only come up with the alternative, he had turned the idea into reality and made Ham's mother accept it. Ham would be forever grateful. Williams had been wonderful, and if he could have remained there for the rest of his life, as a student seeking knowledge and answers to the riddle of existence through reading and reflection, he would have. So far, the role of student was the only truly tenable position he'd ever occupied in his life. He had not wanted to abandon it, and had managed to prolong it through various fellowships, graduate programs, and ultimately a dissertation. But neither the world nor his mother looked kindly on a grown man who wanted nothing more than to be a student in school for the rest of his life. There was always the expectation and the insistence that he "do" something with himself and his education. His mother thought she knew exactly what that should be, but since he himself had never arrived at any viable conclusion about his life's occupation, he thought the best place for him to stay and figure it out was in some fine school far away from his mother. After his breakdown in the third year of law school, she had accepted his proposal to enter the Ph.D. program in English at Harvard. Mr. Laney had apparently put it to her like this: Would she rather tell people her son was in the loony bin, or at Harvard? So at Harvard he had been able to remain reading literature for another seven years. But life did not allow anyone to stay contentedly in one place for too long. The forces of nature moved destructively onward, bringing disruption after disruption until they finally brought the ultimate disruption of death. This seemed the only destination his life had been headed toward for some time. Mr. Laney could not alleviate his adult crisis as he had solved the one of adolescence. Then, it had been the question of where he should go; now, it was the question of what he should do. It had been too much to expect that this one man could produce two such miracles.

Suddenly Mr. Laney swiveled back around, thrust the receiver into the cradle and faced Ham with narrowed eyes. "What's wrong?" he said.

Caught off guard, Ham spread his hands out. No words came out of his constricted throat.

Mr. Laney snatched up the phone again and pressed a button. "Hold my calls," he said, slamming the receiver back down again. "Don't you think you ought to be taking medication?"

Ham was taken aback, having forgotten how quickly Mr. Laney could travel from the trivial to the momentous, from chili cheese dogs to the existential crisis of the human condition.

"Probably," Ham admitted finally as Mr. Laney continued to pierce him with his narrowed eyes.

"There's no shame in it, you know," said Mr. Laney. "And you look like you need something. What's stopping you?"

"It's not exactly a quick fix," Ham said defensively. "It's not like taking an aspirin when you have a headache." He paused to see what effect these words had on Mr. Laney, who was absently putting one French fry after another into his mouth and appeared to be trying to decide whether they were worth consuming. "The drugs take about three weeks to get into your system," Ham continued. "By then, I figure I'm either dead, in the hospital, or somehow managing on my own. So why bother?"

"The point is to stay on them so you don't run the risk of being dead or in the hospital by getting so low in the first place." Mr. Laney temporarily desisted from eating French fries in order to emphasize the importance of this statement.

"They never stopped me from being 'low,'" Ham said. "They mainly stopped me from being able to think. I realize that was no loss to humanity, but it was a loss to me, and it only made me more 'low.'"

"But if the drugs also stop you from thinking about suicide. . . ."

Ham gave a rueful smile. "Thinking about suicide is sometimes the only thing that keeps me going—or prevents me from committing suicide." When Mr. Laney failed to laugh, Ham added more seriously, "I've never really been on the actual brink of committing suicide."

"Really?" said Mr. Laney, crumpling the half-empty bag of fries. "I always wondered. I was too afraid to ask your mother, and your sister believes you should be on medication regardless. Tell me what you think."

Again Ham was taken aback, although he had made the appointment with Mr. Laney precisely in order to have this kind of discussion. But after the way their meeting began, it had seemed too much to hope for. However, now Mr. Laney appeared to have put aside two of his favorite things in the world—his food and his phone—and was prepared to focus his gaze on the problem Ham was bringing before him. Only now Ham didn't know what to say. And just his bad luck, for once Mr. Laney appeared prepared to wait forever for a reply.

"I suppose I agree with Walker Percy on this issue," he said finally. He knew it was lame.

"Agree how?" said Mr. Laney sharply, glancing up at the clock on the wall above Ham's head.

"Well . . ." he began, floundering quickly, afraid of boring Mr. Laney or wasting his time. Yet he also hoped that Mr. Laney had become bored enough to stop waiting for a full-fledged, two-sided conversation. Mr. Laney was quite capable of conducting a lengthy monologue, and often seemed to prefer these. But again, he waited. Ham sighed. "Walker Percy said depression can be a healthy response to a crazy world or a pointless existence," he said.

Mr. Laney leaned across his desk with all the intensity of his colossal body. "Healthy?" he began. "I'm not sure suffering is healthy if it paralyzes you to the point where you can't do a damn thing with your one and only life. You don't look healthy to me. And you look like you're suffering." He leaned back and relaxed into his chair. "You know there are people still alive in this town who knew LeRoy Percy. Practiced law with him. They said he could be charming and cheerful and on top of the world one day. Black as night the next. Bipolar. Back then, they didn't have anything for it." Mr. Laney leaned forward in his chair across the desk again. "But if there *had* been drugs for it, I do believe he would never have taken his shotgun and killed himself in the attic of what is now your mother's lovely home." Again Mr. Laney leaned back. "And Walker Percy would have had an entirely different perspective on depression."

"According to the doctors, I'm not bipolar."

"You're not?" Mr. Laney seemed surprised.

"At least, I have no manic highs," said Ham with a wan smile. "Only lows. It must be what the Victorians called melancholia."

"They had a different name for it at the psychiatric hospital in Boston."

"Yes, they did."

"Well," said Mr. Laney, glancing again at the clock. "All I can say is this." He fixed Ham with a steely gaze which offered neither comfort nor sympathy. "We all know it's a crazy world and only likely to get crazier. If you don't want to take anti-depressants, then you've got to find another way to laugh at the world or live with it. As for life being pointless—so what if it is? If you think life is pointless, but you don't want to end it, then you've got to do something else about it. Give it your own point. That's all you can do."

Ham shifted in his seat and cleared his throat. "Believe it or not, that's what I've been trying to do all these years. I don't appear to be very successful at it."

"Doesn't matter," said Mr. Laney, waving his hand dismissively. "You don't have to succeed. Success isn't the point. The definitions of success are all relative and highly variable. So you just have to try. And as Walker Percy himself said, at the end of the day, you can still enjoy. . . ." Mr. Laney looked around the room and finally seized on the remaining bag from Gus's Hot Dogs, which he picked up and dropped back down. "What was the example he used?"

"Oysters, I think," said Ham, smiling tightly.

"That's right!" said Mr. Laney, looking at Ham like he wasn't such a piti-ful mental case after all. He frowned and gazed into the distance, trying to summon the quotation. "We can still walk abroad on a summer night, see a show and eat some oysters. Close enough?"

Ham nodded, impressed. "Close enough." He smiled less tightly this time.

"Then you know what you have to do." Mr. Laney slammed both of his palms down emphatically on his desk. "If you're not a suicide, then you've got to do a better job of being an ex-suicide. And I'll need a decision by the end of January about that lower level position for next year." The telephone rang, though it wasn't supposed to, and Mr. Laney looked back up at the clock. "I hate to cut things short," he said. "But I've got an appointment with two very difficult parents who I think must just have arrived. Early. Their son is a C+ with absolutely average SAT scores, but they think I can get him into the Ivy League." Mr. Laney sighed and pushed against the desk to propel himself out of the chair. "Used to be, I had to fight to get the boys and girls out of Alabama. Now they all want to get into Harvard."

"Sounds like you fought and won, then," said Ham, rising from his own chair.

"I'm winning," said Mr. Laney, walking him toward the door. "But success only brings a different set of problems. And two of these will be here shortly.

Come back soon," he said, extending his hand. "And let me know as soon as you decide."

Only when Ham was alone in the hallway did he remember that he wanted his visit kept confidential. But the headmaster's door was firmly closed against him, and he could hear Mr. Laney's voice already engaged in another telephone conversation. Surely he knew better than to call Ham's mother, but it was entirely possible he was now speaking with his sister. On the other hand, it was equally likely that Mr. Laney had already forgotten about Ham's existence. Or believed he had summoned Ham for the conference, which would fit with the way he'd conducted it. Meanwhile, the problem posed by the rest of his life—including the next two days—was still unresolved.

Furtively he poked his head out of the corridor into the main hallway. Seeing no sign of his brother-in-law, he proceeded toward the foyer and had almost made it to the double glass entrance doors when someone called his name. He turned around to see Erica Cooley loping in his direction. Her stride was a bit uneven—in fact, she limped—because for some reason he couldn't recall, one leg was somewhat shorter than the other. Was it last month or last year he'd seen her at his parents' house? He couldn't remember that either, but he did suddenly remember that he had promised to contact her. About what? He no longer knew, but he was flooded as usual with those feelings of guilt, failure and inadequacy that defined him to himself.

Nevertheless, she greeted him cheerfully and seemed to bear no grudge or bitter recollection of promises he had not fulfilled. Whatever it was she'd wanted must not have been important. In his experience, people who really wanted something from him usually asserted themselves against his passivity until they got it. And once they got it, they usually discovered that they didn't really want it after all, and gave it back to him.

"What brings you here?" she said, pushing open the front door.

"Mr. Laney," he said, joining her outside.

"Is he trying to get you to teach here too?" she smiled.

"As a matter of fact, yes," he said, glad she had provided such an easy explanation for his presence on campus. Suddenly Erica's own situation came back to him. "Are you . . . ?" he began uncertainly. "Did you decide to take the job he offered you?"

"Not yet," she said, looking at her watch. "Are you parked down the hill?" She indicated the gravel parking lot at the foot of the incline on which the school buildings were located. When he nodded, she said, "I'll walk down with you. I've got a two o'clock class at UAB," she said. "And I'd like to grab something to eat before that. I'm just tutoring some students in French on their lunch break here," she explained. "I thought it would be a good way to help myself figure out if I'd like to spend seven hours a day five days a week working at this place."

"The idea of spending seven hours a day five days a week anywhere sounds hard," he said.

"Yes," she agreed with a grin. "But living with my parents twenty-four/ seven is worse."

Thinking of Mrs. Cooley, he laughed. As they reached the end of the sidewalk at the bottom of the hill, an idea occurred to him.

"I'm sorry I never called you," he said. "But if you'd still like to get together, maybe sometime this weekend . . ." His voice trailed off as his idea petered out on him. He should have thought this through more carefully. There was nothing really he could think of to offer her.

"Sure," she said. Gravel crunched beneath their feet as they made their way into the parking lot. "Why don't I meet you somewhere?"

"Fine," he said, unsure what to say next.

"Where do you live?"

"Oh—downtown."

"I'm just learning downtown," she said, searching in her purse for car keys. "Thanks to these classes at UAB." She held up her keys. "Is there any place you like to go there?"

"I'll bet you know downtown better than I do. I don't get out much."

"Why don't we go to lunch somewhere? Maybe in Five Points. That's not too far from downtown. What about Botteghe Café? Do you know where that is?"

"On Highland Avenue?"

She nodded and opened her car door.

"Okay," he said. "Tomorrow?"

Again she nodded. "We better say quarter till twelve. It gets crowded."

"Okay," he agreed.

He watched as she got in the car and waved at him while driving off. Although his appointment with Mr. Laney had not produced the results he'd wanted, perhaps he had at least solved the problem of tomorrow, if not the problem of the rest of his life. Lunch was the perfect idea—why couldn't he have thought of that and proposed it to her as if he had some brains in his head? Lunch would get him out of bed and force him into action soon enough to prevent the total submersion he feared. Then in the late afternoon, there were his nephews' soccer games. Sunday would be another problem, but at least Saturday was taken care of. He had reached that abject point where he had to take one day at a time and plan carefully how to get through that day without putting his entire life into the hands of the mental health professionals.

~ 7 ~

By Monday morning, Ham knew what he needed to do. There was really only one thing for him to do, and now that he'd stopped fighting it and decided to do it, the sense of relief was so enormous he wondered why it had taken him so long to reach this decision. Even the secretary in the main office noticed the difference in him and commented on how much better he looked than he had on Friday. When Ivy Greer suddenly seized his arm on her way to the mail slots, it didn't even bother him. She pulled him close and muttered in his ear.

"You have *got* to come to the faculty meeting today at ten. Promise me."

Normally, an encounter like this would have destabilized him entirely. Today he was able to agree quite calmly to her request, and even gave the secretary a cheerful smile in response to her playfully raised eyebrows. What did it matter if she developed the wrong idea about his liaison with Ivy Greer? It wasn't like he was going to be around much longer.

The sense of blessed release put such a spring in his step that he was actually among the first to arrive for the faculty meeting. Ivy Greer came in soon afterwards, sat next to him, and pulled her chair even closer so she could murmur in his ear without being overheard by the others who were filing in. He couldn't hear Ivy, either, but that was something else that didn't matter or require action on his part.

Today the chairwoman was accompanied by the dean of Humanities, Mr. Akin, who sat along with her at the head of the conference table. Although Ham had attended no faculty meetings in over a year, he knew this was unusual. He noticed also there were no boxes of Krispy Kreme doughnuts, and none of the chatter that usually took place before a meeting began. When the door closed, the atmosphere in the conference room became charged with a tension that he alone seemed not to feel.

As the chairwoman's voice began to drone, he marveled at how little this affected him also. Formerly, his nervous system would have been activated simply by being in this room, even with the usual Krispy Kreme doughnuts and idle chatter. Today, however, he felt nothing—certainly not the surges of adrenaline that left him weak and dizzy afterwards. It was almost like the sensation of numbness he'd experienced those few times he'd tried the anti-anxiety medication prescribed by a previous psychiatrist. Except this was far better. Instead of feeling artificially anaesthetized, he now felt above and beyond any troublesome reality in a much more real and permanent way. It couldn't touch or reach him. The mere act of making his momentous decision had already enabled him to leave it all behind, just like that.

It wasn't that he tuned out the chairwoman, either. He could hear what she said quite clearly. It was all about the "disturbing data" generated by the new teacher evaluation process in the public schools, and the need for "higher standards" in the English Department at Cahaba College.

Next to him, Ivy Greer raised her hand. The chairwoman was obviously annoyed at this interruption to her carefully prepared speech, but Dean Akin beamed his genial smile.

"Yes, Sister Greer," he said pleasantly.

Ivy had been prepared to launch into her own speech, but she abruptly closed her mouth.

"Actually, it's *Dr.* Greer," she said.

"Of course. Of course." Dean Akin bobbed his head. "I remember. Your mother told me you finished your degree. How is she?"

"She's fine."

"Good. Good. You know we're all pulling for her to get the job. Can't think of a better person to be assistant superintendant of the Birmingham public school system."

A low hum of voices echoed this sentiment. A few of the other faculty members and even the dean himself seemed on the verge of pursuing this topic further. Ham wouldn't have minded learning more either, since up until now, he'd known nothing about it.

"If I could just clarify what we mean by higher standards," said Ivy.

"I was just getting to that," said the chairwoman, eager to regain control of the conversation. Today she was robed in brilliant turquoise, and had jewelry to match it in her ears and around her neck.

"Because when I turned in my midterm grades," said Ivy, locking eyes with her chairwoman, who had opened her mouth a second too late. "You called me into your office. Told me I'd given way too many F's. Even when I showed you portfolios from the failing students. You said F's were too harsh. Would only cause students to drop out of school. And would not serve our purpose of producing college graduates. So what do we mean here by 'higher standards'? Do we mean that failing work can now be given failing grades without teachers being chastised for doing so?"

Although the chairwoman appeared to be at a temporary loss for words, the dean stepped in smoothly.

"Excellent points you've made, Miss Greer," he said amiably. "This actually brings us to the main reason we've called today's meeting." He looked over at the chairwoman. "If I may?" he said, as she nodded somewhat sourly.

The dean proved to be quite adept at public speaking. Ham wondered if the rumor he'd heard last year was true, about the dean being some sort of salesman before coming on at Cahaba College. At any rate, a confident and convincing flow of speech issued forth that did sound somewhat like a sales pitch, promoting in this case something called "Zero Tolerance for Failure." Although the dean discoursed with eloquence and at length about this new administrative policy, the gist of it, as far as Ham could make out, was that instructors in the English Department needed to hold their students to higher standards, and at the same time, make sure that none of their students failed to achieve those standards.

When he concluded, the dean leaned back with a satisfied sigh. Lacing his fingers together, he placed his hands on his stomach and surveyed the faces in the room with his customary beaming smile. Except for Ivy Greer and the chairwoman, the other women in the room were nodding their heads in approval.

"Amen, Brother Akin," one said.

A chorus of "amens" echoed from the group.

The dean's smile broadened. "Are there any questions?" He looked around the table again.

When Ivy Greer raised her hand, his brow contracted just enough to be noticeable. He nodded in her direction. "Yes?" he inquired, lifting his eyebrows.

"How is this new Zero Tolerance for Failure policy any different from the old policy?"

"I'm sorry," said the dean agreeably. "I must not have done a very good job of explaining it." He winked at the women sitting opposite Ivy. They gave him sympathetic simpers in return indicating that his explanation was flawless; the problem was with that new girl. She'd come around in time, get with the program.

"Sounds to me," said Ivy, tapping her pencil on the table. "This so-called new policy will be just like the old one."

"I'm afraid I don't follow you," said the dean. Although his countenance remained cordial, his tone was losing its good cheer.

"Students who turn in failing work will be given passing grades."

A collective gasp came from the table. It was hard even for Ham to believe that she had gone this far. She didn't look like a bomb-thrower. She didn't even look like an adult. In her hooded SPELMAN sweatshirt over the usual jeans, she looked like a pre-pubescent pre-teen who had not yet become interested in makeup, clothes, jewelry, or the latest hairstyles. The other women seemed so much more substantial. Yet Ivy Greer was by far the most commanding presence in the room.

However, Dean Akin regained his composure and sunny disposition. "Perhaps this would be a good time for the head of the department to explain how we plan to achieve results under Zero Tolerance for Failure." He turned to the chairwoman with a dazzling smile.

Although surprised to be given the floor, she recovered quickly and launched into another lengthy monologue. She lacked the oratorical skills of the dean, but her British-accented English offered some compensation. The longer she talked, the more British-accented her English became, and there was no denying the weight or credibility this accent gave to her speech. Apparently "the plan" she was outlining required all faculty members to conduct mandatory grammar and spelling workshops for all students with "below-average skills." Given the minimum eight office hours per week spread out over all five days, there should be plenty of "workshop time" for struggling students.

Again a chorus of "amens" swept around the table, as heads nodded. Ham believed he heard someone say "Righteous." He could only be grateful that none of this applied to him, and hated to imagine how he would be suffering at this moment if he had not already arrived at his breakthrough decision. As it was, he was only a spectator, not a participant, in the scene unfolding around him. He wondered, though, how Ivy was faring. Trying not to move his head, he chanced a sideways glance at her.

True to form, she was flipping through pages in her binder. Meanwhile the chairman was explaining that a detailed memo would be forthcoming in everyone's mail slot.

"If there are no further questions, I think we should adjourn the meeting," she said, looking at her watch. "It's getting close to eleven. I know Dean Akin has another appointment, and many of us have classes to prepare for."

"Actually, I have a question," said Ivy.

No one said a word. The slightest, almost imperceptible exchange of glances took place between the dean and the chairwoman.

"Did you say *mandatory* workshops?" Ivy asked.

Both the dean and the chairwoman inclined their heads.

"We have to do them?"

"Well, really," said the chairwoman slowly. "I think it's the least we can do for our students here. Don't you agree?"

Although this question was directed at Ivy, a chorus of "Yes ma'ams" came from everyone else.

"So we'll get paid two thousand dollars per workshop?" said Ivy.

"Whatever gave you that idea?" the dean broke in indignantly, momentarily losing his unruffled demeanor.

"The Faculty Handbook," said Ivy calmly, unmoved by the dean's sudden combativeness.

"The Faculty Handbook?" Dean Akin looked at her like she'd lost her mind.

Ivy looked down at the binder in front of her and began reading from a place marked by her index finger. "'A full-time faculty teaching load is defined as four courses per semester,'" she quoted. "'Any courses beyond four that a faculty member teaches in a given semester will be compensated at two thousand dollars per course.'" Ivy looked back up at the dean. "If the workshops are mandatory for students and teachers, then that makes them part of the assigned course load. And that means they should be compensated as such."

"Thank you for bringing that point to our attention, Miss Greer," he said smoothly. "We'll look into the matter and get back to our valued English faculty." Consulting his watch, he said, "I see I'm about to be late for my next meeting. It's been a pleasure, ladies, and I thank you for your time. Until we meet again."

Gathering his belongings, he moved swiftly to the door of the conference room and strode just as swiftly through the main office without glancing in the direction of the secretary, who was poised at her desk for an exchange that did not occur. The equally slighted chairwoman followed hurriedly in his wake. Meanwhile, the remaining faculty members heaved themselves up from the table in the conference room with something less than alacrity.

"Girl, am I glad you spoke up," said Lorraine Janson.

The others echoed that sentiment. Indeed, the yes-chorus that had greeted the dean's utterances and the administration's new policies appeared to have been nothing more than an exercise in public relations and personal protection. In the absence of the dean and the department head, the chorus of voices that now prevailed had something entirely different to say.

"Don't pay me enough as it is."

"Just a little change we're getting."

"Got enough work already grading all those papers."

"Think I'd just as soon retire as teach all those workshops."

"On top of four classes already."

In leaving, the women were profuse in their thanks.

"You did us all a good turn there."

"Sure was smart of you, to think of that."

"Never would have occurred to me, not in a million years."

"Surprised that's even *in* the handbook at all, the way they think we're happy to work around here for almost no pay."

Lorraine Janson patted Ivy on the arm as she left. "I sure am glad you're here. Your mama's proud, I know."

Ham was as impressed as the others. He was not the kind of person who would read the Faculty Handbook either. He had never once glanced through it, and didn't even know what he'd done with his copy. It was entirely possible he'd thrown it away.

In spite of all the gratitude heaped on her, Ivy only nodded impassively and collected her materials until all the others had left. She remained seated in the conference room until the chorus of voices had moved beyond the main office.

Turning toward him, she spoke in a low but intense voice with barely controlled rage. "Can you imagine anything more lame-brained than what we just heard?"

Ham took this for a rhetorical question and said nothing, just shook his head.

"What do you think we should do now?" she asked him quietly. "What should our next move be?"

Ham didn't have the heart to tell her that he wasn't in this with her and in fact was preparing to take himself out altogether. "Well," he began timidly, trying to think of some way to help her in the meantime. "How *are* these students going to get prepared for the teacher certification?"

Ivy slammed her palm down on the table. "They aren't going to get prepared!" she said angrily. "They can't learn in a few months what they haven't learned in almost twenty years! The first thing we need to do around here is stop pretending! Our students *shouldn't* pass that test! The seniors I've seen so far are definitely not qualified to go out and be teachers! They're not even good students! How can they possibly be teachers? I for one do not want to send them out into the public educational system to do what they can't do, and then in a few years' time, be dealing here in the college with the results of what they haven't done in the grammar schools! All that does is perpetuate ignorance and keep us down. What we need here is a complete overhaul. A new faculty, a new administration, and a new curriculum. And while they're at it, a new campus! Instead of facing any of these realities, they're just demanding that the faculty perform some kind of miracle. Without pay!"

At that moment the secretary backed into the conference room with a cell phone clamped to one ear. When she closed the door and turned around, she spied them for the first time.

"Oh, my God!" she said, surprised and embarrassed. "I had no idea the two of you was still here. I thought everybody had left. I am so sorry. Please pardon my interruption. I think it's just great the way you two are getting together. Putting your heads together, like this, I mean." She fumbled for the doorknob behind her. Into her phone, she said, "I got to call you back." When the door opened behind her, she almost giggled in nervous relief, and exited quickly.

"Perhaps we should leave," Ham suggested.

Ivy heaved a huge sigh. "Yes," she agreed, looking at her watch. "I've got class in a few minutes, too."

They said nothing as they passed through the main office. Only when they'd left the building and headed toward Module #13 did Ivy break the silence.

"You do agree with me, don't you?" she turned to him.

Agree with what exactly? He'd forgotten. "About the workshops?" he said. "Yes, it's hard to see how those would be enough to save these students in time."

"Nobody's trying to save anything but their own ass!" said Ivy bitterly. "And as for the college itself, it's doing the same thing. Just like any institution. Concerned with its own survival to the point its core mission got thrown out a long time ago. Ours has even got twisted totally around. We're not educating the black race here. We're just part of a rotten system that creates jobs for black people."

They had arrived at the steps leading up to Module #13. Ivy swung at the aluminum railing with her leather carryall, which caused it to vibrate loudly in the chilly November air.

"How do these people justify to themselves what they're doing here?" She thrust her face into his, as if it were his question to answer. "They are betraying and oppressing their own people! And they don't even care! As long as they have their position! As long as they have their pay!"

She looked at him as if he were one of these people, and truthfully, that's how he felt. After all, until recently, he had been clinging to his job here, along with the illusion that he was making a certain—though small—contribution to the public good.

"Look at this!" She stared indignantly at the aluminum railing which was still reverberating. "Have you ever wondered why the teachers are in trailers, the students are in trailers, but the people who run this place are in a white palace?" She jerked her head in the direction of Carver Hall, otherwise known as "the Big House."

Actually, he had noticed the discrepancy, but had not formulated it as a question since there was no one he felt comfortable asking.

"It's a perfect metaphor," she said. "They got theirs, and that's all they care about. The rest of us can just stay slaves who do slave labor for slave wages and turn out more slaves for the system!"

It was not comfortable being a white male while a black female ranted about slave labor and slave wages. Although it appeared she was not angry at him, a casual passerby might not have drawn that conclusion. Fortunately, there were no casual passersby at the moment, but that would soon change. He was certain it was almost eleven. Grabbing hold of the railing, he tried to calm both her and the hollow aluminum.

"The rest of the campus *is* being renovated," he reminded her, taking a tentative first step up the staircase.

"That's what they want you to think," she said bitterly. "But all that scaffolding? The cranes? The dump truck?" She swept her arm in the general direction of the main campus, currently over-run with scaffolding, cranes and other construction equipment. "All those things are just props," she said. "It's just a stage set. Designed to make us *think* the rest of the campus is being renovated. But have you ever seen one single construction worker? Have you ever seen any of this machinery being operated? Have you seen any sign of real progress whatsoever?"

His hand dropped from the railing and his foot slid off the first step as if he'd literally been struck by her questions. Actually, he *had* seen a few construction workers, but only a few, and no sign of any tangible progress in over a year.

"Don't think the white boys down in Montgomery don't know how to play this game," she said grimly. "They make masters out of a few black men, give them their own big house, then say, we got no more money. So the black women and children, they're still slaves, living in the cabins. But the black men are happy—they got theirs. They're not going to fuss about something like their own women and children living the lives of slaves in the cabins, in case their Big House gets taken away from them. They're gonna leave it be. And the black women?" Ivy glanced up toward the module, where some of these black women currently sat, behind very thin walls. "The black women seem content just to be house slaves. They're not going to say anything either, because they're just happy they're not out in the fields. And the children who come into this world slaves go out into this world slaves same as before, just hoping they can get to the point they don't have to work the fields. It's the plantation all over again, only the black men here think they got it made, because they're called 'dean' and 'president,' and the black women think they're doing okay because they're called 'educators.' And the white boys down in Montgomery are just sitting back watching it all unfold according to plan. They don't have to make slaves outa black people because the black people make slaves outa themselves for the price of a shiny new building and a fancy title. And when it gets to a certain point, the white man can just shut it down and say, 'We tried.'"

At this moment, doors to all the modules, including theirs, began opening with a bang and emitting students and faculty. Ham and Ivy stood by and nodded politely as several of their colleagues came down the stairs and headed for the teaching modules. He felt as sheepish as if they had just been caught in the middle of a lover's quarrel, and several of the covert glances they received from the others indicated that this was exactly what appearances suggested. No doubt Ivy's raised voice had been overheard, and the natural assumption appeared to be that the cause was personal in nature rather than academic, intellectual or professional. Ham was the only person he knew who did not see sex in every situation. But for some reason, it seemed, everyone else on earth appeared to believe that sex was at the root of everything. He didn't understand it.

On her way down the staircase, Lorraine Janson grabbed hold of Ham's arm instead of the railing for support. She took this opportunity to whisper in his ear. "I think you all make the cutest couple," she said. "Don't let anybody tell you different. Times have changed when it comes to that, even in Birmingham."

Fortunately Ivy was so wrapped up in her own reflections that she neither heard nor even noticed this exchange. Even after their colleagues had passed out of hearing, she remained listless and motionless, as if lacking the will to mount the steps to her office. Ham felt sorry for her. She was still invested;

she couldn't afford not to care, like he could. He racked his brains for something sympathetic to say.

"Perhaps you shouldn't worry about saving the college," he said quietly. "Perhaps it's best if it's allowed to die." He was afraid his "sympathy" was too colored by his own recent determination, but it was the best he could come up with on short notice. When she remained silent for quite a long while, he became even more afraid that he'd irritated rather than soothed her nerves.

Finally she said, "Don't think I haven't thought of that," before lapsing again into a brooding silence. He was relieved until she turned to him with a piercing gaze and re-doubled intensity.

"Segregation is over," he reminded her nervously, trying to pre-empt her next communication, whatever it might be. "These students can all go to the University of Alabama, or UAB. They don't need a black college in order to get a degree."

For a moment she looked at him as if he'd lost his wits. "Do you know the percentage of black students at the University of Alabama?" she challenged him fiercely. "Do you?"

He shook his head apologetically. It never occurred to him to think in terms of numbers or statistics.

"In a Southern state with one of the biggest black populations of any in the country, what would you expect the percentage of black students to be? At the flagship public university that's supposed to serve the needs of the *entire* state population?"

"I'm guessing that percentage is much lower than it should be," he ventured.

"Less than ten percent!" she cried. "Less than ten percent!"

He had expected to be shocked, but not this shocked. "But why?" he said. "What's stopping black students from going to the University of Alabama?"

"What's stopping them?" she cried, outraged.

"Well, it isn't George Wallace. It isn't Jim Crow," he said, trying to defend his ignorance.

"No, but it's everything else," she countered. "It's the parents, who don't have the money or the vision to encourage their kids even to think of college. It's the teachers who don't teach or care about the future of their students. It's the black kids themselves, who don't learn what they need to or make the grades to go to college, and don't want to go anyway."

She glared at him as if this were all his fault, although for the most part she had accused her own society. Still, he knew it all *was* his fault, if not personally, then collectively, as a member of the society that had flourished at the expense of hers. He lowered his eyes from her steely glare and said nothing.

"Even if a black kid *does* have the grades, the ambition and somehow the parents scrape together the money to send him to college, Bama is usually the *last* place they'd want to go," she informed him. "Unless they're football players," she muttered.

"But why?" he looked back up.

She treated him to a derisive snort of laughter. "You're a Brookie," she said dismissively. "You probably can't relate. Have *you* ever been in a situation where you know you're not wanted or respected?" she asked him accusingly. "Where you stick out like a sore thumb? You're a complete misfit with no hope of being accepted by the society around you? Do you know what it's like to hope you *are* invisible, so you can just slink through the day with no one noticing you? Because if they notice you, they will only make your life miserable in some way?"

"Actually, I can relate perfectly to all that," he told her. "You've just described the life of a Brookie who can't be a Brookie."

He braced himself for a declaration delivered with withering contempt to the effect that the plight of a poor little rich white boy could not possibly be compared to the plight of poor black kids born in a former slave state. Mercifully, she refrained, and instead gave him a look of something like sympathy. He was so relieved he inadvertently voiced his next thoughts.

"I don't think I would have survived at the University of Alabama," he told her. "And if I'd gone through fraternity rush, I wouldn't have made it through the hazing."

Again he waited for her indignant eruption at the mere suggestion of a parallel between the troubles of privileged white children and those of underprivileged black children. Again it didn't come.

"I wouldn't have been happy at the University of Virginia, either," he confided. "It's where my mother wanted to me to go. I'm lucky I had a guidance counselor who found the right college for me. Where I did fit in."

"So you understand why the average black kid would rather not go to the University of Alabama," she said, more as a statement than a question.

"Of course," he nodded.

"Do you know what percentage of black college graduates in this country come from historically black colleges?"

He shook his head.

"One third," she said, reaching out for the railing.

"One third," he repeated. He too grabbed the railing and together they proceeded up the stairs, which were just barely wide enough to accommodate the two of them.

"One third of all black college graduates come from HBCUs," she said, turning to him as they reached the top.

Though this *was* a compelling statistic, he wasn't sure whether it compelled him to believe that historically black colleges were offering better programs for black students, more nurturing environments, or just easier degrees.

"*I* went to a historically black college and got a great education," she said, jabbing her chest with an index finger. Whether she intended to refer to herself, or the SPELMAN written on her sweatshirt, it wasn't clear. "Think of Howard, in Washington, or Morehouse," she said emphatically.

Just as she flung open the door to the module, a gust of November air seized it and slammed it against the wall of the building. She seemed not to notice his struggles in reclaiming the door and shutting it behind them.

"Then there's Xavier in New Orleans," she continued. "Did you know that Xavier alone produces three-fourths of all African-American medical students in this country?" Now it was his chest she jabbed with her index finger. "The point is: Historically black colleges have been part of the solution in the past, and are still part of the solution. We can make *this* college part of the solution, too. I know we can." Suddenly she smiled at him. "I'm so glad you're here. Now I've really got to run."

~ 8 ~

He should have known better than to answer the telephone when he arrived back at his apartment later that afternoon. But usually, he thought in his own defense, his mother left messages—or summonses, rather—on his voice mail. She didn't see the sense of reaching him directly and wasting time while he expressed his own opinion, which was of absolutely no consequence to her.

"I understand you had a *date* with Erica Cooley this weekend."

Clearing his throat, he acknowledged that he'd met Erica Cooley for lunch on Saturday. "I didn't really think of it as a date," he added, because his mother's accusing tone had laid emphasis on that word. "Is that what she told her mother?"

"She didn't tell her mother the first thing about it!" his own mother announced dramatically, as if it were unheard of for a thirty year-old woman to have lunch without telling her parents. "You were seen," his mother explained.

At Botteghe Café, he'd been vaguely aware of several familiar faces whose names he couldn't come up with, and had known there would be an unpleasant reckoning with his mother, who would take him to task for being rude to Mrs. So-and-So or Mr. Thus-and-Such. The fear of running into people he was supposed to know was one of many reasons he didn't venture out much. The main reason, of course, was that he wanted to avoid having to answer the question of what he was doing with his life. People he was just meeting for the first time were as likely to pose this question as people he'd known all his life. So basically, he needed to avoid going out at all and meeting anybody at all. Having lunch with Erica would be safe enough, he had assumed, because her presence would shield him from the intrusions of others. The problem of being spotted together had not occurred to him.

". . . most unstable," his mother was saying. "Virginia is afraid you may just be *using* her. Of course I told her, no son of mine is capable of that."

"Using her?" he echoed. What was he to say to this? He supposed he *had* "used" her, though not in the way his mother meant by the term, which was her generation's code word for an unmentionable act of intimacy outside the confines of marriage. No, he had simply felt himself drowning, and had reached out desperately to grab hold of whatever came to hand to keep himself from going under. Erica is what he'd caught hold of. But if she hadn't previously suggested getting together when he saw her at his mother's dinner party, he doubted he would have had the presence of mind to grasp this lifeline. Unwisely, he pointed out to his mother that Erica was the one who'd proposed the idea.

"What are you telling me?" she cried, scandalized. "That *she* asked *you* for a date?"

He sighed. "I don't think she considered it a date, Mother, and neither did I."

His mother, as usual, paid no attention to what he said. "Virginia has more on her hands than I thought."

"Oh, come on, Mother. Even in Birmingham, I don't think there's anything the least bit radical about two old family friends having lunch together."

"A girl who asks a man for a date is a girl who will do *anything,*" his mother declared emphatically.

What did she mean by "*anything*"? he wondered. Rob? Kill? Or merely engage in sexual relations? He didn't dare ask. "We just had a single lunch date," he said, instantly regretting the use of his mother's loaded word. "It didn't lead to *anything,* and it's not going to."

In truth, however, they had met again the next day at a screening room in one of the UAB college buildings, where the French film society was showing *The Double Life of Veronique.* Erica had mentioned that she would be attending this event at two on Sunday afternoon, if he had nothing better to do and cared to join her. In effect, she had thrown him another lifeline, and he had seized on it. That was all.

"It would be a shame to take advantage of a poor girl who really needs professional help."

At that moment Tink jumped in his lap and meowed for his long-overdue attention. He stroked her back.

"Good heavens!" said his mother. "What was that? That creature's not still in your apartment, is she?"

"Of course she is, Mother. Did you think I brought her into my home just to turn her out in the street?"

"You could have told me she was there with you before we had this conversation."

"What difference would that have made?"

"I would never have discussed her if I'd known she was in the same room with you," she said stiffly.

"What are you talking about?"

"What do you think we've been talking about? Erica. Erica Cooley."

"That was Tinkerbell, Mother," he sighed. "What you heard was my cat. Erica Cooley is not in the room with me."

He was flabbergasted by the portrait of Erica his mother's imagination had constructed. On the one hand, she was a poor girl in need of professional help, and on the other, she was a voracious sexual vixen—or kitten—who might even be in his apartment ready to devour him at that exact moment. He thought it prudent not to add that Erica had never set foot in his apartment, since she actually *had* come in for an hour or two after the movie yesterday to share a cup of herbal tea, which is what he always drank in the afternoon on account of his stomach. Fortunately it was what she'd asked for without even knowing about his condition. She had been intrigued by his apartment in the building catering to UAB students, largely because she thought it was a deliberate statement of rebellion or protest against his Mountain Brook upbringing, and a form of homage to Thoreau's philosophy of Spartan simplicity. Of course it was nothing of the kind, but rather a cheap and convenient place to live that was also small enough for him to keep clean with little effort.

"Well, thank goodness," his mother was saying, greatly relieved. "I think it best to leave the poor child alone and let her try to get herself together as best she can. You know there was some dreadful business with a married man in Colorado. We have more than done our duty by her. Leave it to me. I'll let Virginia know."

"Let her know what?" He sensed that his mother was on the verge of hanging up, and knew that if he looked at his watch, it would be just about that time she needed to go consult with Harry about the final preparations for dinner. She could talk his ear off as if neither one had anything better to do, until she did have something better to do, at which point she hung up abruptly as if he'd been wasting her precious time. It was taken for granted, of course, that he never had anything better to do.

His mother made one of her characteristic sounds of exasperation. "Have you not heard a word I said? Virginia wanted to know whether Erica could expect to hear from you again. I told her I would find out and get back to her. Don't worry—I'll know just how to handle this with tact and diplomacy."

At that point Ham could hear Harry's voice in the background, and his mother ended the conversation by hanging up abruptly with her usual tact and diplomacy.

He poured himself half a glass of Scotch and sat back down on the sofa to resume stroking Tinkerbell. Although he was always left dazed by a conversation with his mother, the one today was especially confounding. While she and her friend suspected he might have some romantic interest in Erica Cooley, his co-workers at the college appeared to believe he had formed an attachment to Ivy Greer. In truth, the idea of being interested in either of these women had never occurred to him. But then again, ideas of this nature never did. Apparently, he was as lacking in sex drive as he was lacking in all other drives that normally defined the males of his species. It wasn't that he was unable to do *anything* with the opposite sex, or incapable of enjoying it, however. In fact, he enjoyed it immensely, and there was often that moment during each occasion when he believed that sex was the single greatest experience he'd known in his lifetime, and wondered why he didn't pursue more such experiences every waking moment. But this sensation was fleeting and left no lingering traces, not even the desire to repeat the experience he had recently identified as the peak of human existence. If he had a woman in his life who wanted sex with him, he was happy to comply, but somehow the idea never occurred to him with sufficient force compelling him to act upon it. According to several therapists, this is what it meant to have "no libido."

It was only thanks to several determined women in his past that he had known extended relations with the opposite sex. There had been a no-nonsense, horse-faced German girl named Ursula who was a fellow philosophy student at the University of Heidelberg. There had been an ambitious Jewish girl at Harvard Law School. And in his Ph.D. program, there had been a girl from Montana who had grown up on a ranch and looked like a lesbian. Before she revealed her interest in him, he had assumed she *was* a lesbian. All of these women had pursued him for reasons known only to themselves. One therapist had suggested that domineering, controlling women often sought out passive, meek, mild-mannered men who could be controlled and dominated. Another therapist had pointed out that his relationship with these women reflected the dynamic of his relationship with his mother. Nevertheless, he had found them all pleasant alternatives to living alone, which he wasn't very good at doing, though he suspected it was his natural condition.

If any one of these women had wanted or suggested marriage, he no doubt would have been married by now. His life would have taken a different turn, and he'd be set on whatever course was mapped out by his wife.

Perhaps he needed that. Perhaps he never would have suffered that terrifying bout of clinical depression and the subsequent hospitalization which haunted him still if his girlfriend at the time had not just left him. His break-up with Rachel was in fact one of the precursors to his breakdown in law school. As she had packed up and moved out, she had commented that he had all the intelligence of an Einstein coupled with all the ambition, motivation, and direction of an amoeba, and she just couldn't stand it anymore. Of course he couldn't argue with her characterization of his ambition, motivation and direction, but none of this was any worse than when she'd first met him and supposedly admired and respected him enough to take off her clothes while he used the bathroom in her apartment after coming back from their first date in law school. It was when she was gone from his life that he took such a turn for the worse as to require hospitalization.

It suddenly occurred to him that his recent close call with another break-down might be some form of delayed reaction to his parting with Jill. There had been no actual break-up. He had simply moved back to Birmingham. Somehow he had assumed that his life in an apartment in Birmingham would not be too much different from his life in an apartment in Massachusetts. But that apartment in Massachusetts had contained Jill, who perhaps had wanted something more concrete from him than his unspoken wish to have her in his apartment in Birmingham. Or wherever. But usually with Jill, if there was something she wanted, she spoke up immediately in order to get it. At any rate, she had been so preoccupied applying to jobs all over the country, the subject of their future never came up. If she didn't raise it, he didn't see how he could. Now, she was teaching queer theory at the University of Nevada in Reno. If she had ever suggested that he accompany her there, he undoubtedly would have done so instead of capitulating to his mother's insistence that he return to Birmingham so he could be near his family in its time of need.

But in the end, all these women had gradually lost interest in him and dropped out of his life. They pursued him, they initiated sex, they invited him to move into their apartments, but they stopped short of proposing marriage. He had never been able to bring himself to do so, and the women had disappeared from his life just as they'd entered, on their own mysterious volition.

The phone rang like a shrill warning sign that pierced his peaceful, Scotch-soaked reverie. He looked at his watch. Six o'clock. His parents would be eating dinner. Surely Ivy Greer wouldn't be calling at this hour either. Tentatively he picked up the receiver, and was relieved to hear his sister's voice.

"I'm fine," he said in reply to her question. Then, "No, it wasn't the flu," he acknowledged. He was forced to admit that what his sister had witnessed last week had not been a fainting spell, but a panic attack. "But I'm fine," he reiterated. "Where were you on Saturday? I didn't see you at the games."

Apparently she had been away all weekend attending a conference, and had just returned home, where an urgent message awaited her from Norman Laney.

"He said—and I quote—that the molecules of your entire body—especially your face—looked like they were stitched together with filaments of spider web liable to give way at any moment."

He laughed. It was an exact description of how he had felt at the time.

"Norman Laney was most concerned," she said sternly. "And so am I. Why didn't you tell me on Thursday?"

"It was just a rough patch after the session with my therapist," he said dismissively. "That's all. It's over now."

"She needs to help you find the right anti-depressant."

"We've been through this before. You know how I feel about it."

"Yes," she said wearily. "But there are plenty of new ones you haven't tried."

"There are plenty of old ones I did try. None of them worked."

"They got you out of the hospital. They worked."

He didn't want to concede the point, but neither did he want to engage in this particular discussion.

"One of these new ones might be able to help you enormously without the side effects," she continued.

"Side effects?!" It not only amazed him—it outraged him—that those who had never once even considered taking a drug that targeted their own brain chemistry could so blithely push them on others, and just as blithely dismiss the results as "side effects."

"You know what I mean," she said.

"I certainly do," he said. The drugs had put an end to his "self-defeating" thoughts by preventing him from having any thoughts at all. His feelings of despair and self-loathing had disappeared because his ability to feel anything at all had disappeared. Why did the world believe that this state of vegetable being was preferable to death? Essentially, the drugs were the equivalent of a complete frontal lobotomy. So far in life, his choice was between being a human paralyzed by depression, or a vegetable paralyzed by the anti-depressants. He chose to be human, and believed it was the right choice.

"Why would you not give something a chance if it could turn your life around?"

"You really think a little pill is the magic bullet I need?" Sometimes he wished he could think so, and believe in the power of a little round tablet to dissolve the problem inside himself. But instinctively he knew it wasn't that simple or easy, that he harbored a multitude of problems that would require a similar cluster of remedies to counteract them and liberate him from the death grip in which he remained a prisoner.

His sister was unaccountably silent. "What did you mean by 'magic bullet?'" she said finally.

"It doesn't matter," he said. "I've come up with my own plan. Go have dinner with your family."

"I'm coming over," she said. "Just give me ten minutes. I'll be right there."

It took him thirty minutes to convince his sister that his "plan" did not involve a magic bullet of a different sort. If he could have told her what the plan was, his task would have been easier, but it was still just a tender, fragile seedling that needed more time in the incubator before it was planted in the open soil and exposed to the full light of day. He was afraid his whole idea might shrivel up and die if he brought it out before it was ready. But eventually his sister was reassured, and said she'd see him on Thursday at the club.

"The club?"

"For Thanksgiving. You haven't forgotten, have you?"

"No, of course not," he lied indignantly. "I'll see you on Thursday, then."

~ 9 ~

Normally on Thursdays he would have been preparing to meet with his therapist, but because it was a particular Thursday in late November, he found himself preparing to eat Thanksgiving dinner at the Mountain Brook Club. He would rather have been with his therapist. Looking around him at the blur of faces that didn't seem a whole lot more festive than his, he wondered how many of these others would have preferred to be at their therapist's office as well. Of course, if given completely free choice, all the men in the room, including himself, would have chosen to be at home in front of the television, watching football. Their faces had a look of glum acquiescence and submission to the will of their women. The children at every table squirmed uncomfortably in their boredom and Sunday best, as he himself had done when he was a child attending events at the club. At the moment, his nephews were squirming on either side of him, impatient for the meal to get underway and get over with. But they were better off than he was: at a certain point in the buffet service, when people were popping up peripatetically from tables all over the room to get seconds or thirds or dessert, the children could pop off and disappear to the usual hideaways and cubbyholes without anyone really noticing or objecting. He, on the other hand, was stuck for the duration, and had to resist the urge to squirm in his own seat.

On the whole, the women seemed the most satisfied to be where they were, showing off their new dresses, dutiful husbands and beautiful children in their literally priceless clothes. But even they weren't exactly happy. Doubt lurked in the eyes of some; too much bourbon already shone in the eyes of others, especially the older women, the grandmothers like Lula Petsinger, who had most of her meals at the club anyway. It was the women who gave off the whiff of guilt and failure that made the whole atmosphere so oppressive and the whole occasion seem so doomed. The square jaws of their mirthless men and the restlessness of the malcontented children begged an obvious question these women could not ignore despite their bright laughter and jangling jewelry. Why weren't they having Thanksgiving dinner at home, where Thanksgiving dinner belonged?

For once in this town where half the streets, including his own, were named "Country Club" Drive, Road, Place, Circle, Lane or Avenue, the Mountain Brook Club was not the place to be. For once, an appearance at the club was the ultimate sign of failure rather than success. This, at any rate, seemed to be the fear haunting the eyes of the ladies: that the people here today were not the people who had made it, or who had it made. These were the people who had come to naught and had not been able to come up with their own Thanksgiving dinner, or an invitation to someone else's. Whether they lacked loyal help or sufficient will, these women had not been able to provide a family meal for an important family holiday in the privacy of their own homes where family events belonged. Instead, they had dragged their beleaguered families out to a public (sort of) place for their private holiday ritual. Those who did not belong to the club, had been turned down or were considered "unacceptable" candidates for membership to this elite pinnacle of the social world, would never have guessed at the air of defeat and decline it could generate. For Ham, this sense of malaise hung over the club at all times, but was most pronounced on Thanksgiving and Easter. It was no comfort to think that it was filled with people just like himself—wealthy, privileged and lost—who would have been better off in their therapist's office.

And it didn't help that the quality of the food was equivalent to what he could (and often did) procure from the frozen food section of the supermarket. Only here he had to wear a coat and tie to consume what was essentially a Stouffer's turkey dinner. The thin slices of mostly tasteless meat had that same layer of gelatinous skin that peeled right off the edges. The cranberry sauce was the usual quivering heap of jelly containing the familiar indentations caused by the ridges of a can. The sweet potato soufflé, which no doubt also came from a can, was not redeemed by its topcoat of marshmallows, which grew soggier and soggier the longer it remained in the steaming chafing dishes on the buffet line.

As he bent over his plate to remove a string of skin he'd neglected to peel from his slice of turkey, he caught the eye of one of the waiters, who gave him a conspiratorial grin. Ham almost laughed as he thought that for once in the city of Birmingham, Alabama, the black people around him had the best of the situation. At least they were getting paid for being there, and afterwards, they would go home to the best Thanksgiving dinners to be had in the city, prepared by the black women who cooked dinner for white people almost every other day of the year. This particular waiter, Ham could tell, was already relishing the moist, flavorful smoked turkey (prepared on a black barrel grill), served with home-made cornbread dressing and gravy that he would go home and enjoy in contrast to the hospital-quality food served on the white bone china with the country club logo. What could these black people here possibly think of this pitiful food they had assembled and served to pitiful white people who didn't really know how to have a good time any more than they knew how to do anything else for themselves?

Maybe it would have been different in a place like Commander's Palace in New Orleans, where there were balloons and jazz, frothy mimosas and world-class cuisine amidst the oak trees of the Garden District. Here, he felt like he was in the conference room of a Ramada Inn. No one could really explain it, and no one wanted to acknowledge it, but the dining room of the Mountain Brook Club occupied the space below ground that was normally called the basement. The view from the single window showcased the outside stairwell leading to the rear lawn, which could just barely be glimpsed from where he sat at the table with his family. There were much grander ballrooms and receptions rooms on the first floor for weddings and parties, but the main dining room was located downstairs, below ground level in a dim, cheerless room with low ceilings and only one window. It mystified Ham how the people who belonged to the Mountain Brook Club believed they had arrived at anything other than a mordant metaphor for their own disordered existence. Here they sat in what was essentially a cellar, and congratulated themselves for being on top of the world.

As disoriented and disjointed as was his own existence, he was at least one step ahead of the rest: he knew how bad off he was. The proud and boastful Old South façade of the clubhouse, conceived and constructed by New South money, did not fool him anymore than did the slightly smaller versions of this house found in the pseudo-colonial residences throughout Mountain Brook. Inside you would find a sad collection of miserable people who didn't like each other, themselves or their lives despite how strenuously they performed the motions necessary to convince the world otherwise. At least he knew it. How much the sham he had been forced to participate in as a child of this particular world had contributed to the shambles of his adult existence—that he didn't know. But being here wasn't helping him. He was more and more convinced of the efficacy of his plan.

His sister prodded him under the table with her shoe while inclining her head ever so slightly in the direction of their uncle, who had apparently been addressing Ham at some length and was now awaiting a reply to a question

Ham had not heard. His mother turned toward her brother-in-law to speak for her son, as she had been doing ever since he was old enough to speak for himself.

"Whatever happens to the college is not Hamilton's concern," she said. "He's leaving after this year and will finally be doing what he should have done years ago."

Ham was actually satisfied with this response to whatever the question was, and saw no need to amend or add to his mother's statement. Fielding a wink from his father, he hoped his uncle was equally satisfied and felt no further need to engage in discussion or impart important information, which to Ham's mother was tantamount to "discussing business at the table" and was therefore taboo. After all, no one wanted to kill the holiday spirit. So it was better to stare at each other silently as if they had nothing to say than to bring up a serious subject which might challenge or engage the intellect.

His aunt Belinda had long ago consumed her usual three mouthfuls and was now sipping her third bourbon while staring contentedly into space. On Thanksgiving Day, his uncle Barry usually got around the problem of both his wife and his sister-in-law by spending most of his time at other tables, shaking hands and greeting friends as was only natural for an Alabama state senator who of necessity spent a good deal of his time in Montgomery and needed to make use of any opportunity to see the people who sent him to Montgomery, where he preferred to be. It wasn't that he had any political ambition or desire for public service. Rather, he had a girlfriend in the capital city he'd more or less lived with for the past twenty years. If Ham's colleague Ivy Greer could have met him, she would have been forced to adjust her perception of "the white boys down in Montgomery," who—judging by his uncle—did not in the least know what they were doing— in the legislature, at any rate. His uncle's main agenda in being a member of the Alabama state legislature was to avoid having to live in Birmingham with his wife. For her part, his wife liked both her husband's money and her husband's absence, which allowed her to devote her time to her Garden Club, her bridge games, and her bourbon and water. There were only a few occasions a year when they had to function publicly as a married couple, and Thanksgiving was unfortunately one of them.

After his uncle's unsuccessful attempt to make conversation with his family, Ham was not surprised to see him rise, yet again, from the table. But then his father rose as well to shake hands with Henry Cooley, who had just arrived in the dining room with his family. Rising along with Mark, he nodded to Erica and peered anxiously beyond her for signs of her sister, who appeared not to be there. It could be hoped that she was in Connecticut with her husband's family. That was a stroke of luck. Mrs. Cooley was otherwise engaged at another table; having snagged her purse on the corner of a chair, she was using this trifling accident as the occasion for her usual hullaballoo. Everyone in the room would now be aware that she was in it. Still, he could be grateful that she was exploiting another table for this purpose rather than the one he occupied. But just at that awkward moment when he was halfway between standing and sitting back down while looking behind him to make sure of his chair, he heard his name being declaimed from across the room.

"Hamilton Whitmire!" cried the voice. "Just the man I want to see! You're the only philosopher I know of in Birmingham, and I need a philosopher! Can you please please please tell me the difference between a rotation and a repetition?"

People laughed as they inexplicably always laughed at whatever Virginia Cooley said. But this time, he feared, it was possible they were laughing at him. He certainly felt foolish enough, having whipped his head around at the sound of his name, but was otherwise too paralyzed to straighten up into the erect posture of either a man or a philosopher, neither of which was an accurate description of his state of being, especially at the moment. On the contrary, he felt as if he'd been caught with his pants down, about to sit on the toilet. He also felt as if all eyes were now on him, including Mrs. Cooley's, which were coming closer and closer as she moved toward him from across the room. When she was putting on one of her acts, her eyes always had a way of bugging out like giant orbs on stems in a cartoon character. Indeed, the whole scene was beginning to feel like a frame from a cartoon. But today for the first time, he noticed that these popeyes of hers were not trying to commandeer him and press him into her service. Instead they were begging him. Also he noticed there were strands of gray in the shoe-polish black of her hair. With dawning horror he realized that this aging prima donna ballerina had just taken a flying leap into the air and was expecting him to catch her and then guide her as she pirouetted across the stage of the Mountain Brook Club's dining room carpet. As a seasoned performer, she should have known better than to choose him for a partner. He had no talent for this sort of conversational ballet. What was he to do? He knew he was supposed to supply some witty and clever rejoinder which would make her own initial sally seem all the more witty and clever than it had been. But he'd long since forgotten her opening line. The only thing he could think of to do was firm up his posture and say "Happy Thanksgiving" with a strained smile. If nothing else, he could just play the straight man.

By now she was upon him, towering over him and seizing both of his wrists. "You must give me the benefit of your philosophical wisdom!" she proclaimed.

Benefit of philosophical wisdom? he wondered. What was that? "I don't think there *is* any benefit," he told her. "At least, I haven't noticed any in my own case." This was quite true: whatever understanding he possessed of complicated schools of philosophical thought appeared to have no practical application whatsoever, including to his own daily existence.

Her back was turned as she greeted the others. "Seriously," she said, facing him again. "I'm reading Walker Percy for my book club, and I just don't get this business of rotations and repetitions. We are *dying*—I mean *dying*—to have you come lead our discussion." This time she seized both of his arms with her long, tapering hands and clutched as fiercely as if he and he only had the power to save her from the certain death she had referred to. "Please say you'll do it! You just have to say yes!"

"But I don't get the business of rotations or repetitions either," he said.

She threw back her head and whooped with laughter. "Oh, you darling man!" she exclaimed, suddenly letting go of his arms and throwing her own long limbs around his neck. "You are as much the soul of modesty as you are a genius! I love you Hamilton Whitmire! I love you! We'd be so lucky to have you as our speaker!"

"What's the book?" he inquired politely.

"Book?" she said, thrown off course and momentarily confused. "Oh!" She recovered quickly. "It's *The Moviegoer*. I just read the most wonderful line right before we came here. Henry had to literally pry the novel out of my hands and frogmarch me to the car."

To his horror, Mrs. Cooley proceeded to deliver the line as if she were a famous actress from the Royal Theater Academy performing Shakespeare on a London stage. Addressing an invisible spot in one corner of the ceiling, she went into a trance-like state and quoted verbatim, projecting her voice: "It is not a bad thing to settle for the Little Way." Turning back toward the table, she recited, with the appropriate air of philosophical resignation: "Not the big search for the big happiness, but the sad little happiness of drinks and kisses, a good car and a warm deep thigh."

Elsewhere in the room, someone clapped and whistled. "I like that part about the warm deep thigh!"

It was a predictable response from Big Julian Petsinger, otherwise known as Big Pet, who was of course no one's idea of a pet. Norman Laney called him the biggest barbarian in Birmingham. If not for his vast wealth and social standing, others might have called him a redneck. Although the Petsinger family had been one of the original "Big Mules" of Birmingham's iron and steel industry and amassed a tremendous fortune, the money and status Julian Petsinger had always known had not succeeded in making him what Norman Laney called "a civilized being." Big Pet routinely walked out of Libba Albritton's dinner parties before dinner was served so he could go get "some good American food" at the country club. The only reason she invited him was because his only son had married her daughter. He went for the same reason, but could never be prevailed upon to stay for the meal. His poor pitiful wife whom everyone adored put up only the most token resistance to what Mr. Laney called her husband's "barbarity." Her nerves had been shot to pieces years ago from the daily stress of living with her husband. He was indeed a big man, also red-faced from his steady diet of red meat and Scotch, and full of what he may have thought was good-natured bluff and bluster. But there was a crushingly iron will behind it which had immediately reduced Lula to a nervous wreck within a year of her marriage. She came from that generation of Mountain Brook women who had never once—in their entire lives—washed their own hair. A woman who had never had to wash her own hair was not a woman who could go up against Big Pet. The loveliest debutante of her year, she could have picked anyone, so the story was, but had unexpectedly settled on Big Pet, who even then was bigger than he should have been. Whereas she was immeasurably more refined, delicate and cultivated, he was quite measurably more rich. Many wondered if her family had pressured her into this unfortunate choice as a way to reclaim their own past, in which the deBlanchard family had been the biggest of the Big Mules in Birmingham until the Petsingers became even bigger and eventually bought them out. Whatever the case, Lula had learned to make a life out of Scotch and cigarettes, while her husband made his out of Scotch and rib-eyes.

"Let's hear more about those warm thighs!" he yelled from across the room.

Mrs. Cooley had finally found a real opening from a man who was neither the soul of modesty nor a genius. A gleam came into her eye as she prepared to take immediate advantage of her latest cue.

"Say that again!" called out Mr. Petsinger. "Let's hear that fine speech one more time!"

At this point Mr. Cooley began tugging gently on his wife's arm. Ham braced himself for the worst. He couldn't stand it when people spouted literature any more than when they quoted Scripture. Sacred texts deserved respectful consideration in places of sanctity, like the church, the classroom, or the privacy of home. Otherwise, the wisdom found in the texts should be quietly observed and followed to the extent possible in the given individual. Under no circumstances should a sacred text be put to vulgar uses.

While Lula Petsinger was laying a restraining hand on her husband's own very warm thigh, and Mr. Cooley explained to his wife that everyone really wanted to eat their turkey and get back to the football games, Erica took the opportunity to tell Ham that there *was* going to be a movie on Sunday after all. The announcement after last Sunday's film about a hiatus during the Thanksgiving weekend had been incorrect.

Mrs. Cooley obviously had antennae all over her body to feel for any available material she could possibly work with. She whipped back around.

"What's this?" she crowed with a delight that even sounded genuine. "I didn't realize the two of you were *seeing each other!*" she said, with just that sort of stage whisper designed to convey intimacy and at the same time carry to the farthest corners of the room.

"Oh, Mother, really," said Erica, blatantly rolling her eyes. "You are so transparent. And if you think you can get away with that old-fashioned trick, you are living in the wrong generation. Come on. Let's go eat."

Mrs. Cooley was momentarily flustered, since the naked truth was not her usual medium. "Oh, hush," she said. "You are really the most impossible child. All I meant was—"

"All you meant was to plant the idea in everyone's mind that Ham and I are dating. Did you hope the idea might occur to us? Or that we'd be forced into it by public expectation? Let's go eat," she urged again. "Ham's not interested in me. He likes the films; that's all."

"Of course he's not interested in you!" her mother shot back gaily. "Why would he be? You've got nothing to offer—no looks, no accomplishments, and only a few warped brains in your idiot head. I never dreamed he *could* be interested in you! But that doesn't stop me from being interested in him! I want him for my book club and I'm going to get him!"

"Come on, Virginia," said her husband fondly. "Let's allow these folks to eat their dinner, and go get some of our own." While he exchanged a wink with Ham's father, Mrs. Cooley shot Ham's mother a look that said "See? My impossible child is worse than your impossible child" before allowing herself to be led away. From the pucker of his mother's lips, Ham could see what conflicted joy she derived from having the lesser grievance. And now Virginia Cooley had succeeded in placing Adelaide Whitmire in her debt. She—Mrs. Cooley—had called Adelaide's son a genius, a philosopher, and above all—a darling man. She had said she loved him and had to have him—for all the world to hear. It's true that Adelaide had invited her dratted child over to dinner last month, but Virginia Cooley had more than paid her back, and now Adelaide owed her. She owed her.

"I suppose you'll have to do it," said his mother grimly, her mouth now a thin line without benefit of lipstick.

He felt himself blushing as he groped for his long-lost chair and finally sat back down. "Do what?" he said.

"The book club, of course," said his mother impatiently.

Mark leaned across the table. "The Cooley book group isn't so bad," he said under his breath. "They actually read the books."

"What's that?" said his mother-in-law, who belonged to a different book club comprised mainly of elderly ladies who seldom read the books.

While Mark was busy covering the tracks of his indiscretion, his sister Valerie turned to him. "You're blushing," she observed.

"Just getting hot," he explained. But he was actually in the throes of a beet-red, red hot blush which suffused his whole body much as the sudden memory of last night's dream had just suffused his brain. He may not have been "seeing" Erica Cooley, but he had certainly had a vivid dream about her last night. This dream was in no way erotic, and he couldn't even remember its actual substance. But somehow the very experience of dreaming about her made him now feel as if they had engaged in a form of intimate relations. His mind had taken possession of her, and she had embraced and saturated his unconscious, where they had commingled in his bed. While the content of the dream had nothing to do with sex—he was certain of that—the dream itself had been an intensely sexual experience. A second wave of blushing swept over him at the memory.

His mother was waving her hand dismissively to brush aside Mark's words as inconsequential and of no account. This also happened to be her opinion of her son-in-law himself, who was an "absolute nobody" from "absolutely nowhere," despite being tall, handsome, a loving husband, an excellent father, a well respected educator and the author of a book which had been reviewed in the New York *Times,* the Washington *Post,* and the *New Yorker* magazine. But as a "no-name" from a "no-account" place in the Midwest, now nothing more than a mere teacher, which was a job for women, he was an embarrassment as a son-in-law to Adelaide Whitmire. She would have traded his looks, his accomplishments, his good reputation and perhaps even his love and devotion to her daughter and grandsons for someone "known" in Mountain Brook. Then it could have been said that Adelaide Whitmire's daughter had made a good marriage. But his last name of "Ellis" meant nothing in

Mountain Brook. She didn't even bother to look at him while silencing him with a wave of her hand.

"There's no need for you to call," she said to her son. "I'll find out everything you need to know and give you the details."

"I'd rather you told Mrs. Cooley I can't do it," he said. "Tell her I'm too busy."

"I can't lie to Virginia," said his mother, who believed that no one but herself was a truly busy person. "You'll have to do it just this once."

He'd heard those words before, when asked to lead his mother's book club in their "discussion" of Thomas Mann's novel *Buddenbrooks*. Unfortunately, he had been under the mistaken impression that they wanted him to expound on German culture, with which he was somewhat familiar, and the philosophy of Nietzsche, with which he was even more familiar and which informed important aspects of the novel. Only after he realized that at least one elderly lady was snoring did he realize that many others were also asleep. And only then did he realize that he was there to entertain, not educate. (Later his mother explained that he was only there because Norman Laney couldn't make it.) But in a desperate attempt to entertain the ladies, he had self-deprecatingly compared himself to the last pitiful gasp of the once-great Buddenbrook merchant family—a weak, sickly, artistic dreamer, incapable of continuing the family business or even the family itself. In his nervous desperation, he couldn't stop talking, and had gone on to point out that although it was clear that Hanno Buddenbrook would never marry or have children, it wasn't quite clear if the author intended him to be homosexual. Most of the ladies had finally awoken upon hearing the word "homosexual," but he was afraid he'd succeeded only in making his mother's friends suspect he was referring to himself.

"I'll make it clear to Virginia that she cannot count on you for *anything* else," his mother was saying. But we do owe her this."

Strangely, Ham also had the feeling that he owed something to Mrs. Cooley, but it didn't occur to him why until later in the evening, when he re-played the scene at the country club in his mind. "I love you, Hamilton Whitmire!" Mrs. Cooley had proclaimed. Of course, this absurd declaration was as false as everything else she ever said. Still, Ham couldn't help but savor the words: it was the first time in his life he'd ever heard anyone utter them.

~ 10 ~

The next day, Ham had an appointment with his therapist, thanks to a holiday from school which meant that his day was free and several of Lauren's Friday patients were out of town. At the beginning of the week, he had decided to unveil his plan to Lauren at this time. She was the one, he realized, who could help him muster the courage to put his plan into action against protestations from any family members, namely his mother. For the first time since he'd been going to Lauren, he'd enjoyed the process of rehearsing his opening monologue and actually looked forward to delivering it.

But he was no more than a few seconds into his spiel before he realized that it wasn't going well, as Lauren shifted uncomfortably in her chair and tugged at her miniskirt to make sure it covered the upper reaches of her thigh. Just that suddenly, he lost all the conviction necessary to continue with his speech. Nevertheless, he blundered ahead, stumbling and faltering frequently throughout. She remained nothing but patient and impassive as he dogged on to the end. Afterwards he nervously awaited her verdict while she said nothing for what seemed like infinity. Finally she frowned. His heart went into freefall, and he felt like he needed to bend over and scrape it off the floor.

"I don't understand why you think you need another degree," she said eventually.

She had missed his entire point; he felt almost angry.

"Why could you possibly want to pursue another degree? This—whatever it is?"

"MFA."

"MFA," she repeated skeptically.

"Master of Fine Arts," he filled in hopelessly.

"Isn't that the same degree your brother-in-law couldn't get a job with?"

He nodded.

"Then I fail to see what possible good it could do you."

Hadn't he just explained at great length?

"You've already racked up three degrees in higher education already," she went on. "Almost four. Let's see." She began ticking them off on her fingers. "A bachelor's in English from Harvard," she began.

"Williams," he corrected miserably.

"Williams," she nodded. "Thank you. A master's in German from the University of—"

"Heidelberg," he supplied, not bothering to point out that the master's was in philosophy.

"A Ph.D. from Harvard—also in English—and almost a law degree—again from Harvard."

They stared at each other.

"What is the point of yet another degree?"

His lips were dry. "A few weeks ago you asked me why I didn't just quit my job at Cahaba College," he said haltingly. "I-I thought you'd be more pleased that I had decided to do this." He also thought he deserved more credit for proposing to buck his mother, who had insisted he return home on account of his father's health, which actually appeared to be okay.

Lauren sighed. "But this is the first *real* job you've ever had. This is the first time in your adult life you haven't been a student at some elite university. The first time you've stepped foot into the real world, as it's called. Surprise! It's a mess. Just like the college where you're teaching. And what's your first instinct when you encounter the problems of the world? You want to run away." She leaned forward. "I think this is your whole problem. We've talked about it before when we've discussed your tendency to procrastinate. You allow yourself to run away and duck the issues when you need to stand your ground and confront them. You have to *engage*. You have to grapple with the mess of the world in one form or another, whether it's Cahaba College or something else. The world needs you—of all people—with your intelligence and education—to engage with its problems. And more importantly, *you* need that engagement with the world."

She didn't look at all like a violent person. She was actually rather petite, with a head full of strawberry blonde Shirley Temple curls and dimples on her face to match. Yet he felt as if she'd just seized a dagger and plunged it into his chest. As if that weren't enough, she proceeded to twist it.

"You have *got* to wean yourself off the approval and admiration you get from teachers," she continued. "It's only a substitute—and not a very good one—for your mother's approval and admiration, which has never been forthcoming and probably never will be. Because degree programs come to an end. And you cannot keep hopping from one program to another, perpetually postponing the issues of adulthood, and expect to achieve a full-fledged existence. You must supply your own validation. 'This is who I am; this is what I do,' and let the world—your mother—be damned. You've got to stake your claim as an adult in this world. All else flows from that."

She was ruthless. He didn't expect the world to feel sorry for him. But he did expect that his therapist would take some pity on him, because he was paying her to do so. However, instead of being shored up by her sympathy, he was coming apart at the seams.

"Remember what you told me about your breakdown in law school?"

He nodded unhappily.

"I know there were several contributing causes; there usually are. But one of them was the rejection of your manuscript by your cousin's publisher. Remember telling me that?"

He nodded again, more miserable than ever and pained as ever when he thought about the fate of his novel. He'd had such high hopes. Not only that his novel would get published, but that its publication would mean he was a writer. And if he were a writer, it wouldn't matter that he wasn't a lawyer. He would be established as someone doing something no one—including his mother—could argue with. Otherwise, he was just a worthless failure, scribbling anonymously away in inconsequential notebooks. Publication would allow him to do what he most wanted to do with the world's respect, approval and perhaps even admiration just in the nick of time, when he would be graduating from law school with no plans for taking a bar exam or entering practice.

He didn't see how his novel wouldn't get published. His cousin's books were amateurish, hodge-podge concoctions filled with as many clichés and conventions of so-called Southern literature as James could cram into each one. There were race riots and lynchings in some; others had jolly black mammies in the kitchen and letters from dead Confederate soldiers in the attic. Despite his Alabama heritage, James had never encountered any of these aspects of his heritage in his whole life, and it showed in his writing. The collection of stories written by his brother-in-law Mark and published by the same company were much more "finely wrought," as one of the blurbs had noted. Still, they were rather slender pieces of writing, and Ham was not surprised that Mark had so far been unable to produce the novel the publisher wanted next.

Ham had every hope that his own novel would find a ready reception. Instead, it had been rejected with surprising swiftness. To this day, Ham could still quote the words of the rejection letter. Despite praise for the lyrical writing style and the philosophical insights provided by the story, the editor had failed to "fall in love" with any of the characters. It was apparently of no consequence that Ham had not intended for that editor—or any reader of his novel—to "fall in love" with any of the characters. These characters were not intended to be lovable; they were intended to be like real people.

"In response to this rejection," his therapist was bulldozing brutally ahead, "what did you do? Continue to pursue publication?" She paused in case he wanted to fill in that blank. "No, you decided to enter a Ph.D. program. I think it was a dodge." (She made it sound like it was a murder.) "Same with the university in Germany. Same with law school. Same with the MF—whatever you're talking about now."

He cleared his throat. "But I'm afraid I'm the kind of person who needs structure to my day," he said nervously, ashamed to add that he also needed a barricade against the bombardments of his mother.

"It's not simple structure to your day—like some kind of scaffolding—that you need," she said. "It's more like infrastructure for your life. And that only comes from engagement in the world."

She lifted her eyebrows in case he wanted to interject at this point. He did not.

"If you want to pursue your writing, by all means, do so," she said. "But that does not mean you need to pursue another degree. You can work on your writing during your summers off, during the days you don't teach. You do not need to turn your back on either your family obligations or your professional commitments. And in fact, you should not do so."

Switching gears, his therapist rattled onwards. "Changing the subject," she said briskly, "I must bring this up before we run out of time." Pausing ominously, she consulted her watch and looked back up. "Under the arrangement we have with your sister, she called to let me know what happened last month, when I challenged you about your job at Cahaba College." She paused again. "She said you fell apart, had a panic attack which she personally witnessed, and otherwise came dangerously close to having a breakdown, as was observed by another close family friend." She paused yet again, presumably to see if he wanted to contradict anything she said. He didn't. "Your sister believes you should have been placed on anti-depressants like—ten years ago. I'm not so sure I disagree.

"Now, I've shown you the respect of pushing you even harder today than I did last month; I think you can take it. But I want you to return the favor and try some of these new drugs that have come out since the last time you took an anti-depressant. It's all a matter of finding one that does what you need it to without unacceptable side effects. We may have to go through a period of trial and error. None of these drugs is perfect, and none of them is *the* answer. But it might be a help. It could be part of an answer. What do you say? How about it?"

He nodded dully, trying to remember what Mr. Laney had said about how he looked like he was held together by nothing but spider web filaments liable to give way at any moment. Well, the fragile cobweb holding him together had been dealt a devastating blow; its filaments were disintegrating and would soon be mere wisps on the wind. It didn't seem to matter much anymore that he maintain any stoic principle about the integrity and sanctity of a brain that had so clearly failed him. The most he could do was maintain a stoic silence as Lauren's voice droned on and on about the drug she thought was his best choice, optimistically called "Well" something or other, which had been one of four anti-depressants given to various patients of hers and other psychiatrists who had recently taken part in a clinical study conducted by UAB researchers. The report of the results had actually just been published in a pharmacology journal, and she could give him a copy if he cared to read it. Meanwhile, she handed over a large box of samples and a written prescription, while launching into detailed instructions about how to take the drug and what to expect from it. As he distractedly accepted the box of samples thrust upon him, he had a sickening sensation of déjà vu, as when he'd thought he'd written a great novel and was sure to receive an offer of publication, but the editor had offered only to shred his copy of the manuscript instead of spending anybody's money on return postage. Here he'd thought he'd arrived at a momentous and life-changing breakthrough, only to discover that he was simply repeating a self-destructive pattern to which he'd been completely oblivious.

Stumbling out of Lauren's office, he was in such a fog of distress that he almost collided with a woman in the waiting room. Although tear-stained, her face was unmistakable; nevertheless, he couldn't think of her name.

Fortunately she recognized him immediately, called out his name and broke into her enormous trademark smile, which triggered his memory of who she was.

"Dooky?" he called out, incredulous.

She hugged as quickly and easily as she smiled, tears notwithstanding. Dooky St. John was one of three sisters who all went by nicknames given by their black maid when they were babies. There was Dooky, for Dorothy; Mookie, for Marian; and Pookie, for Patricia, he believed. Or was it Pamela?

He couldn't remember. All the sisters had attended Mountain Brook High School, whereas he had attended a small private school whose students rarely interacted with those from the public high school. All three St. John sisters were beautiful golden girls who perfectly exemplified what it meant to be a Southern belle. Dooky had a radiant smile which literally went from the middle of one cheek to the middle of the other in a nanosecond, filling the room with her dazzling cheer as it had when she first noticed him a moment ago. There was nothing calculated or forced about either the smile or the high spirits, and it was probably this buoyant vitality that accounted for her beauty more even than the blonde of her long hair, the blue of her big eyes or the length of her full dark lashes, which all seemed as unstudied and unforced as her smile. But it wasn't her beauty that made her the ultimate Southern belle. It was the sweetness emanating from the very core of her being. Although she had the kind of world-class looks that could have turned her into a world-class bitch, Dooky was sweeter than sweet tea, as they liked to say in the South. It wasn't saccharine either, but the real thing. Steel magnolias were another matter, but in a true Southern belle, the greater the looks, the sweeter the woman. This was the real secret to the power of the Southern belle, and Dooky possessed it. There was not one smidgeon of either reserve or hauteur in her open, guileless manner. Out of the endless bounty of her carefree good nature, she offered up her beauty and her gaiety to anyone she met.

Still, she was the kind of girl who had always intimidated Ham from the time he was a bookish teenager at a nerdy private school whose students were rarely invited to take part in the fraternity or sorority activities at the high school. Dooky St. John had been president of TKD sorority. That was all Ham needed to know when he learned he had been assigned to escort her to the debutante ball his mother insisted he attend because the daughter of one of her friends was being presented. At the time, Ham was then a Phi Beta Kappa junior at a small Ivy League college; Dooky was a Kappa Gamma at the University of Alabama. These were the logical extensions of their very different high school experiences. He had expected Dooky to scorn him as a geekish, awkward and pitifully short specimen of manhood who was utterly unfit to be by her side. Instead, she had greeted him with a warmth and sweetness which suggested they'd known and loved each other all their lives. It wasn't long before he felt this was actually the case, and surprised himself by thoroughly enjoying the Ball of Roses. Many of his former high school classmates were there as well; it was thrilling to see them again with the loveliest girl in the room on his arm.

Dooky didn't just suffer his presence; she welcomed it, and by the end of the evening he understood why. In violation of the rules of the debutante society, she was already (secretly) engaged to Louis Lankford. If her engagement were known, she would not be allowed to be presented at the Redstone Ball, which was the most prestigious and exclusive of Birmingham's three debutante balls. Also, her parents were worried about Louis, who was a bit of a rake and had come quite close to getting expelled from Bama for his drinking and failing grades. Even worse, he had already been kicked out of his Phi Gam fraternity for reasons that were not at all clear, since drinking and failing grades were part of what it meant to be a Phi Gam. There was no question about what Louis would do when he—er—graduated, as the Lankfords owned three Buick dealerships, two BMW dealerships, and the only Porsche dealership in town. Louis himself favored Porsches, which were replaced on a regular basis whenever he crashed one. He and Dooky had agreed that it was best to keep their engagement a secret until the following year, when he would hopefully graduate along with Dooky and they could get married. With her charming candor, Dooky made no secret of what she wanted from Ham: a companionable escort for all the debut balls and parties who understood that her affections were already engaged. It had been the best summer of his life.

A year later he was embracing Dooky at her wedding reception at the Mountain Brook Club. He rarely saw her after that, but assumed that if anyone were going to have a charmed and happy life, it would be Dooky St. John Lankford. He heard she had three handsome sons in rapid succession. Later she surprised everyone by joining one of the mega-churches out by the interstate and becoming a solo vocalist for their Christian chorus. Together with the choir, she recorded an album of Christian music that was supposedly a best-seller on the mega-church circuit. Yet on the whole, this turn of events somehow seemed entirely in keeping with Dooky's wholesome Southern sweetness. She was the last person he expected to see going into a therapist's office.

"You didn't hear?" she asked him dubiously.

"Hear what?"

"I think the whole town is talking about it," she said. Her face puckered and threatened to cry. What could possibly have happened? He'd never seen her look like this and was deeply shaken. He racked his brains. The only thing he could think of was—

"Louis?" he asked.

She nodded.

He winced with shock and disbelief. "Oh, no," he said. You can't tell me there's another—" He just couldn't bring himself to say it.

"Another woman?" she said.

He nodded fearfully.

"It's not another woman," she said.

He breathed with relief. Let Louis lose his dealerships, turn into an alcoholic or even get a rare fatal disease. But don't let him strike at the lovely heart of Dooky St. John. He waited to hear what it was.

"It's another man," she said.

He was so thunderstruck that he simply stood there in shock, unable to utter one word of solace. Only when Lauren opened the door to summon Dooky for the appointment did he snap out of it and begin awkwardly taking his leave, trying all at once to apologize for what had happened to her, for the inexplicable behavior of the male species, for the unexpected twists and turns of life and his own inadequate response to it. He was certain that not one bit of coherent substance could have emerged from his incoherent stammering, but hoped he had at least managed to convey his heartfelt concern.

She flashed her Julia Roberts smile and hugged him again. "You are so precious," she breathed into his ear. "Running into you has done me a world of good. More than any therapist could ever do. Call me," she squeezed his hand and waved gaily in farewell, her vivacity heroically restored.

Even when the door closed behind her, Ham remained in the waiting room, as if transfixed and unable to move. Of course, marriages fell apart all the time, but that wasn't supposed to happen to Dooky St. John. She was supposed to be exempt from any pain or problems. Because she was the golden girl. The quintessential Southern belle. The absolute incarnation of everything she was supposed to be. And she had done everything she was supposed to do. First and foremost, she had married the golden boy who was equally everything he was supposed to be, down to his ruddy complexion and the blond of his hair, which was always manfully windswept from his Porsche convertibles. Even his brief period of wild youth was somehow in keeping with what Louis was supposed to do as the son of a wealthy, prominent family. The scrapes he'd gotten into only emphasized and demonstrated his family's wealth and prominence, which were needed to get Louis out of his scrapes and reinstated as a college student. And it was all the normal, perhaps necessary, preface to a life of settling down with his lovely wife and taking over the family business.

They were the preordained couple. Their community depended on them for its self-preservation. For this reason, society celebrated them wholeheartedly and *they were supposed to be spared any tragedy.* Even he would never question why Louis would get a girl like Dooky. Ham might have been smarter, nicer, harder-working and more accomplished, at least academically. His family's wealth and prominence were probably equal to the Lankford's. Yet unquestionably, Louis Lankford deserved Dooky St. John. Louis Lankford was able to do the one thing Ham Whitmire could not do, and that was—take over the family business. Let him have a last fling of youthful freedom, and then he would be ready to become the man society could count on to do what it needed done. He would marry the golden girl. He would take over the family business. He deserved the golden girl—and Ham did not—because he was going to take over his family's business—and Ham was not. Ham had always accepted this simple calculus without protest. He had never felt that he deserved the happiness of marrying the golden girl—or any happiness at all—because he was not able to take over the family business.

But now that society's preordained couple had fallen from its pedestal, he didn't know what to think. The figures of the bride and groom were toppling off the five-tiered wedding cake and shattering not only themselves, but also somehow his sense of himself and the world he lived in.

* * *

Back home in his apartment, the voice mail on his answering machine contained the news that his father had just suffered a massive stroke and was in the ICU at UAB Hospital.

~ PART TWO ~

~ 11 ~

It was during the first of January, soon after Christmas and before the new semester at Cahaba College that Ham received the phone call from Harry. He had just returned to his apartment from the Spain Rehabilitation Center where his father had been transferred to undergo intensive physical, occupational and speech therapy. For his mother, who had met him there, it was a longer journey back to her house, and Harry had taken advantage of her absence to place the telephone call to her son, whom he said he needed to see about something important. Harry showed a similar desire for discretion in conducting this meeting, which he wanted to happen when Ham's mother was "out the house." At first, Ham didn't know how to go about arranging this, but Harry's many diffident but repeated observations about his father being "out the woods" finally struck Ham as a suggestion that they get together during hospital visiting hours, which his mother attended without fail, if not without complaint. It wouldn't make too much difference if Ham missed one visit, Harry was hinting. Accordingly, they agreed to meet at two o'clock the next afternoon, when his mother was sure to be gone.

"Thank you, Mr. Ham-elon," said Harry in his characteristic way of uttering the initial syllable distinctly and clearly, and swallowing all the others. For the first time, it occurred to Ham that his nickname of Ham might have derived from Harry's garbled pronunciation of Hamilton. The idea appealed to his sense of justice. His mother could be utterly disparaging and disdainful of Harry at the same time she relied upon him completely. Somehow it was only fitting that he be the one who truly named her only son.

When Ham arrived at the house the next day, Harry was already waiting outside the door of his father's study, holding his baseball cap in front of him out of deference to the occasion. Ham wasn't used to seeing Harry without the cap on his head, and was surprised at the amount of gray in his hair. He didn't even want to think about how old Harry was, but realized he must be getting on in years: he and Ella had begun working for the family when Valerie was a baby. Then he was struck by a terrible thought: What if Harry wanted to announce his retirement? This would be a calamity second only to his father's recent stroke. In fact, Ham reflected, it would be an even worse calamity: Harry's labor was much more important to his mother than her husband's was. She could deal with her husband being out of the house and in the hospital, but she wouldn't last long at all without Harry. In the moments of brutal honesty to which she was given, she had no trouble expressing this either. "While your father was at the office," she would say dismissively of her husband and his work, "Harry and I took down the Christmas tree. It was really the work of two men, but Harry got it to the street right before they came by to pick it up." Harry did the *real* work that was most important to her and her sense of well-being, while her husband escaped to the office to avoid such hard labor and enjoy the diversions afforded by his business.

As Ham led the way into his father's study, his own nervousness began to mount, especially as Harry himself seemed subdued and began fingering his baseball cap with increasing agitation. Of course he was planning to announce his retirement. What else could it be? And what would any of them do without Harry? Of course it was he who had kept their mother together—not just during their father's long hospitalization—but during her whole married life as a wife and mother. He and Ella had begun working for her soon after she first married, and when Ella's rheumatoid arthritis had forced her to stop, his mother had simply gone out in the yard where Harry was trimming the boxwoods and said: "I guess you'll have to see about our dinner now." Over the years he had proved to be an excellent chef. Indeed, he was actually a better cook than Ella, though Mrs. Whitmire gave only grudging respect to his efforts and naturally took all the credit when the compliments flowed. To her, it was no less than she deserved, with Ella having quit on her like that. "Lots of people have arthritis," she would sniff, "and it doesn't stop them from performing their duties." She could never be made to understand, despite repeated explanations, that there was a substantial difference between everyday, run-of-the-mill arthritis and the rheumatoid version that afflicted Ella.

Harry stopped respectfully in front of Mr. Whitmire's desk, and appeared to expect Ham to sit in the chair behind it. Perhaps he was following the protocol of some ritual that had evolved over the years; Ham wouldn't know. But he walked around to the other side of the desk and sat down in his father's chair, bracing himself for the worst.

132

He cleared his throat. "What did you want to see me about?" he said, nodding toward the chair behind Harry. "Why don't you have a seat?"

"Oh, nawsuh," said Harry, fingers drumming on the bill of the cap. "And I do apologize for takin' up yo' time."

He went on to make many further apologies before stating the nature of his business. Meanwhile, Ham's mind was racing to come up with inducements sufficient to convince Harry to change his mind about retiring. He was thus unprepared to hear Harry say, "I needs to get paid."

The shock on his face must have alarmed Harry, who immediately embarked on another round of apologies. Interrupting with an apology of his own, Ham said, "My mother has so much on her mind right now. I'm sure she just forgot."

"Your mother don't pay me, Mr. Ham-elon," said Harry. "Mr. Whitmire he mail my check every month."

"Of course, of course," said Ham, trying to recover quickly. He should have known that his mother wouldn't be the one to disburse payment for services rendered. As an immensely wealthy woman, she was accustomed to a sense of complete entitlement, which included the privilege of not actually having to pay for anything. Since it was a well-known fact that she could afford whatever she wanted, it always struck her as rude and ridiculous when she was asked to prove it by actually paying for something. Ham could still remember from when he was a boy how she would mutter darkly while rummaging through her purse for her wallet as the cashier seemed to insist stubbornly on receiving money for the groceries. "Of course I have plenty of money," his mother would assert, as if this mere fact were enough to procure her whatever she wanted without having to engage in the vulgar and actual transfer of cash from one hand to another. That business was beneath her. He should have known.

Clearing his throat, he asked Harry, "How much is it we owe you?"

"Well, it's like this, Mr. Ham-elon," said Harry, clearing his own throat before falling silent.

Ham waited patiently for several moments as Harry appeared to draw courage from contemplating the floor.

"Like this" turned out to be a generous monthly sum that probably would have staggered his mother, who prided herself on paying the lowest wages in town. Apparently she had no idea what she was really paying Harry since she wasn't paying him at all. His father was. He should have known. And the monthly wage—slightly higher than what Ham made as a professor at Cahaba College—was only part of it. The previous month's check would normally have included an equally generous Christmas bonus, which Harry apologized for needing in order to pay for the repairs to his truck. Although Ham had no trouble agreeing to this, Harry still stood there nervously shifting his weight from one leg to another and hanging his head.

"What else is there, Harry?"

After further prodding, Harry produced from his back pocket two sets of papers which had each been meticulously folded into squares. These were the renewal forms for the health insurance policies that his father had apparently been paying for on Harry and Ella's behalf. It embarrassed Ham to realize that he had never once even considered this issue, but was thankful that his father had done so, especially considering Ella's serious and chronic illness. He reached over the desk to take the documents, which had already been filled out, signed and dated. Obviously Harry must have given these to his father at the beginning of each year, and his father wrote the necessary checks before mailing it all in.

"I'll take care of it, Harry," he said.

Still Harry waited.

"Anything else?"

There was Lois; Harry had promised to speak for her. She also needed her check.

"Of course, of course," he said.

Harry named a sum that was naturally a good bit less than what he made, but still would have surprised Ham's mother, who for some reason wanted to believe she was practically a slave mistress who paid her help next to nothing at all.

This time Harry shook his head when Ham inquired if there was anything else, but he remained standing in front of the desk. Ham didn't know what to say or do at this point.

"Well, if that's all, Harry . . ."

But Harry just fingered his cap and looked down at the floor.

Suddenly it dawned on Ham that this poor man actually needed his money, just like he'd said. That was the whole reason they were in his father's study. "I'm as bad as my mother," Ham thought to himself. "No wonder I'm full of self-loathing." It wasn't money in the abstract, theoretical sense that Harry needed; it was cash in hand. What was Ham to do? At the moment, he didn't have anything in his wallet other than the odd ten or twenty.

"Would a check be okay, Harry?" he inquired tentatively.

Harry nodded with relief. "That be fine," he said. "Be fine."

But this solution posed another problem, as Ham didn't begin to know where his father's checkbook was. His own checkbook was in the car, in his briefcase.

"Would you excuse me a minute?" he said, rising. "I'll be right back."

It was the least he could do, he reflected as he went out to his car. A moment ago, he had been trying to figure out how to entice Harry to stay with the family for the rest of their mother's natural life. Paying the man's monthly wages was a good way to start.

Back inside, he wrote out two checks for Harry: one for Lois and one for himself. "And I'll take care of this right away," he said, nodding at the insurance forms on the desk.

Harry thanked him profusely, and said "I do apologize," before leaving the room.

What would happen at the end of this month? Ham wondered when left alone. His father's life was no longer in danger, but for the moment he was unable to walk, talk or move his arms. The look in his eyes indicated he was mentally alert and aware, and the neurologist's findings had so far corroborated this impression and provided hope for future improvement, but for the time being his father was utterly incapable of communicating. Ham could not even seek any answers, let alone assistance from his father. For now, his father's job was to re-master the tasks of infancy and childhood. And Ham's job? His job was to become the man his father had been—whatever that was—at least as far as a few isolated individuals were concerned—and hopefully for a very limited period of time. Fortunately, his father had the kind of office which more or less ran itself, along with the business. It shouldn't be too hard to write a couple of checks each month to his mother's household help. Hopefully that's all his task would amount to before his father came back home.

The soft chiming of the clock on the wall brought him to with the realization that he better take care of those insurance forms before his mother returned. In doing so he had to push aside a pile of unopened mail that had accumulated on his father's desk. There was quite a lot of it. As he wrote out the necessary checks, he wondered if there was anything urgent in the stack. Should he go through it? he wondered. Or would that be a violation of his father's privacy? In the end he decided to skim through the letters for anything that might require immediate attention.

To his great consternation, he quickly discovered that every single item in the stack of mail required immediate attention, as it consisted of bills needing payment. Some of the envelopes even had SECOND NOTICE printed in bold black capitals on the front. Apparently his mother took NO NOTICE of any bills that needed to be paid, but she would certainly take notice if she suddenly had no power, water or telephone service. Examining more closely, he saw where some of the bills—like from Rosemary's or Rich's—were actually addressed to his mother, but she clearly had not believed their contents had anything to do with her. That was for her husband to take care of. The fact that her husband could not even feed himself at the moment had not shaken her conviction that he should and would take care of paying the bills. This lowly chore had always been done by her husband in the past, and she obviously didn't see why it shouldn't continue to be done for her despite her husband's incapacitating stroke and her oft asserted claim that she was the one responsible for "running the household." Why had he taken her at her word? He of all people should have known that his mother's words could not be trusted or taken at face value. Yet he of all people had done just that.

At least he knew better than to believe that his mother would shoulder the burden of the unpaid, overdue bills as soon as they were pointed out to her. Although it was only a small clerical matter of opening the checkbook and filling in the blanks with the appropriate names and amounts, his mother would no doubt expect someone else to do this just as always. Who would do it? He naturally thought first of his sister, who was seven years older than he and had always been the competent, take-charge type he wished he could have been. Picking up the phone, he glanced at the clock to figure out where his sister would be at this hour. It was 3:35. Probably she was still in clinic. If she was seeing a patient, he wouldn't be able to reach her. He'd have to wait until she got home, although when she did get home, she'd have the boys and their homework and the dinner to prepare. She had enough to deal with; she didn't need anything else.

Neither did he; but heaving a sigh, he realized he could not have made a good case for exempting himself from duty. The new semester at Cahaba College was still a week away. The only other burden he had to bear right now was the lifelong one of his own hopeless self, which was clearly too much for him. Yet it became increasingly apparent that he would be expected to deal with the bills, and he figured he might as well stay on at the house and try to get it over with in one sitting. The worst part about it all, he thought, was that he'd have to encounter his mother on her own home turf. She was a much less malign presence on neutral ground mediated by the presence of innocent bystanders and official onlookers like doctors and nurses. It was also helpful if there were another main object of attention, such as his father's inert body in the hospital bed. But on her home territory she could be at her most brutal and today there would be no mediating presence. To her, Harry didn't count; he was the invisible man.

It behooved him then, to get started right away in order to minimize the time he'd be alone at the house with his mother. He was also somewhat worried about the two manila envelopes from Blue Cross, which looked similar to the ones Harry had given him earlier. Were these his parents' own premiums, which needed to be renewed? Or was it something more complex that would necessitate a conference with his mother? He decided to address himself to these first to allay his fears.

An hour later, by the time his mother had arrived back from the hospital, he had opened all the mail and taken preliminary stock of the situation on his father's desk. Fortunately there were no unpleasant surprises, although there were indeed several surprises. One of these was the statement from a credit card issued in Harry's name. Ham had not realized that his father gave Harry a Visa card, but it only made sense because Harry was apparently the one who filled up the cars with gas, did the grocery shopping and made all the necessary purchases from places like the hardware store, the garden center, the pharmacy and Wal-Mart. No wonder his mother was able to say she had never once set foot in Wal-Mart and had no idea where it was. She didn't need to; Harry was the one who went to Wal-Mart. Ham had always supposed that his mother ran all the household errands for the simple reason that she was always complaining about having to run all the household errands. But judging from her own credit card statement, the errands she did pertained mainly to the beauty salon and the dress shops. What then did she do with herself? She didn't seem to be running any other errands and she certainly didn't take care of the household expenses. But at least as far as these were concerned, he saw no major problems. There was interest on some of the unpaid balances and late fees for the utility bills. That was the worst of it.

And fortunately, when his mother returned, it was not with the full force of her usual personality. For many Mountain Brook ladies like his mother, going downtown was like taking a long, arduous trip to a distant, dangerous, third-world country. And his mother seemed to have spoken the truth about one thing at least: the daily hospital visits were indeed "taking something out of" her. There was much to be thankful for in that, he realized, as she grumbled only briefly about why he hadn't told her he'd meet her at the house. Instead of answering, he mentioned the pile of unpaid bills on his father's desk.

"I was wondering when that was going to be taken care of," she said.

The use of the passive voice astounded him. What form of royalty did she think she was that she didn't have to take care of it herself and didn't even have to ask someone else—politely and respectfully—to take care of it for her? She could just assume it would be done without having to think about it at all.

"If you'll just show me where the checkbook is," he said.

"In the desk where it always is, I guess," she said, offering no further suggestion about where that might be. "I suppose you'll want Harry to bring your dinner in there like he does for your father," she stated gruffly.

This was an unexpected gift, and he accepted it with alacrity. He thought it best not to question his mother further regarding the whereabouts of the checkbook and return to the study with equal alacrity. A few moments later, Harry knocked softly and entered carrying a drink in a crystal tumbler on a silver tray. Who had remembered that he preferred Scotch to bourbon? His mother or Harry? Probably Harry, he thought, accepting the drink gratefully. He had no trouble finding the checkbook in the top drawer of the desk, and when Harry reappeared an hour later with his dinner on a tray, he was about half-way through the stack of bills. If not for the meticulous documentation he thought prudent, he might even have been finished by dinnertime, which was six o'clock at his parents' house on account of Harry needing to get home. On the whole, however, he was glad of the excuse to have his dinner on the TV table Harry magically conjured and noiselessly assembled next to his chair. Was this an everyday ritual, he wondered, or just something his father did when he needed to pay the bills? He'd always assumed his parents ate dinner together, but he'd also made other assumptions which had proved to be inaccurate. Taking his leave, Harry thanked him again for his "help."

The only matter which presented a problem were the insurance forms which inexplicably asked for information such as dates of birth and social security numbers which surely the company must already have on file. Of course he knew his parents' birth dates, but their social security numbers were another issue. Not wishing to disturb his mother—leave Grendel's mother alone in her lair was ever his motto—he went rummaging through his father's desk for a document that might contain the social security numbers. He had no luck in any of the drawers, but there was one large bottom drawer which appeared to be locked. Hadn't he noticed a key in one of the pockets of his father elaborate leather checkbook cover? He had. This key did indeed fit the lock and the drawer opened. It contained a stack of magazines which appeared to be pornographic and were filled with pictures of nude males in erotic poses suggestive of oral and anal sex acts with other nude males.

Seeing this was like being struck by a bolt of lightning which caused an immediate and complete loss of power in his brain. He was utterly incapable of forming any thoughts or any response at all to what he was seeing. He also lost any sense of time and had no idea how long the power outage lasted in his brain. It could have been ten minutes; it could have been two hours he sat there incapable of thought, speech or motion, much like the state his father was in at the hospital. The sudden surge of power that brought his mental processes flickering back to life also seemed to have overloaded his circuits. He was now capable of thought, but not capable of putting multiple thoughts together into a coherent whole. On the one hand he believed that someone else must have had access to his father's desk and left magazines there. On the other hand, he realized his father was a homosexual.

The next disordered thought that popped chaotically into his scrambled brain was that he must tell his mother the news immediately. This notion was soon displaced by the equally illogical notion that he must do something about all of this at once. He closed and locked the drawer and pocketed the key. That would take care of the magazines for now. But what to do about his father? Absent-mindedly he picked up the dinner tray to return it to the kitchen, where he expected to find his mother. It could be hoped that she might inadvertently provide some hint or clue that would offer guidance and direction about the course of action he needed to take. She was not known to be shy about expressing her opinion on this subject at any other time. Of course this was just another disconnected thought in his foggy brain, and his mother was nowhere to be found.

The dirty dishes from his mother's dinner were already in the sink. He added his to the stack, unable to determine if the load in the dishwasher had already been run. His mother belonged to the generation which insisted that all dishes be sparkling clean before being placed in her spotless dishwasher. Pots containing the butter peas and new potatoes were still on the stove. Lifting the lids, he wondered what to do about the leftovers. A brief search of the obvious cabinets produced no Tupperware or storage containers. Did his mother just leave the leftovers for Harry to throw out in the morning? It was entirely possible. On the whole he thought it best to forget about the food and go find his mother. She was probably in the den.

He crossed back through the living room and re-entered the private wing of the house. His mother wasn't in the den, but a TV table indicated that she had eaten her dinner there in front of the television. Did she eat her dinner there alone every night and watch TV while his father ate dinner in the study and read his—magazines? As if in reply to his question, a sudden snore erupted from his parents' bedroom. He looked at his watch. It was 7:30. Was it possible that his mother was just an old lady, and not some she-dragon? Supposedly the evening still lay before him, along with the rest of his life. But somehow he had the feeling, punctuated by his mother's snores, that it was all over. At least, he thought irrationally, at least he had the key.

~ 12 ~

The next day he was supposed to meet with his colleague Ivy Greer. His first instinct was to postpone the occasion, but when he started to do so, he realized it would probably be less stressful just to go through with the meeting than to make the necessary explanations and rearrangements. In fact, meeting with Ivy was not stressful at all these days anyway. Ever since his father's stroke, she had become something more than a colleague demanding his help. She had become something he hadn't had in a long time—a friend. When she learned the news about his father, she had gone out of her way to be kind and solicitous. Based on experience with her own father, who fortunately was in remission at the moment, the sympathy she offered was meaningful and insightful. Three times she'd insisted he come over for dinner at her apartment during the holiday break, and not once had she raised the subject of Cahaba College or what she wanted him to help her do there. And one time, when his car was in the shop, she'd given him a ride to the rehab center. She'd even withstood the withering gaze of his mother, who unfortunately approached the entrance just as Ivy had arrived to give him the sunglasses he'd left on the front seat of her car.

"Your mother must have thought I was your girlfriend," Ivy said later. "Because she looked none too pleased at the idea of me."

"Don't worry. She was more likely to think you were a maid at the hospital," Ham had replied without thinking.

Luckily Ivy was not offended; on the contrary, she burst out laughing. Before he knew what was happening, he was laughing too. He laughed harder than he'd laughed in a long time, and couldn't remember a time when he'd ever been able to laugh so freely at his mother.

But today he and Ivy were scheduled to discuss a plan they could take to the administration for offering remedial instruction to all incoming freshman students during the summer before they started college. After everything Ivy had done for him in the past few weeks, he really wanted to return the favor and be of some assistance to her for a change. However, something about the look on his face must have betrayed him as soon as she opened the door.

"What's wrong?" she said as he entered her apartment. "Has your father taken a turn for the worse?"

He hadn't planned on telling her; he hadn't planned on telling anyone after recovering from the initial shock of discovery. But in short order he was blurting out everything he had learned yesterday at his parents' house. The relief in doing so was enormous. The one thing he managed to keep to himself was the amazing fact that his parents' servant Harry, who had never finished high school, earned a higher income than they did as professors at the college. Otherwise, he poured out everything.

She didn't seem at all taken aback to have him spilling his guts right there in her living room. He wondered if girls routinely did this with one another— if this, in fact, was what girls were doing when they spent so much time talking to one another. He'd never before understood how girls could do this. How could there be that much to say? Or talk about? But if what they did was anything like what he had just done . . . it was like a therapy session, without having to make an appointment or pay a fee. He could definitely see the point of that.

"Do you know what I think you should do?" she said, as soon as he'd finished.

He waited.

"You need to go right back to your parents' house," she said. "Go through that room with a fine tooth comb. Every drawer. Every cabinet. Does your father have a computer in there?"

He tried to remember. There wasn't one on the partners' desk, but he couldn't recall if there hadn't been one at all. "I'm not sure," he said.

"Then you need to make sure," she said emphatically. "And if there *is* a computer, you need to go through every file. In case there's *anything* your father wouldn't want the rest of the world to see."

"Oh, my God!" He clutched at his hair. "You're right!"

He couldn't believe he hadn't thought of this himself. What he had stumbled on yesterday had been so shocking he hadn't been able to imagine there was anything worse. Or anything more. But of course, he could simply have come upon the tip of the iceberg. There could be a lot more. And it could be a lot worse. In a sudden spasm of panic, he nearly jumped off the couch.

"Don't worry about this business with the college," said Ivy, rising from her own seat. "You need to take care of family business first. Family comes first. I totally get that."

She went into her kitchen and retrieved something from the refrigerator as he rose slowly from the sofa. He hated to let her down for today, but really, she was right. In any case, he wouldn't be much help to her until he set his mind at ease. When she returned, she handed him a sandwich in a plastic container.

"I made us these ahead of time so we could work through lunch," she said. "Why don't you take it with you and go do what you gotta do."

It was not a question but a command, which he reluctantly obeyed.

"Go on." She turned him around and prodded him toward the door. "I can do what I gotta do just fine without you. Would've been more fun with you, but I can hammer this proposal out on my own."

On the threshold he turned around. "I'm sorry," he said.

"Don't be ridiculous." She almost pushed him out the door. "Call me tomorrow and let me know what you found."

On the drive over to his parents' house, he realized he really *was* sorry, not only because he'd rather spend the day anywhere but at his parents' house, but because a part of him had actually looked forward to drafting the proposal. He wasn't entirely lacking in writing ability, and enjoyed crafting something out of words. It was just his luck, he sighed to himself: the first time he actually wanted to assist Ivy with her efforts, she told him not to bother.

* * *

The "library" in his parents' home, where he had spent yesterday afternoon and evening, was his favorite room in the house. It looked much like it might have in LeRoy Percy's day back in the 1920s, (thanks to Norman Laney), with its polished mahogany partners' desk, books from floor to ceiling filling all the shelves, and stately reading chairs placed in front of the windows facing the street and the Birmingham Country Club.

As a boy Ham had spent a great deal of time in this room during the long summer days when his father was at work and his mother was tending to her meetings and "errands." Back then, there were no day camps such as his nephews enjoyed now during the summer. No tennis or golf camps, no zoo camp, and no organized sports leagues for the months of summertime, when families supposedly took their big vacation, which in his family's case, meant two weeks at the beach in August. In his childhood, when almost none of the mothers had jobs or careers, there was supposedly no need for any summer programs to keep the children occupied. But unfortunately, his mother had done nothing to address the boredom and tedium of the long summer days during which he'd had nothing to do. "I have way too much to do to waste my time trying to entertain you," she declared. His sister, seven years older and a teenage girl, was similarly uninterested and unavailable. He didn't remember what she'd done during the summers, but she hadn't been at the house with him. And Ella, the one technically in charge of looking after him, definitely had too much to do to stop and play with him. He didn't live in the kind of neighborhood where boys ran around outside and played together, and even if there had been neighborhood children, his mother would no doubt have forbidden such unsupervised running around in the sweltering hot sun of June, July and August. He felt as lonely and forsaken as an only child, wandering forlornly throughout the empty house.

He had gravitated toward the "library" at first because he liked to climb up on the big reading chairs and gaze longingly out the window at the Birmingham Country Club, where the world of fun and happiness existed beyond his grasp. Gradually he began exploring the nooks and crannies of the room, and over time became intrigued by all the books on the shelves. In search of something amusing, like illustrations or photographs, he plucked a few books down. The words on the pages usually failed to register, like the meaningless blur of a foreign language.

But one afternoon, while perusing a volume containing a few drawings, he began reading and found himself absorbed by the story, about a mistreated orphan named Oliver Twist. Although both of his own parents were alive and well, he felt like an orphan anyway, and had a similar sense of being unloved and ill-used. It was on page fifteen, next to a picture on page sixteen, that he'd first begun reading. Before long he went back to the beginning and read from start to finish. Afterwards he'd searched out all the books by this guy Charles Dickens. Many were too long and complicated to hold his attention, but he learned how to go through the books and find the ones that weren't. That first summer in the library, he also came up with *Treasure Island, Swiss Family Robinson,* and *The Wind in the Willows.*

In some ways, this had been the beginning—the beginning of his adult existence, of who he was. He learned how to delve into books for the stimulation and pleasure not provided by the outside world or any of the other people in it. And what was this outside world after all? Nothing but a few cars passing on the street or the drone of the vacuum cleaner in a distant room. The outside world did not have much, if anything, to offer him. Books, by contrast, had everything to offer him. There were exciting adventures in other places he could project himself into; there were other children he could imagine as his playmates or friends. Above all, books gave him the best gift of all—the gift of himself. Through reading, he was able to go inside himself and begin to recognize his own thoughts and understand his own feelings. Books were everything; the outside world was nothing. In a way, he had built the rest of his life on this premise. As others might ignore their interior world and fail to cultivate an inner self, he ignored the external world and cared nothing for developing an outer self who interacted with others. He thought it preferable to live entirely within his own interior world, and become nothing but his own inner self.

The discovery he had made as a child in this library had changed his whole life. Accordingly, he loved this room as he believed no one else did, and had always thought himself the one in the family most intimately familiar with its contents. But last night, he had made another earth-shattering discovery of its contents, and this discovery was threatening to change his life again, by pulling him in the opposite direction, back into the outside world and its people who had failed him in the past.

Today he noticed for the first time an enormous armoire that did in fact contain a computer, along with an entire miniature modern office, as shelves sprung out to create desk space for all the latest technology and equipment. Remembering Ivy's advice, he knew he needed to go through every drawer and every file. He spent three hours just going through the computer. Fortunately, his mother had a one o'clock hair appointment, and visiting hours at the rehab facility began at two. According to his mother's rigid rulebook, a wife had to be there for the start of visiting hours and for the duration, or she was not worthy of being called a wife and deserved only the harshest condemnation from all the doctors and the hospital staff.

Even more fortunate, there was nothing the least suggestive or suspicious about any of the email correspondence or attachments on his father's computer, and not the slightest scrap of evidence to indicate that his father had arranged assignations or conducted "improper" relationships. Even the files marked "Personal" contained only family documents, keepsakes and mementoes. The only shock Ham received from his painstaking search through the computer came from all the spreadsheets, financial statements and legal documents he found there. He'd never thought of his father as a businessman, and didn't know why so much data of this type would be on his father's personal computer at home.

And then he was struck by a terrible idea. His father had another office. Away from home. With a computer. A desk. Drawers. Cabinets. He knew he needed to get over there, and it couldn't be soon enough. His father had been gone from the office for over a month. His recovery was going to be protracted, and there was even the possibility that he would not be able to return to work. If there was anything at all compromising among his father's personal possessions or office effects, Ham wanted to be the one to find it. He cringed at the thought of a well-meaning secretary hunting through his father's office for some necessary item and coming across a stack of magazines like he'd found yesterday.

At that moment he heard his mother calling for Harry as she entered the house. He was so possessed by his fears that he didn't even think twice before going out of the room to meet her. He urgently needed a name and a phone number.

"Oh, it's you," she said. "I need Harry to go get the things out of my car, unless you can do it." She unwound a scarf carefully from around her neck so as not to disturb her freshly fixed hair. "Why weren't you at the hospital? This is the second day in a row you haven't come."

"Who is the office manager at Dad's office?" he asked her.

"You mean Gerald?" she said, unbuttoning her coat. "Gerald Blakely?"

"That's it," he said, remembering the name now. "Thanks. Do you know if there's a phone number for him?"

"Haven't you already called him back yet?" his mother grumbled.

Shots of adrenaline pierced his lungs. "Called him back?" Ham managed.

"Well he called for you several weeks ago," reproached his mother, with the usual hauteur indicating her complete confidence that she was above reproach herself, although she had never once relayed to her son any message from her husband's office manager.

Ham knew it would be pointless to point this out, so he simply asked for the phone number.

"I don't know," she said querulously, in the tone he knew would soon become a grumble. "Your father has a little blue book on his desk where he keeps all the numbers."

"Thanks," he said, and darted off as if he were in a hurry, which in fact, he was.

It was after five, and he feared Gerald Blakely and anyone else would have left the office by now. But Gerald picked up immediately when Ham dialed the number he found in his father's book.

The first part of the conversation was handled easily, as Gerald was full of questions and concerns about his father, although somehow he had managed to become as informed as Ham himself was about his father's current status. But then Ham found himself becoming flustered, as he didn't know how to ask Gerald if he could come in and ransack his father's office.

"I hope I'm not bothering you," he said nervously.

"Of course not," said Gerald. "In fact, I was planning to call you in the next day or so to see when you were coming in. But I didn't want to rush you. What with the Christmas season on top of the family emergency, I know you've been pushed to the brink. At least you've had a break from your teaching schedule. When does the new semester begin?"

"Next week," Ham managed, staggered that this man whose name he had forgotten and hadn't seen in at least a decade could somehow know all these details about him and his family.

"Excellent. Just let me know what's convenient for you," said Gerald.

Ham wasn't sure what he had expected when he picked up the phone to call Gerald Blakely, but it wasn't this. However, it certainly made the task he needed to perform at his dad's office easier.

"How about tomorrow?" he said.

"Wonderful. I'll be here at eight o'clock."

Eight o'clock! Ham was suddenly possessed by fear as he hung up the phone. What did that mean? Why all the urgency? Had Gerald Blakely made a discovery similar to the one Ham had made yesterday? Was he too late? And what should he do? What should he say? Who could help him?

His sister was the obvious choice. But she would be tired from her day at the clinic, and then she had her family to take care of. He was tired too, he realized. And he really could not withstand the trauma of reliving what had happened yesterday as he recounted it to his sister. Also, the whole idea of protecting his father meant keeping his sister out of it.

He picked up the phone to call his colleague Ivy Greer. Luckily she was at home, free for the evening and willing to meet him for dinner. He thought of something else.

"Bring the draft of your proposal with you," he told her. "Maybe I can help you today after all."

~ 13 ~

Whitmire Realty occupied a modest, nondescript location in Mountain Brook Office Park, where Ham arrived a little before eight, hoping to enter unnoticed by any staff, and to escape with similar anonymity later in the day, after his task was complete. Instead, he walked into a busy room already buzzing with activity and people who were fully expecting his arrival and prepared to greet him effusively, as if he were a beloved native son on a kingly visit back home to his humble origins. This was not at all a role he was suited to perform; he felt immediately confused and overwhelmed by all the welcomes, introductions and inquiries after his father.

He was relieved when Gerald Blakely materialized at the edge of the corridor to escort him into his office. But the man his mother had always called "the office manager" led him to a door labeled Chief Financial Officer. Then, the fifteen minute conversation Ham had anticipated lasted more or less the entire day. During the course of this, he managed to gather that, contrary to what he had thought his whole life, Whitmire Realty was not just a moribund family firm or limited holding company that managed a few valuable parcels of land in downtown Birmingham. It was an immense real estate empire encompassing the whole state of Alabama, with tentacles reaching in all directions throughout the Southeast.

In partnership with Cooley Construction, Whitmire Realty specialized in purchasing defunct commercial property that could be turned into shopping centers and strip malls. Cooley Construction generated the building plans and constructed the development, usually a shopping center "anchored" by a supermarket, and Whitmire Realty managed the leases and the tenants. The man (his father), whom he'd always known as a kind, quiet, unassuming and ineffectual blank (compared to his mother), was in actuality a visionary business tycoon, a powerhouse leading a vast commercial enterprise. And his son Ham, a panic-attack-prone depressive who'd recently had trouble getting out of bed in the morning, was his father's power of attorney. Of course it had never occurred to Ham that he had this or any other power.

Assuming Ham knew all this already, Gerald Blakely neither explained it nor gave him a chance to absorb it. Instead, Ham had to struggle to take it all in as Mr. Blakely discussed the latest venture which required his immediate attention as well as his signature on various documents.

At the moment, a deal was pending for a tract of land in a blighted area of downtown Memphis containing rows of derelict warehouses. Whitmire Realty, in conjunction with Cooley Construction, proposed building an up-scale outdoor outlet mall studded with heavy landscaping, "green space," and "interactive water fountains," along with al fresco cafés, bistros and gelaterias. The city council members of Memphis were unanimous in their enthusiasm for the proposed development, which they hoped would not only reclaim a dilapidated section of the downtown area, but would lead in turn to the gentrification of the surrounding neighborhoods of run-down bungalows which had become a magnet for drugs and crime. If the development took place, it was likely the city could obtain grant money for renovating the bungalows into affordable housing and mixed-income neighborhoods. His father's stroke had complicated the negotiations for the sale of the property and slowed the whole process, but after Christmas the deal had regained its momentum and was likely to be successfully concluded in the next several weeks, provided Ham felt comfortable signing off on the deal during his father's incapacitation.

So the man his mother couldn't seem to rely on to move a potted plant from her patio had been busy lifting entire communities out of their economic doldrums.

Mr. Blakely folded his hands on his desk. "I'm happy to answer any questions," he said.

Ham cleared his throat. "I suppose I should consult my father's attorney," said Ham, hoping he wasn't being stupid or making a gaffe.

"Absolutely," concurred Mr. Blakely. "Mark Newcomb got back from Europe two days ago, and is expecting your call. Henry Cooley and Hugh McNamara told me to tell you they can come in either tomorrow or Friday to go over the Memphis plans and answer any questions."

As Ham nodded, Mr. Blakely pressed an intercom buzzer. "Rita? Do you have that file ready for Wilmer's son?"

"Yes, sir," came the reply.

"Bring it in, please."

They spent the remainder of the day going through this file, which contained loan documents, lease agreements and various other paperwork pertaining not only to "Memphis," as that project was called, but other properties as well. At noon the receptionist brought in sandwiches and iced tea. At four in the afternoon, Ham made calls to Mark Newcomb and Henry Cooley and arranged appointments for the next two days.

These took place in his father's office, behind a door labeled **Chief Executive Officer.** As he greeted the men, Ham found himself grateful for the first time in his life for Birmingham's small town effect, which had always caused him anguish since he preferred to be anonymous and invisible. But now he was glad that the businessmen he needed to deal with during his father's illness were essentially old family friends he'd known forever. He'd seen Mark Newcomb and Henry Cooley at parties and the Mountain Brook Club for as long as he could remember. He had a lifetime's familiarity with both of these men, and found himself happy to see them, especially since they were neither at a party nor at the Mountain Brook Club. Yet Ham knew these men as Mr. Cooley and Mr. Newcomb. He was taken aback when they insisted on a first-name basis, and as the meeting progressed, found himself floored that these solid and successful men were treating him as an equal because they sincerely considered him to be one. Mr. Newcomb had a granddaughter and Mr. Cooley had two daughters who were all close to him in age. It was inconceivable to him that he could be their equal.

As Mr. Newcomb, his father's attorney, was closing his briefcase in departure, he said, "I'm afraid your father's stroke is going to speed up the timetable for finding a new CEO. You know he was planning to retire even before this happened?"

Ham nodded uncertainly. He could have known this, if he had made the appropriate inquiries. And he should have known this, if he had listened with even one ear. Worst of all, he did know this, but had blocked it from his mind.

"Do you know what his wishes were on the matter?" he said.

"Well," Mr. Newcomb began carefully. "As you know, Wilmer's deepest desire was for you to take over. But he had no intention of imposing on you," Mr. Newcomb hastened to add. "He always wanted you to choose your own path on your own terms without pressure or interference."

Ham blinked. "What about Gerald Blakely?"

"Gerald would be great," Mr. Newcomb acknowledged. "He's the obvious choice, in many ways. But Gerald doesn't want to do it." Mr. Newcomb chuckled. "I always joked with your father that he paid his people too much. When the CFO doesn't want to be the CEO, you know I'm right."

Ham did his best to echo Mr. Newcomb's chuckle while his heart raced uncomfortably.

"But really," Mr. Newcomb continued. "This is still a family business, and if Gerald took over, there would be complications. With your uncle. Your mother. Your cousin. Understandably, Gerald doesn't want to get into that. And we don't need to get into that just yet either," concluded the lawyer, lifting his briefcase from the chair. "The doctors are giving us every hope that your father will recover, and you can consult with him then about the company's future leadership."

Ham nodded.

Mr. Newcomb thrust out his hand. "I hope I've given you what you need to feel comfortable acting on your father's behalf, in accordance with his wishes."

"Oh, absolutely," said Ham, shaking his hand.

After his meeting with Henry Cooley and his son-in-law Hugh, Ham felt even more confident that he could execute his father's wishes on "Memphis" and anything else in what he hoped would be a short interval before his father regained some power of communication other than the ability to nod or shake his head. Over the weekend, he would take over to the hospital a list of yes or no questions that his father could answer in just this fashion. Then on Monday, which was Martin Luther King Day, he figured he could devise his course materials for the classes he'd be teaching at Cahaba College, starting on Tuesday. Although he had planned to work on his syllabus preparation during this past week, he didn't see why he couldn't get it all done in one day. He was also hoping he could squeeze in an appointment with his therapist, whom he hadn't seen in several weeks because of all his trips to the hospital. The three-day holiday weekend meant that many of her usual Monday patients would be out of town, so there were openings in her schedule and much he needed to discuss, namely, that nothing was what he'd thought it was, including himself. The world was a different place, and the people in it, including himself, were entirely different people from what he had supposed. He figured he could use some professional help with this.

Just as he was preparing to leave, someone knocked on the door. Unfortunately, this was not his father's secretary, but a different assistant he hadn't yet met named Lacy DeMille, who managed his father's "charitable giving" and kept track of his obligations for the half dozen or so boards on which he sat. In view of his father's illness, she was hoping there was some time she could meet with Ham to conduct the "review and renew" sessions she usually had with his father every January. The first of the year, she explained, was when many charitable and non-profit organizations tried to renew their pledges or obtain increases in the amounts. Ham looked at his watch and wondered if this were a discussion that could be completed in about fifteen minutes. He was so worn out he didn't think he'd be able to go see his father in the hospital on his way home.

"How many are we talking about?" he asked. He'd never known his parents to be big donors to anything more than the Brook-Haven School and the Birmingham Museum of Art. This was all his mother boasted of, at any rate. If there were others he felt sure she would have boasted of those too.

"How many what?" Lacy looked taken about. "How many millions, do you mean?"

"Millions?" he echoed. Now he was the one taken aback, inadvertently letting go of his briefcase, which fell to the floor with a dull thud. Reaching down to retrieve it, he tried to process the implications of "millions." Primarily he realized that the discussion with Lacy was not something that could be completed in fifteen minutes. Sighing, he asked if she could meet with him on Monday morning, hoping that she couldn't. But when Lacy readily agreed to the Monday morning meeting and left the room, wishing him a nice weekend and sending regards to his father, he sat back down at his father's desk to call his therapist.

Fortunately Lauren did not seem upset or concerned about his cancellations; she mainly wanted to know if he'd continued to take the anti-depressants she'd prescribed. As a matter of fact, he *had* been taking them, primarily because he still had plenty of the free samples and had not noticed that they made any difference whatsoever to his brain chemistry. He had never expected a pill to solve his problems, but at least these didn't appear to be making his life worse, as the others had. So he was happy to take them and hoped there would be a placebo effect—not for himself, but for anyone else—like his sister and therapist—who believed they would bring about his deliverance.

As he finally left his father's office, it occurred to him that he had never even begun to undertake the search that had brought him there in the first place. He'd forgotten all about it. But somehow, he knew that this search had become unnecessary, and that what he'd found was something he hadn't even known he was looking for: his father.

~ 14 ~

Wilmer Whitmire came home from the rehabilitation center in the middle of February. His mother insisted that Ham and his sister be at the house to greet their father and welcome him home. However, she did not want their father to be taxed or fatigued by the occasion. So as usual, she created a no-win situation for those who had to carry out her wishes. It was only inevitable that she would not be fully pleased, and equally inevitable that her condemnation would be swift and severe. But it was ever thus, he had realized lately. She set people up for failure, and then pounced viciously on them when they failed. He had hoped and expected to have a well-defined role in his father's homecoming. It seemed only natural that he should be the one to drive his mother to the stroke center to pick up his father, help him into the car and drive him back home. But when he'd alluded to doing this, she had looked at him like he was crazy.

"Mother, you need someone to go with you," he had said.

"Of course I do."

"Well, don't you think it's better if *I* go with you, instead of Valerie? I mean, getting Dad into the car may not be easy, and then, all his things. . . ."

"Yes, it will be a job for a man," she had agreed, echoing his own thoughts.

"Well, that's settled then."

"So Harry will take me while you and Valerie wait here at the house."

The discharge from Spain Rehabilitation was scheduled for a Monday. Valerie had taken the whole day off work, and Ham had no classes thanks to his Tuesday/Thursday schedule this semester. They installed themselves in the house before their mother even left with Harry. That way, she could be certain of their presence upon returning and had one less thing to grumble about. Ham watched from the dining room window as Harry led his mother down the front walkway toward the Cadillac that was waiting for her, already running so that it would be plenty warm when she got in. Because of the rain last night and the unexpected early-morning freeze, there was a thin layer of ice on the flagstones, and Harry took Mrs. Whitmire's arm as he led her to the car. He was dressed in what must have been his Sunday suit, and his employer was wearing her mink coat against the winter weather. With his church-going hat on and his hand buried in the fur of the coat, his skin nowhere visible, Harry did not look like a black man, but simply a man. From Ham's vantage point, a stranger would have thought he was looking at a married couple walk arm in arm toward their car.

And in a way, Ham reflected, Harry was indeed the man in his mother's life. She had said as much, although of course, she would have scornfully disavowed such a sentiment if it had ever been quoted back to her. But she had spoken the truth, even if, in her characteristically perverse way, she still didn't know the truth. It was the truth nevertheless, and at least he knew it.

For one thing, Harry looked so much the part of a man—well over six feet tall, his back still straight and un-stooped though he was getting on for seventy just like his employers. In contrast, Ham and his father were both short men of somewhat slender build. Ham's mother was actually a bit taller than either of them, and with her rather stout shape, even looked like the more masculine form. But beside Harry's towering figure, she now seemed more dainty and petite. She looked more like a woman. Did she feel more like a woman, when he was around?

Impatient with her slow progress on the icy walkway, she reached for the car door handle a bit too soon and one of her heels lost traction underneath her. Harry's firm grip on her left arm supported her entirely as she flailed out wildly with her right pocket-booked arm for balance. Harry's own arm, Ham well knew, bulged with muscles thick and strong like ropes underneath the skin. Ham and his father could never achieve such muscularity even if they worked every day to acquire it.

He didn't realize his sister was beside him until she clucked in dismay at the scene they had both witnessed.

"Just what we need," she said. "Dad recovering from a stroke while Mother gets a hip fracture."

"Dad will get a hip fracture too if he comes up the front like she plans."

For a moment brother and sister exchanged a silent look of mutual distress.

"That's not going to happen," said Valerie firmly.

"You know how Mother has planned this whole thing out," he warned. In theory, his mother disdained the use of the kitchen door leading to the garage as the "servants' entrance," although in practice, she used that door herself except for special occasions. Her husband's homecoming after almost two months in the hospital was deemed just such a special occasion calling for the use of the front entrance. Plus, there were no steps to the front door as there were from the garage into the kitchen. And her children's two vehicles were in the driveway now as well. When his mother had originally planned it, the front door seemed a logical choice at the time. No one had counted on ice in Birmingham.

"Please," said Valerie. "Forget what Mother wants. Her nonsense cannot be allowed to control this situation. We've got to call the shots or they'll both be going back to the hospital."

It was surprisingly easy to do. When Ham went out to the car, he spoke with Harry, not his mother, and simply noted that because of the ice on the walkway, they needed to change the arrangements for bringing his father into the house. While they were at the hospital, Ham was going to move the other cars out of the way and park them on the street, so that Harry could pull up next to the kitchen door where there would be help on hand to get his father safely up the steps. As a reasonable and intelligent being, Harry affirmed the wisdom of these changes to the elaborate homecoming agenda his employer wanted him to follow. As an unreasonable and—Ham now realized—essentially unintelligent person, his mother unleashed a torrent of protest. He paid no attention to the actual substance of her objections because he now understood there was no substance. (Parking their vehicles on the street would not be a crime, even if it might be a temporary eyesore blocking the view of the country club.) Likewise, Harry didn't even turn around to respond to her before rolling the window back up and driving off, as his employer sat there stone-faced, with her lips tightly pursed and her hands fiercely clutching her pocketbook. They had both simply ignored her as if she were no more than a stubborn and willful child who perversely insisted on her own way just to see if she could get it. Unfortunately, she had succeeded in getting her own way during much of her life, but it had been remarkably easy to treat her words and wishes as inconsequential and of no account—just as she had always treated his. For far too long, he had made the mistake of assuming that her sharp tongue implied an equally sharp mind behind it. Now he had a better understanding of the limitations of that mind, and it had become a whole lot easier to turn a deaf ear to that sharp tongue of hers.

It didn't take too long to move his own car, his sister's car, and Harry's second-hand Cadillac to the street in front of the house, where his mother hated to see any of her family automobiles, as if they were "white trash in a trailer park." He and his sister agreed that his father's car could remain in the two-car garage on the side furthest from the kitchen door.

As he passed back through the kitchen after re-parking the vehicles, Ham caught a glimpse of the morning paper lying on the counter. "TEACHER'S COLLEGE FAILS TO MAKE THE GRADE," blared the headline.

Shaking his head, he returned to the dining room to wait for the car bearing his father home. He pulled out a chair from the table and sat down behind the window facing the driveway. As a child he often used to do this exact same thing at this exact same window. His mother had Ella feed him and his sister their supper, and—when he was very little—give him his bath before she left work. When he emerged from the bathroom, still dewy from Ella's scrubbing and dressed in the little boy pajamas that Ella had carefully ironed, he would come stand at the dining room window to wait for his father to get home from the office.

Partly because he was simply his father, and partly because he was a somewhat shadowy, vague and mysterious figure, his father was then the most exciting and compelling presence in his life. As a boy he had not understood why his father had to be gone so long every day. His mother explained it was "work," "the office," and "taking care of his family." As far as he knew, his father might just as well be out slaying dragons in some dangerous land full of obstacles and perils that needed to be confronted on a daily basis for the sake of the family's welfare.

Later when he understood there were no dragons like the ones in his childhood storybooks, he still didn't have a good explanation for what his father did when he left home. It was most likely, he realized now, that his mother had passed along no comprehension of the work his father did simply because she'd possessed none to pass along. And his father, he now knew, had deliberately withheld any lengthy explanation of what he did because he had not wanted to force anything on his son as he had perhaps had things forced on him. Ham had no idea how his father felt about "the family business"— whether he had wanted to take that on and enjoyed doing it, or whether he'd simply felt he had no choice. It was one of the many questions he wanted to ask his father if he ever had the chance.

But it was now clear that his father's marriage was probably not a result of his own deepest needs and desires. And he had not wanted to put his son in the same position and set him up for a lifetime of—what? Misery? Anguish? Torment? He felt tears prick at his eyelids as he continued to stare out the window. He looked furtively around to see if his sister was in a position to observe him. Fortunately, she was nowhere to be seen, and he thought he could hear her back in the master bedroom discussing the new configuration of furniture with Lois. Quickly he raised a finger to the corner of his eyes and wiped away the tears.

At this point, Ham felt he owed his father decades of gratitude and apology. It had been his mistake and misfortune to absorb his mother's dismissive attitude toward his father and his work without even knowing it. Appearances had deceived him as well. For one thing, his father had none of the braggadocio or machismo that would have given him the usual personality of a successful entrepreneur. For another, his parents had never enjoyed all their money as they could have, so he had never realized quite how successful or profitable his family's business was. His parents never took "fabulous" trips to Europe or New York—or anywhere, for that matter. They didn't own a second home. When they went out for the evening, it was usually to a wedding or a party they felt obligated to attend. When they went out to dinner, it was usually to the country club. They owned no flashy or fancy automobiles, and his mother possessed no real jewelry he could think of, except perhaps for pearls, which she rarely wore unless there was a wedding or a funeral. Their house was beautiful, he supposed, but it was hardly palatial. Of course, he had always known that his family had "plenty of money," to use his mother's phrase; and he'd been told as a teenager about the trust fund his grandmother had set up for him. But nothing close to the full extent of his family's wealth was in evidence around him, in his family's possessions or in the way they lived. And it wasn't as if his family communicated about important matters or really talked to one another in a meaningful way—either at the dinner table or at any other time. Of course, he and his sister had been rigorously instructed in the rules of manners and polite conversation. Once, when he was eight years old, he'd even been driven back to a birthday party after admitting he'd forgotten to thank his friend's mother. But on the other hand, there had been no real communication in their family; if anything, they'd been taught not to communicate as the key to social survival. The duration of his parents' marriage was a testament to that lesson.

Their household had been as lacking in laughter and happiness as it had been lacking in communication. This was one reason he had looked so forward to his father's homecoming every night. This event would uplift the whole family just as his father would lift him up in the air as soon as he walked through the front door—where the man of the house—his mother insisted—should enter his own home like he owned the place. He should not come straggling and shambling around a side entrance like a simple servant. She had tried, and failed, to make a man out of her husband in the way she most wanted him to be a man. In her frustration and defeat, had she then turned on her son with a vengeance, and tried even harder to make a man out of him, while all the time convinced that he, too, would fail, just as his father had before him? If so, she had nearly succeeded in emasculating him even as she tried to make a man out of him. In trying so desperately to make him what she wanted, she had nearly unmade him entirely.

Meanwhile, as Ham had grown older, his father had retreated more and more to the sidelines, as if he were indeed the nullity his wife's attitude suggested. As a young man, Ham had been disappointed to learn this "truth" about his father. And it was true his father didn't play any sports, like other fathers played golf or tennis. He didn't coach any teams, like the other fathers had coached Ham's soccer, basketball and baseball teams. He rarely even came to the games, which were on Saturdays, when he still went to the office—Ham now knew why. But he had been a great father nevertheless. He had come home every night and tossed his boy up in the air like a bundle of joy. He had taken his son into the "library" every night after dinner to read from the books that later gave his son that necessary sense of his own self, his own life and his own work. He had come in every night after his son was put to bed to lay his hand on his son's almost sleeping body and impart a love that was never spoken. And he did not, like Walker Percy's father, go up in the attic to shoot himself in the head, although he might have had every good reason to do so.

Ham hoped it was not too late to get to know his father, to start showing him the love and respect he now felt so keenly it was like one of those familiar sharp pains in his gut.

When he saw the nose of his mother's Cadillac edge into the driveway, he left the window to inform his sister. Together they went to the kitchen and opened the door leading into the garage just as Harry pulled up into it. Honoring his mother's detailed instructions, he went to open the car doors for her and his father as Valerie waited in the house and Harry came around to get his father out of the passenger seat in front. This had been deemed the most delicate and dangerous part of the whole homecoming operation, not just by his mother, but by the occupational therapist who had previously come out to the house to advise the family on the special accommodations needed to make his father's return both safe and conducive to continued recovery.

And yet Ham was initially struck by how normal his father looked in the front seat of the car. It was a relief to see him sitting upright in everyday clothes in everyday surroundings, rather than wearing a hospital gown and lying in a hospital bed. Now he looked no different than he had before the stroke, although he still suffered some serious deficits. He could speak only with excruciating effort, and his delivery was still so slow and slurred as to be incomprehensible to the unpracticed ear. As for his body, the stroke had primarily affected his right side, and while he could now walk with a cane, his right leg dragged heavily and could not support its share of body weight, so that any forward motion was unsteady and unbalanced. His right arm and hand were only minimally functional. According to the physical therapist, arm and hand function were often the last to return, could take as long as a year to regain normal strength and coordination, and might never fully recover.

Ham made way as Harry leaned over and reached into the front seat as if to lift a baby out of the car. He put his left arm around his employer's waist and his right arm underneath his knees. With grace equal to his strength, he gathered the frailer body and deftly hoisted it up from the seat and out of the car in one smooth, unbroken movement. As an elder in his church, Harry had claimed to have much practice in helping wheelchair-bound old ladies out of their cars for the Sunday services. It was immediately clear that he had not overstated his skills. Keeping his arm around Mr. Whitmire's waist, Harry waited for him to achieve equilibrium while standing before they moved forward.

Ham stole a glance at his mother, who was standing grimly beside the right rear door of the Cadillac, carefully scrutinizing the proceedings with her mouth set in an even more pronounced scowl than usual. For as long as he had been aware of his mother's appearance, all her ill temper, evil humor and utter scorn for the rest of humanity had been written plainly on her face for everyone to read as easily as a billboard advertisement. Had she been born this way, he wondered, or had she acquired this look in the course of her married life? He also found himself wondering what she was thinking and feeling at the moment. Was she upset that her orders had been flouted? Was she thinking that her husband's body was even more lame and . . . impotent . . . than ever?

His mother's thoughts and feelings were usually territory that his imagination had never dared to enter. With an exterior so cross and crabbed, she must possess an interior even more mean and ornery; he had never desired to become familiar with it. Now he questioned his assumption. Perhaps she was simply a hugely disappointed and dissatisfied woman who did not even realize or understand the ways in which her life had failed to fulfill her. After all, she was Mrs. Wilmer Whitmire, wasn't she? She was everything she was supposed to be. But somewhere, somehow, the world and the other people in it had not been what they were supposed to be, and as soon as she found out how—and why—who exactly had not done what—there would be a monumental reckoning. But until then, she lived in a permanent state of disgruntlement. He actually felt sorry for her. In one sense, she may have had it all; in another sense, she had nothing and didn't even know it. She was probably even unaware of her own deep discontent.

Ham reached into the car to retrieve his father's walking cane, while Harry assisted Mr. Whitmire through the few short paces to the steps. Reaching down from the kitchen, Valerie grasped her father's good arm while Harry more or less carried the rest of him up the steps and into the house. Then Mr. Whitmire dropped his daughter's arm, looked around and reached out for his cane. Ham stepped forward to supply it, and his father gave him a lopsided smile.

"Dad, would you like to sit down?" said Valerie.

Her father frowned and shook his head. Ham thought he could read it. The frown said: "I just got up. Why would I want to sit back down?" Carefully his father took a few tentative steps across the kitchen as everyone stood by and held their breath. He had been quite adamantly opposed to a wheelchair, but every onlooker now wished he were seated in one. Valerie tried to take her father's right arm—the debilitated one—but again he frowned and shook his head. He wanted to walk on his own.

"Why don't we show you the new arrangements in the bedroom?" suggested his daughter.

Her father nodded, and slowly they all made their way through the kitchen and living room, into the private wing containing the bedrooms and library. Valerie remained by her father's side as he made his slow, laborious progress through the house. Everyone else followed just as slowly behind, in a silence even Mrs. Whitmire maintained out of respect for the gravity of the occasion. Yet Ham became quite hopeful as he watched his father make his way across the floor. Once he achieved his own rhythm of walking, with the cane and the dragging right leg, he was actually quite confident—if not fully steady—on his feet, and didn't seem in imminent danger of falling.

On the recommendation of the therapist who had come out to the house, Harry had installed grab bars in the shower and bathroom, and hand rails along the bedroom walls. The master bed had been moved, and in fact, all the furniture had been rearranged to accommodate the rails and make for a safer passage from the bed to the bathroom. Middle of the night trips to the bathroom were especially treacherous. Although Ham remained intent on his father as Valerie explained and demonstrated everything—the call button and the pull-up device around the toilet—he could hear his mother muttering darkly to Lois about the inconvenience to herself. Without even a decent grace period, she was already re-directing the focus of her faultfinding. Before, it had all been about the enormous stress of an absent, incapacitated husband, leaving her alone and unprotected at the house at night, while during the day, she had to shoulder the heavy burden of going downtown and visiting him in the hospital. Now, Ham could tell, it was all going to be about the demands placed on her to look after her husband, take care of his handicapped needs, worry constantly about his safety and well-being, and above all, adapt to having unsightly hospital-grade hand rails in her bedroom and grab bars in her bathroom. Where before she had complained about her husband being gone, she was now prepared to complain about having him back home. If nothing else, she was a genius in the art of complaint. The way she had evolved it, the complaint was practically a literary genre, and if it had been eligible, she would have won a Pulitzer Prize by now. At the same time, he understood that she simply needed some way to channel the sense of grievance stemming from her deeply felt but confused sense of disappointment with her life.

Even after the tour of the bedroom and bathroom, Mr. Whitmire still did not want to sit down and rest, not even in the special chair that had been newly purchased and strategically placed for his comfort in the bedroom. He shook off his wife's and daughter's entreaties to try out its many ingenious mechanisms and began making his way out of the room. When he looked at Ham and lifted his eyebrows, Ham knew to follow. Sensing correctly that they were no longer needed for the moment, Lois and Harry left quietly to perform the many other tasks Mrs. Whitmire had laid out for the day. For once mother and daughter were in accord on a subject: they both seemed to think Mr. Whitmire should either lie down or sit down and give them, if not himself, a little rest and peace of mind. Ham could hear them murmuring to this effect as he accompanied his father down the hallway leading to the library.

His father could speak more than he was doing, but didn't like to because his speech was still as garbled as a drunkard's. He waited when he reached the door of the library for his son to open it. Ham turned the knob and pushed the door open, making way for his father to enter first. He could see his mother and sister watching them carefully from the doorway of the master bedroom, but then his father turned around, raised his walking stick and shut the library door. The look he gave his son suggested he would have winked in his customary way if he could have. Apparently, his facial muscles were not yet coordinated enough for that.

He went first over to the reading chairs placed by the windows facing the street and the country club. Then he looked at his son and opened his mouth to begin the protracted process of forming words. Ham thought he knew already what his father was going to say.

"Should I get Harry to move the new chair from the bedroom into here?"

Happily his father closed his mouth and nodded. During his long hospitalization, he'd asked for several books to be brought from home and had spent all the time between his various therapy sessions re-reading the works of Southern history he'd studied as an undergraduate at the University of Virginia before going to the business school. His father had always remained a bit of a Civil War and Southern history buff. With his cane, he pointed to a book high up on the shelf—*The Burden of Southern History*, by C. Vann Woodward—while Ham slid the ladder across to fetch it down. He put the book on the table between the two reading chairs, and his father nodded in thanks.

Next he moved over to the massive partners' desk and stared at the chair behind it.

"Do you want to sit down?" asked Ham.

His father nodded.

"Should I go get Harry?" he asked nervously.

This time his father shook his head. Father and son could handle this alone, he seemed to be saying. Ham had in fact done this many times in the hospital, but then there were nurses or aides and sometimes therapists standing by full of advice and ready with assistance. Here it was just the two of them. But sitting down was much easier than getting up. It was mainly a matter of careful positioning and a graceful collapse into the chair.

Ham had laid all the bills, papers, letters and other mail in neatly categorized piles in a row across the edge of the desk. He'd also compiled a ledger detailing the bills paid and the checks written. His father listened attentively as Ham explained the itemized list and the contents of each pile in front of him. His father nodded, and with his left hand, picked up the checkbook lying on top of the stack of paid bills. Ham indicated where he'd noted all the checks he'd written in back of the checkbook as well.

It might have just been his imagination, but he thought he could see his father pressing with his thumb to feel for the key Ham had replaced in the interior flap of the leather checkbook cover. Sometimes he thought he'd even imagined the magazines which lay in the drawer locked with that key. His therapist wasn't convinced that they constituted conclusive proof of anything even if they did exist. But they definitely did exist—Ham had taken one last look before locking the drawer and putting the key back where he'd found it. Over the last month he'd thought long and hard about what to do with both the key and the magazines. Finally he realized there was nothing he needed to do. He had made good use of the key, had found the hidden truth and secret knowledge he needed to unravel a large part of the riddle of his own existence.

Again it could have been just his imagination, but he believed his father would have winked at him if he could have. Somehow this was only appropriate, as his father had always communicated his most important messages through the twinkles and winks of his eyes. For Ham as a boy, this had never seemed enough, but now, it seemed almost exactly right. They need never speak of the hidden truth lying in the locked drawer of the desk. And though he had given it back, in another sense, Ham would now always have that key.

~ 15 ~

The following month, on a Saturday night in the middle of March, Ham found himself sitting with Dooky St. John at Highlands Bar and Grill. He wasn't sure how he came to be in that position, but knew it wasn't his own doing. Nevertheless, he was quite content to be there, though this was by far the most conspicuous public place he'd been with her since they'd renewed their friendship a few months earlier. Tonight she was, in a way, making a different sort of debut from the one she'd made two decades ago, and somehow it seemed only fitting that he should be her faithful escort for this one just as he'd been by her side throughout the other one.

It was almost six months now since Louis had been discovered in a compromising situation with another man at his family's hunting lodge, when one of his brothers arrived with a group of friends a day earlier than expected. The brother had thought it wouldn't make any difference if they got there Friday night instead of Saturday morning; on the contrary, many lives had been changed forever. Louis was now on an extended "religious retreat" in California. His three sons had transferred at the beginning of the spring semester to the Brook-Haven School, which promoted tolerance and diversity as well as academic excellence. In the Mountain Brook public school system, where discrimination based on race, religion, social status and sexual orientation was as rampant as in the society it served, the boys had been subjected to brutal torment. Norman Laney had been able to "guar-an-tee" Dooky that would not happen at Brook-Haven, and so far, it hadn't. Thanks to Dooky's generous, forgiving nature, divorce proceedings were amicable, and primarily a matter of arranging the financial settlements. These were complicated only because there was so much money and so many assets involved. But everyone would be well provided for. Dooky's only problem was deciding what to do with the rest of her life. For now, she had decided that keeping a low profile was no longer necessary or desirable. So tonight she was making her debut as a divorcée.

Highlands Bar and Grill was not only a great restaurant but a popular place for those trying to launch a new identity or a new life. For anyone suffering a devastating reversal of financial, professional or marital status, the country club was often a very uncomfortable place to be. But with its location on the Southside of Birmingham and its nationally recognized chef—a James Beard award winner—Highlands was part of the larger world which welcomed those whose lives did not necessarily follow the trajectory of the usual Mountain Brook existence. Tonight it was packed.

The table for two reserved for them in the back of the restaurant would be out of the way as soon as they arrived at it, but meanwhile, they had to pass every other table to get to it. Dooky was greeted and embraced by many as they threaded their way through the crowd of high-spirited diners. The waiter leading them stood patiently aside as Dooky never failed to introduce her date. Ham had met many new people through Dooky ever since she had called him to offer condolences about his father and ask if there were a time they could get together to discuss his alma mater, the Brook-Haven School, where she was considering enrolling her boys. Ham was surprised at how many people he didn't know were nevertheless aware of his existence, but after his recent immersion in **Whitmire Realty,** he believed he knew the reason. Fortunately, meeting new people or running into former acquaintances or classmates was no longer the nightmare it had once been. No one was interested in how or what he was doing; all inquiries were about his father. It was extremely gratifying to experience the high regard and esteem in which his father was universally held, especially as these perceptions were automatically transferred or projected onto him in his father's absence. Somehow he felt even taller as well as better about himself in general. And it was a ready-made conversation he could produce without hesitation or stammering: His father was receiving daily visits from three different therapists; had regained some use of his right arm; was walking with more and more assurance every day; was talking some though he still couldn't speak with ease. Nothing appeared to be permanently paralyzed, and the outlook was hopeful that he would continue to progress. This information made everyone happy, and there was rarely time in a small-talk situation for personal inquiries into his own life. By the time people got to "And how are *you?*" their eyes were already darting toward other objects of attention and their bodies were beginning to edge away. The most perfunctory of replies would suffice.

As a consequence, he no longer dreaded going out in public, and being with Dooky St. John was as much a thrill as it had been twenty years ago. Indeed, it was even more so, because then he had been simply filling in for Louis Lankford, who was destined to take his place. But Louis Lankford had proved unfit for this position, and now Ham was taking *his* place. The pleasant sensation that he was now doing that which Louis Lankford could not do was just one of the many changes wrought by that fateful day when he had encountered Dooky St. John right before his father suffered a massive stroke.

"I always thought you two made the best couple! Maybe this was meant to be!"

A woman who looked vaguely familiar had her hand on his back and was reaching out with her other to give Dooky's arm a squeeze. An expert signal from Dooky's eyes reminded Ham to rise from the chair where he had just sat down.

"Ham, you remember Kelly Moreland, don't you? She was president of ADPsi. We made our debuts together. She's Kelly Fitzpatrick now."

"Of course," he was able to say, thanks to Dooky's masterful cues, which had the same desired effect as his mother's more heavy-handed promptings. Fortunately, Dooky's subtle and graceful signals managed to preserve what little sense of manhood and dignity he had left after a lifetime of his mother's unsubtle and graceless telegraphings, which were delivered with the finesse of a bullhorn and geared to the level of an eight year-old boy.

"How are you, Kelly?" he said, utterly confounded by a face he did not at all recognize. She looked ten to fifteen years older than Dooky, and no longer had either the face or the figure that got a girl elected president of a sorority at Mountain Brook High School. Dooky still looked every bit the president of TKD sorority, if not more so. The very durability of her completely intact looks made them somehow more substantial and real. However, Kelly had one thing Dooky currently did not possess, and that was a large diamond wedding ring that flashed with blinding brilliance as she gesticulated throughout her reminiscence of the mishap involving the hot air balloon on the golf course at the Birmingham Country Club during the Ball of Roses twenty years ago. Ham began to wonder if the sole point of the story was to give Kelly a chance to wave her ring around in front of their faces. He also wondered if he was supposed to remain standing, but Dooky was giving rapt attention to her friend's performance, so he tried to follow her lead and do the same.

After Kelly left, enthusing yet again on what a great match the two of them made, Dooky leaned across the table and whispered, "I feel so sorry for her!

Her husband has had one affair after another and she has just *let herself go*."

Ham had assumed it was the other way around—Kelly had felt sorry for Dooky, and had come over to the table on a mission of mercy—but he had long since given up trying to understand the women of his society. For one thing, they all seemed to feel sorry for each other.

At any rate, Kelly's visit proved to be the trigger for a parade of visitors to their table. While most of those dining in the restaurant were totally unfamiliar to Ham, they all seemed to know Dooky. It was exactly like this, he remembered, during the summer of her debut. Dooky was always besieged by adoring multitudes of people he'd never seen before in his life. Except for the lapse of two decades, she might still have been the sorority president receiving affectionate tributes from classmates and sorority sisters. Back then he had enjoyed the throngs of people Dooky always attracted. It was his first and only taste of a heady kind of high school popularity that wasn't even possible at the small school he'd attended. Tonight the phenomenon was more irksome, as he kept needing to pop up out of his chair while in the process of reading the menu, ordering his dinner or trying to eat it. But he could tell Dooky was enjoying herself immensely for perhaps the first time in months, and the outing was serving its intended purpose. Dooky was re-introducing herself to society as an available and beautiful woman; society was taking notice and responding with enthusiasm.

Toward the end of the meal, which Dooky had barely pretended to eat, he recognized from the look on her face that their table was being approached yet again. This time when he stood up and turned around to greet visitors, he found himself confronted by the entire Cooley clan. Fortunately it was Ginger's husband Hugh McNamara leading the way rather than Mrs. Cooley, who was up to her usual trick of lagging behind and laying siege to occupants of another table, the better to make a grand entrance after others had prepared the way by dispensing with the polite formalities. He could see her long arms swirling dramatically around her head already in service to whatever theatrical presentation she had decided to launch. Meanwhile, he shook hands with Hugh, whom he'd come to like a lot during the past two months. In order to conclude the deal in Memphis, they had spent considerable time together, including a brief trip to the city itself to meet with the sellers again and walk over the site one more time. He had not realized that **Whitmire Realty** and **Cooley Construction** shared the expense of owning a small private plane, which made the trip that much more pleasant. Thanks to his Tuesday/Thursday teaching schedule, they had been able to leave late on Thursday and come back the following Friday afternoon.

In the course of the excursion, he discovered that he knew Hugh's first cousin, Taylor McNamara, who had been with Ham in the same freshman dorm at Williams. He had liked Taylor a lot and found that he also enjoyed Hugh's company. Considering that Hugh was Ginger Cooley's husband, he hadn't expected to like him any more than he liked Ginger. He was also impressed by the plans **Cooley Construction** had devised for the development of the Memphis property; it was a highly detailed and carefully thought-out piece of work. Hugh appeared to have similar respect for Ham, probably because he had no choice in the matter. When the Memphis deal was being concluded, Ham had still been his father's power of attorney; that was all Hugh needed to know when he'd needed Ham's signature on all the closing papers. Ham was still the stand-in for his father as head of **Whitmire Realty**; it was Ham Hugh had to deal with in person at the moment. Hugh couldn't do otherwise than respect him.

Hugh's wife Ginger was busy telling Dooky that she absolutely *must* become active again in the Junior League, and that she, Ginger, as president of the Junior League, would personally see to it that Dooky got reinstated right away and placed on whatever committees she wanted. It would be just the thing, Ginger said, to make everybody including Dooky forget about what had happened to her marriage and get Dooky "out there." This was classic Ginger, following the playbook devised by her mother, the pro at socially acceptable self-aggrandizement and self-promotion containing cleverly concealed put-downs of others. While supposedly offering to do Dooky a tremendous favor, Ginger had also managed—for the benefit of everyone in the restaurant—to identify herself as the current president of the Junior League in Birmingham. She also reminded everyone of Dooky's misfortune, and somehow implied that Dooky's inactive status in the Junior League was at the root of all her self-inflicted troubles. Once that wrong was put right, Dooky's life would come together again.

"You are so sweet," said Dooky, without a trace of irony. She really seemed to believe that everyone else was as genuinely sweet as she was, even when they had just put her down and referred to the scandalous break-up of her marriage. Ham hoped Ginger could be content with these accomplishments and call it a night. These hopes were dashed when she turned around suddenly and cried,

"Ham!"

She sounded just like her mother, with a voice that could carry to all four corners of a room, no matter how crowded or loud.

"I've been meaning to call you! You know my roommate from Yale? She was an English major? Then she went to Harvard Law School? I guess this would be after you dropped out! But she finished her degree and practiced law in New York! You would love her! She hated it! Now she's decided to join a literary agency and is looking for clients! Didn't you have a novel or something that never got published?"

It was a fascinating performance, encapsulating her degree from Yale, and his failures to graduate from law school or find a publisher for his novel.

"If you want to help your friend, the last thing she needs is my novel," he said, under no illusion that Ginger wanted to help anyone but herself.

"I'm going to get it out of you," warned Ginger, wagging her finger in his face. "I always get what I want. And what's the worst that can happen if we send it to New York? So what if it gets rejected again? What do you have to lose?"

Nothing but the few scraps of pride, self-respect and self-esteem he was clinging onto.

"Ham's got a lot more important things on his mind right now," said Hugh, taking his wife by the arm. "I'll see you Monday?"

Ham nodded. "Two o'clock," he confirmed, shaking hands now with Mr. Cooley before suddenly being overwhelmed by Mrs. Cooley's embrace.

"We have been *so* worried about your father!" she exclaimed. "And who is this gorgeous girl you've procured for the evening?"

"Oh, Mother," said Ginger. "You've met Dooky. Louis Lankford's wife."

"Dooky St. John," introduced Ham, as Dooky rose from the table with her extraordinary smile.

"Louis Lankford?!" exclaimed Mrs. Cooley, turning around and ignoring Dooky. "*That* Louis Lankford? The one I've been hearing about?"

No one, not even Ginger, wanted to corroborate this unfortunate fact. Ham spied Erica deliberately hanging back behind her family group. When he caught her eye, she shook her head to deplore the follies of her mother, and gave him a look of commiseration.

"I went by to see your father yesterday," said Mr. Cooley, leaning over and speaking in an undertone. Over the years he had learned not to interject substantive conversation too forcefully while his wife was doing her thing.

"My mother told me," Ham nodded. "We appreciate it."

"I think he looks a lot better."

"The doctors do too. We're very hopeful."

". . . considering all you've been through, you poor thing." Mrs. Cooley concluded a backhanded compliment to "Louis Lankford's wife."

"And you," she wagged her finger in his face just as Ginger had. "You are a sly one. Adelaide is convinced that you are a hopelessly confirmed bachelor, and here you are, the man about town. Two-timing my own daughter, though I can't say I blame you one bit." She looked around for that daughter just as this daughter stepped forward in dismay.

"Mother, you are so melodramatic. Ham isn't two-timing anyone." She thrust her hand forward shyly and introduced herself to Dooky.

"Oh, I'm sorry," said Ham. "I thought you knew each other."

"How would they know each other?" cried Mrs. Cooley. "Erica is at least *ten years younger.*"

"Ignore my mother," said Erica to Dooky. "She'd like to make something out of the fact that Ham and I both go sit in a UAB classroom to watch French films on Sunday afternoons."

"I love your earrings," said Dooky.

"Oh, I can't stand that ridiculous gypsy jewelry!" declared Mrs. Cooley. "I *would* say that Erica looks like a hippie, but I've seen hippies better put together than this." She waved her hand scornfully to dismiss her daughter's sloppy appearance. "Erica, I hope you're taking notes. This poor woman has *three teenage children,* is going through a *dreadful divorce,* and is *still married* to a *lousy cur* who *used* her *horribly.* And yet look how beautifully she has turned herself out! She recognizes her *main chance* when he's right there in front of her, and she *makes herself up* accordingly." Mrs. Cooley turned around to the others. "Erica obviously believes that someone is going to love her for her *natural self,*" she explained.

"No, Mother," said Erica cheerfully in her flutey, girlish voice of iron resolve. "You long ago convinced me that no one was ever going to love me. I just thought I could get away with being my *natural self* during my own birthday celebration."

"This could be straight out of Tennessee Williams," said Ginger. "I think it's time to leave."

Ham leaned forward to embrace Erica. "Happy birthday," he said.

"I hope we haven't upset your date," she murmured. "I feel so sorry for her."

"I feel so sorry for her," said Dooky when the Cooleys had taken their leave. "Is she the one who had the affair with the married man in New Mexico?"

"Colorado," he said, trying to recall the scant details Erica had given him. Supposedly it wasn't actually an affair. Rather, her boss, the publisher of the alternative weekly, had made unmistakable overtures to her on the night of his birthday celebration at the newspaper's office. As a married man twenty-five years older than she, he didn't appear to be offering anything other than his middle-aged body in its midlife crisis. And all he was asking for in return was the chance to screw up her life. None of this was in keeping with the newspaper's mission of promoting greater spiritual and physical health through careful attention to the energy taken into and put out of our sacred minds and bodies. Although Erica's job of writing the book and movie reviews wasn't at all related to this mission, the incident had been the catalyst forcing her to re-think her Colorado existence and ultimately led to her return home.

Dooky was stifling a yawn, and Ham decided there was no need to share this story. Rather, he needed to pay the bill and get Dooky home. The time he had lately been spending in her company had already made him more adept at reading social situations and handling them appropriately.

"Why don't you come in?" Dooky suggested as she always did when they arrived back at her house.

It certainly wasn't the first time he'd been inside, but the first time he'd been alone with her in her home, he realized. Usually there was a sitter, or Mr. and Mrs. St. John along with the three boys, ages fifteen, thirteen and eleven. But it was the week of Spring Break, and the children were with their grandparents in Seaside, Florida. Dooky's big house, normally filled with the noise and commotion of three energetic youths, now seemed unnaturally empty and quiet. The still, silent rooms called out for activity to fill them and justify their existence. As Dooky led him back to the sunroom, he could feel prickles of discomfort on the back of his neck, and his insides lurched in a way they had not been doing for a while, he realized now. Although it wasn't uncommon for him to enjoy periods of intestinal calm, he wouldn't have expected this to occur in the aftermath of his father's stroke. Perhaps he'd simply been so busy that he hadn't noticed the usual turmoil, which he felt keenly now. Was he expected to introduce an activity which would fill the house—or at least one of the rooms—with noise and motion?

Dooky herself seemed completely at her usual ease as she reached for her customary diet Dr. Pepper from the mini refrigerator at the wet bar.

"Help yourself," she offered, kicking off her shoes and tucking bare feet underneath her as she sank onto the tropically patterned sofa covered with fuschia parrots and green palm fronds. He caught a glimpse of her gaily painted toenails—the same color as the parrots—before they disappeared from view.

Fortunately the bar was fully stocked and contained an excellent selection of choice single malt Scotches, which Dooky knew nothing about because essentially she did not drink. Although she never declined a drink in public and always sipped a beer or glass of wine when others were drinking, her beverage of choice was diet Dr. Pepper. During the summer of her debut, Dooky would be as fresh-faced and unspoiled at two or three in the morning as she was when he'd picked her up nine hours earlier, because the most she drank was a diet Coke with the merest splash of rum. She indulged in this only so she could say "rum and Coke" when asked what she was drinking. Dooky could never lie any more than she could drink, say a mean word or do a cruel deed. Meanwhile, most of the other girls were puking gin and tonic on the 18th hole at one o'clock in the morning. "I think that's why I was TKD president," Dooky had told him once. "The girls knew I'd never get drunk and embarrass the sorority." This was classic Dooky in all her genuine modesty: the reason she had been elected president of TKD was because she was the most gorgeous girl the planet had ever produced. Also the sweetest.

The bar in her house was primarily "for show" and for her parents, who frequently babysat and naturally expected not to have to bring their own bourbon. A well-appointed Mountain Brook house was expected to have a full array of expensive liquors, even if the head of the house was trying to control a serious drinking problem. But Louis had been going to AA for years, and his drinking had tapered off. However, Dooky had recently confided, she'd since begun to wonder if Louis had been going somewhere else besides the meetings, and engaging in activity for which the drinking had once been a substitute. At any rate, the bottles of Scotch had been mostly decorative until Ham had begun to help himself as he had lately.

Usually he enjoyed himself immensely as he sipped Scotch in Dooky's flower-filled sunroom, which had the look but not the feel of a greenhouse, all windows and plants. Mrs. St. John always stayed and chatted, and of course wanted all the latest details of his father's ongoing recovery. Like her daughter, Mrs. St. John was the essence of sweet. Her concern was genuine and her sympathy was boundless. She was probably the only one in the world who had used the expression "dear Adelaide" with complete sincerity and no hint of sarcasm. The time he had spent with Dooky and her mother on the parrot-covered sofa and armchairs drinking excellent Scotch and basking in the comfort of their warm company and conversation had been the best antidote to the traumatic events of the last several months. In fact, the best times he'd had since he'd been back in Birmingham had been in Dooky's house.

Even the constant interruptions of the boys, who were all supposed to be in bed, were enjoyable and welcome. The boys were good-looking and intelligent, and above all, seemed like happy and cheerful children. Their father's abrupt, ignominious departure from their lives and the taunting they'd supposedly endured in school had not taken any toll that Ham could see. Of course he knew he was seeing just a miniscule portion of the tip of the iceberg and couldn't judge by that; nevertheless, there seemed to be so much love radiating from Dooky and her mother and circulating throughout the house that he could only think this love would carry them through any turbulence. His own fate would have been different, he knew, if he'd grown up with a mother who was kind and nurturing like Mrs. St. John, presiding happily over a house filled with children's games and laughter. Perhaps he himself would even be presiding over just such a household, filled with his own happy children and a wife who was as sweet and loving as Dooky. He'd never before entertained the image of such domestic contentment, and it was enormously appealing.

But tonight he couldn't seem to get comfortable in the chair he usually sat in next to the corner of the sofa Dooky preferred. For the first time it was occurring to him that perhaps he wasn't intended as a mere stand-in until a more suitable candidate emerged on the scene to take Louis's place by Dooky's side. Perhaps he was Dooky's choice. Mrs. Cooley appeared to think so, and therefore, the idea wasn't unthinkable. From the way she had berated her daughter, she even appeared to consider him something of a catch, which he would have considered another unthinkable idea, given that he was short, balding, almost middle-aged, professionally unaccomplished and socially inept. The mere fact of his maleness seemed to be enough. Of course, his family name and the money that came with it didn't hurt either.

Yet Ham wasn't feeling especially male as he sat alone with Dooky in her sunroom. Did she expect him to attempt something with her? Did she want him to? An even trickier question was also bothering him: Why didn't he want to attempt anything with her? Since the discovery in his father's desk and the thorough examination of his father's belongings, he had embarked on an even more thorough examination of himself to see if he shared his father's—inclinations. He had not yet had the courage to ask his therapist if she thought he might be more than just a miserable failure. Of course, if he *was* a homosexual and didn't realize it, perhaps that was the reason he was such a miserable failure, and why the fundamental truth or purpose of his existence remained unknown to him. But he had found nothing inside himself that connected with the magazines inside his father's desk. Why then, was he so uncomfortable rather than overjoyed and, well—excited—to find himself in an intimate situation with Dooky St. John?

"Is anything wrong?" she asked him softly.

"Oh, no," he said emphatically, shaking his head. Wrong? What did she mean by that? Wrong with him? As a man? "I think I'm just tired," he explained, before it occurred to him that Louis might have used this exact same dodge.

"Of course you're tired, you poor thing," she said. "All you've been through with your father in the hospital, looking after his affairs, teaching your classes. It was bound to catch up with you."

Ham didn't know what to say or do next. Fortunately the telephone rang to give him a brief reprieve.

"Excuse me," said Dooky. "That will be my mother, reporting on the boys."

She moved to the other corner of the sofa, next to the end table where she picked up the phone. As he watched her murmuring into the receiver, gently nodding and occasionally laughing at something her mother said, he wondered how on earth he could be expected to approach this perfect woman with his clearly imperfect self. She was complete in her beauty; he would be like a mosquito that deserved to be slapped away if he had the temerity to land on her body.

It wasn't just that he felt unworthy, however. He felt *unable*. If he attempted the effort, he knew his very fingers would prove incapable of even unbuttoning the back of her shimmering silver dress, the color of moonlight. Without question, other parts of his body would fail to perform as well. But even beyond the performance anxiety, there was something else, something even worse. *He did not even want to unbutton her dress.*

Something had to be wrong with him, he knew. She was one of the loveliest women he had ever seen in his life, and at her invitation, he was alone with her in her own home. What would any "normal" man be doing in this situation? Probably, any "normal" man would have already done it by now. Done that which "normal" men do when alone with a beautiful woman who had made herself available and accessible. The ringing of the telephone just a minute ago would have been an unwelcomed interruption and would have gone unanswered. It would be stupid to say he wasn't attracted to her. How could anyone not be attracted to a woman who was both the sun and the moon, with hair of gold and a dress of silver? There was only one answer: He must not be a "normal" man, then. He burned with shame at the thought.

Hanging up the phone, Dooky was seized with a yawn which she covered charmingly with the back of her hand.

"I'm sorry, Ham," she said, yawning again. "A minute ago I was fine; suddenly I'm exhausted."

Was this the truth? Or a skillful ploy designed to shift the burden of failure away from him and onto herself? It would be just like Dooky, he reflected as he drove back to his apartment, to spare his feelings, give him a way to save face, and keep the status quo of their relationship intact. No doubt she had done this throughout her marriage, and it had become second nature. Unlike his former girlfriends, Dooky would never take matters into her own hands, so to speak, and instigate a physical relationship. She was much more likely to do the one thing they hadn't done, and suggest marriage. Not in so many words, of course. It would be like the way he had found himself at Highlands tonight without ever having asked Dooky for the date. In the same way he could find himself walking down the aisle with her. But that image he'd conjured of domestic contentment would never materialize, because eventually the in-laws would go home and the boys would go to sleep. He'd be left alone in a room with Dooky, and he would be expected to do that which he could not do with her.

He'd be in the same wretched situation his father had endured with his mother for almost fifty years. And he would live forever with the guilt and the sense of failure and inadequacy of being with a woman for whom he could not be the man she needed or wanted. This precisely described not only his father's relationship with his mother, but his own relationship with his mother. When he wanted so badly to escape what his father did, he wondered, was it more the expected marriage to the right girl than the business he had been running away from? For the first time it occurred to him that perhaps it wasn't so much the family *business* he had wanted to avoid, but the *family* business, as represented by the kind of sham marriage his parents had.

He thought of all the forced faces he saw at the country club: his aunt and uncle's, Big Julian and Lula Petsinger, who had made her unfortunate choice of life partner when she was eighteen, at the end of her debutante season. Belonging to a generation of women for whom getting married was everything, they had nevertheless gotten this one all-important thing so terribly wrong. It wasn't just his parents' bad marriage, but all the bad marriages made by young people way too young to make good choices or avoid the pernicious influence of their society. The toll it had taken was enormous. He was one of the casualties; the bad marriages of his parents' generation had created a toxin which poisoned his outlook, made all of life seem joyless, doomed and not worth living. Or was he just rationalizing, yet again? Undoubtedly the time had come to find out. Was he gay or what? At his next appointment, he'd have to ask his therapist.

175

~ 16 ~

Two weeks later, on the first day of April, the end of the school year was only about a month away. Five weeks, to be exact. It was hard for Ham to believe that the semester was almost over; it felt as if it had only begun. The previous semester seemed to have lasted forever without end, whereas this semester had flown by despite a workload that was several times heavier because of all he was doing with the family firm.

There was a sense all over campus that the semester was winding down, and everyone was breathing a sigh of relief and winding down with it. This had been a stressful year for the college, with the public exposure of its deficiencies—broadcast in the *Birmingham News*—and the public outcry that had erupted for the college to simply shut down or be shut down. As a result of his father's stroke, Ham's attention had been diverted to other fronts which commanded his first loyalty. It was almost as if the pull of the white world into which he'd been born was inexorably claiming him for its own. He'd had no time or energy to spend on the college's troubles and had barely been able to fulfill the numerous responsibilities of his four courses. But he had not shirked his teaching duties or resigned from them unexpectedly: that in itself was an achievement.

Unfortunately, it was the only achievement he had managed for Cahaba College. After he and Ivy Greer had submitted their proposal for the remedial education of incoming freshmen—to which the administration had never responded—Ham had not had time to take further part in his colleague's crusade to save the college. Although he knew she was still engaged in this heroic mission, he had no idea what she was doing about it, not only because she was Monday/Wednesday/Friday and he was Tuesday/Thursday, but also because his social life had been taken over by Dooky St. John. The friendship that had blossomed between himself and Ivy had no room to grow at the moment since he had little interaction with her on campus or off.

But today Ivy Greer came storming into his office, her eyes blazing and her body snapping with furious energy. He tried to conceal his impatience; he really needed to finish marking the stack of papers in front of him before his next class, and if possible, he wanted to take a stab at writing that recommendation he'd promised Tameika Young.

"Did you get your letter?" she demanded, without preamble.

"Letter?" He looked at her in bewilderment.

"Offering you a contract for next year." She plunked down without invitation into one of the (brand new) chairs facing his desk.

"Oh, yes," he said, remembering now. "I believe I did." He thumbed through the pile of paper he'd pulled from his mail slot that morning. "Here it is," he said, holding it up. "Did you not get yours?"

"I got a letter all right," she said, glowering at him across the militantly folded arms on her chest. "My letter informs me that my contract will not be renewed for next year."

"What?" he cried, in disbelief. "There must be some mistake."

"There's no mistake. I've just come back from talking to the dean."

"Well, what did he say?"

At that moment, his cell phone rang and he excused himself while he answered. She nodded and her eyes filled with tears as she rose to leave. Frowning, he shook his head and motioned for her to remain seated. His caller was Hugh McNamara; there was some glitch with the permits for the demolition of the warehouses in Memphis. Since the wrecking crew was scheduled to begin work in a matter of days, this issue had to be resolved without delay. The conversation with Hugh lasted long enough that he'd lost the thread of his discussion with Ivy by the time he ended the call and turned back to her.

"I'm sorry," he apologized. "You were saying . . . ?"

"The dean was saying," she corrected him bitterly. "I'm just '*not a good fit*' for the college."

"Not a good fit," he echoed in bemusement. "I guess that's true. You're intelligent, you're experienced, you're qualified, you have excellent credentials—including a Ph.D—you're committed to what you do, and you even love doing it. And incidentally, you're also very good at doing it. So I guess you don't fit in here at all." He paused, but his attempt at humor had not lifted her spirits. "That's it?" he asked her. "You weren't given a reason?"

"That's it. He thanked me for my year of service to the school, wished me luck, and showed me the door."

Ham fell back against his chair. "Can they do this?"

"I guess so, because they just did."

"But they have no legitimate reason. You're the best teacher in this department by a long shot. Probably the best in the whole school."

"They have their own reasons. And those reasons don't need to be legitimate. I guess it didn't help that my mother isn't going to get that promotion." Ivy gave a mirthless laugh. "The fact that she was up for it could be the main reason I got this job in the first place. They may have thought it was strategic to have an ally in the public school system where we send most of our graduates. But now that she's out of contention, I'm out of a job. I guess I caused too much 'trouble.'"

"But isn't there-? Don't you have-?" He groped for the proper terminology, which was escaping him if he'd ever known it in the first place. "Is there no. . . . recourse?"

"There's no grievance process, if that's what you mean. There's also no faculty governance. Instructors have no way to protest when the administration does whatever it wants. Don't forget this place is allowed to operate by its own so-called rules. White folks let black folks run their own show here, and the black folks have run this place into the ground because they don't care about serving the college's mission. They're only serving themselves. Show up for work, collect the paycheck, don't rock the boat. This is what human nature can sink to when nobody holds your feet to the fire."

"But now the college *is* being held accountable," Ham argued. "And they need you," he said. "You of all people. How do they think they're going to re-invent themselves without people like you? There's obviously a lot this place needs to do differently if it wants to survive, and without people like you to help lead the way, they don't stand a chance. What they need to do is to clone you, not get rid of you."

"Well, they've got Miss Mombasa," she said, referring sarcastically to their chairwoman. "Obviously, they're not planning on turning over a new leaf," continued Ivy quietly. "They're just going to try to find a new way around the same old problems. And they don't want someone like me here to call them out on it. Did I tell you what I learned—do you know how our dean—who just showed me the door—got his job here?"

He shook his head.

"He was terminated—terminated—from his position at Toogaloo when he couldn't account for what had happened to the money that was supposed to be in the travel fund for academic conferences. Apparently none of the teachers had actually applied for money to attend a conference until three years ago. They had a new hire—from Morehouse—who wanted to go present a paper, applied for travel money, and the ten thousand dollars that was supposed to be in the fund couldn't be located."

He shook his head again. "How do you know all this?"

"One of my professors from Spelman. The black college circuit has a very active grapevine," she sighed. "Anyway, Dean Akin had to go back to his first love of shoe sales. Until another dean from Toogaloo became our president here. And our president's wife is first cousins with Dean Akin's wife. So it goes," she sighed.

"Toogaloo?" he said. "What in the world is that?"

"Another black college," she explained wearily. "In Mississippi."

Ham gave a wry chuckle. "Is it just me?" he ventured tentatively, hoping he wasn't putting his foot in it, "or does the name 'Toogaloo' inspire something less than total respect?"

She gave a curt bark of something that might have approached laughter. "Believe it or not," she said, "Toogaloo is a very well-respected HBCU. But who knows what that means? It could mean, thirty-five years ago, they produced some civil rights leaders. Great. But what are they doing today? Possibly the same stupid things we're doing here."

"Could it be as crazy as this place, do you think?"

"Well," she considered, "we literally got some of the same bozos. Because we got the bozos they got rid of."

He shook his head yet again, this time in disgust. "Perhaps," he concluded timidly, "it could be for the best. This place is obviously reaching the end of its line." He racked his brain for further words of comfort, and came up with something someone had said to him recently. "Why stake your future on a place that has no future? There are other ways to . . . do what you want to do."

"Don't think I haven't looked," she admitted. "But there are no openings at either UAB or Birmingham-Southern."

"What's that other place?" He tried unsuccessfully to come up with the name of Birmingham's community college.

"Shelby State?" she said, heaving a sigh. "I looked there too. And they *do* have some adjunct positions. But even if it paid enough—which it doesn't—I don't see myself. . . . Don't get me wrong: I have nothing against suburban white students. But that's mostly what they have there, and it just isn't . . . it's just not. . . . I know I could find another job somewhere else, in another city or state, but I really don't want to leave my dad."

He nodded in keen appreciation of her plight. The doctors weren't willing to predict how long her father would remain in remission, but the consensus appeared to be that it would not last. Ivy wanted to be with her father during whatever remained of his life, and she wanted to be there with him and the rest of her family during the final crisis. Ham now knew exactly how she felt. But he didn't know what to say, or how he could help with her predicament. It wasn't as if *she* had a trust fund that would allow her to remain in Birmingham with her family without having a job.

"What are *you* going to do?" she said, nodding to indicate his own letter, which was offering him the contract now denied to her, though she was the one with the truest dedication to these students and the fiercest commitment to their common cause. "You're not coming back, are you?"

"No," he confessed, shaking his head. "With my father's stroke, and the company. . . ." He faltered, not having planned on broaching this topic today.

"What exactly will you do?" she persisted. "Are you going to work for your father's company now?"

He didn't know what to say. He hadn't exactly answered this question for himself, and had so far even refrained from putting the question to himself in so many words, in such a direct fashion. And yet at the same time, he felt he was arriving at an answer with each day he showed up at the offices of **Whitmire Realty**. For the moment, he was supposedly only filling in until his father could return. In reality, however, it was becoming clear that his father would never return to work full-time—not as the CEO, at any rate. At the moment, his father was still too preoccupied with his various therapies, and his power of speech was still too limited, to warrant his presence at the office for any amount of time. So Ham stood in for him during the day, and afterwards, brought the necessary papers, messages, issues and questions home to his father. They went through these together in the late afternoon and early evening. Ham had always been adept at reading his father's thoughts without needing them translated into words. In this situation, he became skilled at asking the right questions that enabled his father to communicate through a nod, a shake of the head or the minimum of words. He looked forward to the day when his father could return to the office and instruct him more fluently. But with each batch of documents or memos he took from home and ferried back to the office, he knew the baton was being passed on to him, and that he was accepting it.

It remained an ongoing revelation to learn that what his father did, as exemplified by the Memphis project, was a lot more interesting, challenging and stimulating than he ever would have imagined. And most probably, he might never have discovered this astonishing truth if he hadn't been thrust abruptly into the middle of it all by virtue of his father's stroke and the power of attorney he had given his son. The emergency role he had been called upon to play in helping to launch this new development had actually been—well—fun; whereas a simple, self-deprecating overview of the business delivered by his humble-minded and unpretentious father would have had the same numbing effect as his boyhood tours of the office. He would have come away thinking that what his father did was extremely boring, just as he had assumed when he was a boy. He would have failed to perceive how interesting and even meaningful his father's work could be.

The Memphis project would create something of value and even beauty in the midst of urban desolation. It would generate employment and tax dollars. If it had the desired ripple effect, the black community there stood to regain one of its lost neighborhoods, now given over to drugs and crime. Not to say that the enterprise was about high-minded ideals and open-handed generosity, but it was a lot more akin to what his sister did as a physician than he would ever have supposed. In a way, a group of cancerous cells—the derelict warehouses—was going to be destroyed, and the health of a blighted area might be restored.

On the other hand, he had learned through painful experience that even the supposedly noble and pure profession of teaching could harbor its own kind of corruption and iniquity. As an instructor at a black college, he had in a perverse way probably perpetuated the ignorance and poverty of the black population of his native city more than he had alleviated it. However unwittingly, he had helped to put unqualified teachers in the public school system. And he himself had not been successful at teaching black college students from the public schools in Birmingham what they hadn't learned in the public schools in Birmingham. Now *that* was a task beyond his powers. Running a multi-million dollar company was much easier.

For that matter, anything would be much easier than trying to teach underprivileged, disadvantaged descendants of slaves what they needed to know in order to take their place in a society still largely controlled by those who objected to their very existence. His dismal and failed attempt to do so had ironically helped him to recognize and take his own place in that society. He had not helped them at all, but in trying to do so, had ended up helping himself enormously. One day, he hoped, he would be in a position to return the favor. One day, perhaps he would be able to offer some means of redress to history's victims from the largesse he possessed as one of history's beneficiaries. But for now, Cahaba College's battle with itself and its detractors would have to be fought by others.

For a variety of reasons, he had learned he was not ill-suited to "the family business." His own legal knowledge was actually not without some practical application, although, ironically, he often found himself wishing he had an MBA as his mother had once wished. However, the look he could easily imagine on his therapist's face if he told her he'd decided to go back to school for an MBA, rather than an MFA, was enough to convince him he simply needed to go forward now with the education he had. It was enough, at least for right now, which was all he had time to worry about. Meanwhile, he had the weird sensation that many of the pieces of his life were falling into their proper place, and oddly enough, this involved his own place within "the family business."

He *did* feel bad about leaving his colleague Ivy Greer in the lurch. He felt even worse for their students, who deserved so much more than they were ever going to get from either the college or the world they had been born into. At the very least, they deserved Ivy Greer and others like her in their college classrooms. But he had no confidence that the apathetic administration would scout for the best possible candidates to do some of the hardest and most necessary work of all in their classrooms. On the contrary, they would make sure to find more compliant and passive personalities—like he had been when he first came on board—whose chief attribute was a desire not to rock the boat. Unfortunately, he didn't know of anything he could do about it at the present moment.

"I understand," she said softly, as if reading his thoughts. With another sigh, she rose to go. "When will you tell them?"

He hadn't thought about that. The sooner the better, he supposed. "Today, I guess," he said.

* * *

The dean was not at all surprised. "And of course, there's the company," he added, after Ham spoke at length about the complications of his father's stroke.

"The company?" said Ham, taken aback. Other than Ivy Greer, he had told no one at the college about his family's business, and had even gone to the trouble of obscuring his family name itself by shortening this to "Whit" on campus.

"Whitmire Realty," said the dean smoothly.

"Yes," said Ham, uncertainly.

"I imagine they'll really need you on a full-time basis at the office at this point."

Not only did they know exactly who he was, along with the nature of his family's business, it appeared to be common knowledge that he had already been working at this business, at least on a part-time basis. The irony was a bit much: in the past, faculty at many historically black colleges had second jobs—in used car or real estate sales—to supplement their substandard salaries. Earlier in the year, Ivy had explained that the eight hour office hour requirement—to be spread out over five days of the week—was intended primarily to prevent any instructors from having second jobs, which were prohibited by the Faculty Handbook and considered grounds for dismissal. Ham had not only had a second job—in real estate sales—but the administration had been fully aware of it.

"I hope you won't forget about us here at Cahaba College in our time of need," the dean continued pleasantly.

"No, no. Of course not," said Ham, preparing to leave.

The dean made no move to rise, and remained seated with his elbows on the desk and his fingers forming a temple which supported his chin as he gazed intently ahead. "And I hope you can see your way to doing something for us, as your uncle suggested two years ago, when he recommended you for the job here."

"My uncle?" said Ham, arrested in his slide toward the edge of the seat.

"Barry Whitmire," said the dean, nodding. "As you might imagine, we always receive a great deal of interest from the community whenever we have a faculty position open here at the college. Your uncle called on your behalf, after you applied for the job, to assure us of how much we stood to gain if we offered the position to you."

And Ham thought he'd gotten the job by virtue of his Harvard Ph.D. Of course he should have realized the appointment would have gone to one of the legions of lesser-qualified applicants with social, family or political ties. In this case, *he* had happened to be the one with the strongest political tie. The fact that he was actually qualified rather than unqualified had been beside the point.

He settled back in his chair as an idea took shape in the back of his mind, triggered not only by the dean's words, but by a conversation he'd had recently with Lacy deMille, about the treatment facility in Montgomery for troubled youths his father had been giving large sums to every year, largely at the behest of his brother's girlfriend, who worked there. Serious and, unfortunately credible, allegations of abuse at the facility had surfaced in the Montgomery newspaper, and in January, Lacy had advised that they withhold the usual donation until she could find out more. Yesterday she had informed him that the facility was under investigation and might be closed down even if it was cleared of all charges. She suggested that the money be allocated elsewhere.

"As a matter of fact," Ham told the dean, "I *am* prepared to give the school a large grant."

The dean nodded calmly, as if he had fully anticipated this very announcement. Ham proceeded to name the exact, princely sum his father had been giving to the treatment facility. The dean blinked once. Improvising as he went along, Ham said he intended the grant to be used for funding remedial programs in grammar and composition for incoming freshman students, like the program he and his colleague Ivy Greer had outlined to the administration earlier in the semester in the proposal they'd submitted. These programs would help the students as well as the college itself become better equipped to provide the competent teaching force needed in the public school system. However, there were certain conditions that must be met. First of all, he was disturbed that the chairman of the English department at Cahaba College did not have the appropriate credentials for this position, and he would not feel comfortable giving any grant money at all for any purpose unless this problem was rectified immediately. This could be easily done, he pointed out, since there was currently a member of the English faculty with a Ph.D., and in their year on the faculty together, he had come to respect and admire Ivy Greer a great deal. She was an important new addition to the campus, and he would be entirely comfortable with her as chairman of the department to implement and oversee the remedial program. He got along well with her, and could easily foresee a continuation of their "working relationship," in which Ivy was a "conduit" for his ideas [and money] for the college. With her at the helm, he would guarantee the funding for two years, and then would re-evaluate the effectiveness of the program. Future grants would be contingent on how well the program was succeeding and how quickly the college as a whole was moving toward a "more qualified" faculty. If the administration demonstrated its good faith and moved quickly to address his concern about the chairmanship of the English department, he would also be happy to speak to his uncle about the "long-term viability" of Cahaba College.

His uncle, he now realized, was someone else he was going to have to get to know better. There was a lot he was going to have to get to know. As it was, he knew practically nothing, despite his years of education and his various degrees. Fortunately, he seemed to be learning quickly. After just a few short months in the business world, the language, tone and manner he used on the dean had come surprisingly easy. Of course, it was the money that was really talking, and the dean had listened. He assured Ham that the administration valued Ivy Greer as much as he did, and had already been involved in discussions about elevating her to the chairmanship of the English department.

Back at Module #13, he almost ran into Ivy Greer as she came down the stairs carrying a box of books so large she couldn't see in front of her.

"What are you doing?" he asked her.

"What does it look like?" she said irritably. "I'm cleaning out my office of course."

"I wouldn't do that right now if I were you," he said.

"Why not?"

"I think you'll find that your contract is going to be renewed after all."

It was on this day that he fully realized how much he appreciated his family's business.

~ 17 ~

A few days later, on the following Friday, Ham woke up at five-thirty as he had been back in the habit of doing for the past several months now that he was essentially working two jobs. This morning was no different, although for some reason, it felt different. The fact that it was Good Friday meant little to him: the offices of **Whitmire Realty** would be open today, and there were one or two matters he needed to deal with. What was it then, that made today feel so different? Perhaps it was simply that hint of spring in the air. And for whatever reason, he had slept particularly well the night before. It had been one of those profoundly deep sleeps that makes yesterday seem like a century ago. Yawning one last time, he stretched out his arms, and his left hand collided softly with the body of Erica Cooley, who was sleeping beside him. The memory and reality of what had happened last night crashed into his mind like a mack truck. The sudden impact of the stark truth, lying there next to him, was utterly devastating.

It was the same shock he used to have as a teenage boy, when he suddenly understood that the unbelievable sexual experience he had just enjoyed actually involved another human being—one who might have wants, needs and ulterior motives totally opposite to his. And what's more, that claim on him might clamp down sooner than he could run away from it. A speedy retreat was of the absolute essence. In the idiocy and amorality of male adolescence, this was what he had called a date, and he'd had his fair share. He would slake his desires with whatever girl went out with him without much caring who she really was, what she really wanted, or the consequences of his urgent behavior. But as soon as the lust was released, he would realize with horror that he had committed a most intimate act with a virtual stranger, a girl he didn't even know and didn't want to know. His first and only thought was to get away and distance himself as quickly and completely as possible from any hint of the intimacy that had occurred, as if it had been a terrible, terrible mistake best handled as if it had never happened. This was easy enough to do in high school, when the girl had a curfew and parents who expected her to sleep in her own home. What had happened when you took her in the woods behind John Bynum Field after the movie could recede into the background like a fantasy that had played out only in his feverish adolescent male imagination, and had never been a reality. The girl's feeling or needs were never considered. In other words, he was a typical teenage boy: sexually driven and emotionally immature. Later, in college, his approach to girls had changed drastically, not so much because he magically matured but because a crippling depression descended on him which had smothered his desire for anything, including relations with the opposite sex and even life itself.

But last night, with Erica Cooley, he had suddenly and unaccountably behaved like a teenage boy. He had fucked—there was no other word for it—the daughter of his father's business partner and an old family friend. Afterwards, he'd felt as if he'd purged every particle of himself in the process. It was no wonder he had slept so well and felt like a new man this morning.

But now what was he to do? Hoping not to wake her or preclude his escape, he looked over at her out of the corner of his eye without moving his head even a millimeter. She was lying on her side, with her back facing him and several strands of her hair trailing across the pillow like tentacles reaching out to grab him. What in the world had come over him? How and why had he landed himself in such a predicament? Rubbing his eyes, he began to go over in his mind the events of the previous evening.

He had given Hugh a ride home from the airport at about six o'clock yesterday evening. They had gone on a quick turnaround trip to inspect the process of demolition and debris removal that had just gotten underway at the Memphis site. It was a Thursday, because Hugh wanted to be with his family on Good Friday; his children had a holiday from school. Ham's students also had an official holiday on Friday. They hadn't exactly protested when he'd announced the cancellation of Thursday's classes.

When he dropped Hugh off at his house, there was a pouring, drenching April rain which probably accounted for why Hugh forgot to grab one of his cases from the car before dashing into the house. Ham ran after him with it, but it was Ginger he encountered at the front door, on the lookout for her daughter, who was supposed to be returning from a neighbor's house in all that pouring rain. Fortunately, the rain began coming down even harder than before, giving Ham a perfect excuse not to stand there chatting with Ginger, who thought she probably ought to go call the neighbors and tell her daughter to stay put until the rain slacked off.

With neither an umbrella nor a raincoat, Ham had simply lowered his head and charged like a bull through the sheets of rain. He could barely see the walkway and didn't see the girl at all—he'd forgotten the name of Ginger's daughter—until he'd almost run into her. She was limping badly and sobbing uncontrollably underneath the hood of her raincoat. It was obvious something terrible had just taken place: she must have had a very bad spill on the slick pavement or even been struck by a rain-blinded car.

The arms he'd thrown out to prevent himself from slamming into her ended up enveloping her as she barreled heedlessly into his chest. He tried as best he could to comfort her, find out what had happened and determine if she was badly hurt. Would she need to go to the hospital, he wondered, in all that impossible rain? She didn't respond to anything he said; it was likely she didn't hear him or understand what he was saying over the pounding of the rain. Instead she burrowed her face further into his chest as she clung to him and continued to heave with sobs. Soon she was as thoroughly soaked as he was despite her raincoat. Only when he partially succeeded in extricating himself and pushed back the girl's hood did he realize this was not Ginger's daughter. This was Ginger's sister Erica, who spasmodically managed to convey that she'd just had a terrible fight with her mother and left the house to seek solace from her sister.

Why would she go straight from one viper's nest to another and think she'd get anything more than another snake bite? Poor girl. He could not bring himself to escort her to the front door. But they had to get out of the rain. He took her arm and led her over to the curb where his car was parked.

At his apartment, he found her some dry clothes and changed out of his own wet things. This wasn't the first time she'd been in his apartment, and it came naturally to make her a cup of herbal tea like they always enjoyed after the French films. He poured a cup for himself as well instead of the Scotch he'd wanted earlier. As they sat down on the sofa, he listened abstractedly to the tale of woe and abuse involving her mother. It was an extremely familiar story; he felt as if he'd heard it all somewhere before, and couldn't stop himself from mostly tuning it out.

What mainly intrigued him was her choice—from the pile of possibilities he'd given her—of his nine year old nephew Paul's (clean) tee shirt and soccer shorts. They seemed to fit her well enough, except the shorts were a bit too large and the tee shirt was perhaps a bit too tight. Her (wet) nipples pricked at the fabric. Her breasts were not at all large as breasts tended to be these days, but on her scarecrow frame, even her minimal endowment was not inconsequential. It had an impact that had nothing to do with size. These breasts were brave little things that stood up with proud nipples. Sort of like Erica herself, they had more to them than you expected. He found himself wanting to caress them like he'd caressed Erica herself earlier when he thought she was a crying child who needed soothing. He also found himself wondering what she had done for dry underwear, since he hadn't been able to supply that.

And that's when he became like a teenage boy, when whatever the girl was saying became only a meaningless drone in his uninterested ear, and all he could think about was when and how he could take off her equally meaningless clothes and get between her legs. Soon enough, this had happened, when she put her face in her hands and convulsed again with sobs. Setting his cup of tea down on the coffee table, he moved closer beside her on the couch. He put his arm around her, stroked her hair, and when she turned toward him, he'd kissed her wet, tear-stained face. The next thing he knew, they were in bed together. He didn't remember exactly how matters had progressed so rapidly. Perhaps that partially explained what happened. He hadn't thought about what he was doing, geared himself up or willed himself into action. It had just happened. The experience was quite satisfying, and he didn't think it was at all unsatisfactory for her, thanks to the precise, detailed and emphatic instructions his last girlfriend Jill used to give him.

But now what? He rubbed his eyes again and sneaked another look at the sleeping body next to him. It hadn't moved. His alarm clock showed it was six A.M. He still didn't fully understand what had happened and had no idea how to get out of it. In a way it was his therapist's fault, he thought only half-jokingly to himself. At his last session he had finally mustered the courage to ask her the question that had been weighing on his mind since January. "Do you think I could be gay?" he had asked her, with the same dread another kind of doctor might be asked "Do you think I could have cancer?" He had sat there anxiously awaiting her verdict. Instead of delivering this with all due speed, she had cruelly prolonged his agony by asking an absurd and excruciating series of questions. Had he ever had sex with men? Had he ever wanted to have sex with men? Had he ever been attracted to men? Did he have fantasies of sex with men? Did he often dream of having sex with men? Did he ever find himself seeking situations to be around nude men—at the Y or the gym? Did he linger in bathrooms or locker rooms longer than was necessary?

"Of course not," he had answered indignantly and impatiently.

So then she had simply shrugged and said "If you're being honest with me, it doesn't sound like you're gay."

"That's it?" he'd said in disbelief. "You're not going to probe any further into this? After what I've discovered about my father? After all you've said about my sexual dysfunction?" It had cost him enormously to bring the topic up; he was not about to be cheated of any benefit. "What if I'm gay and don't know it? What if I'm repressing it?"

In response, she had laughed—laughed—while he sat there with white knuckles. Quickly she had sobered up and explained in her best professional manner: "It's been my experience that most people can't really repress a sexual attraction. What tends to get repressed is the acknowledgement or acceptance of what such an attraction means, along with the impulse to act on it. Although you'd be surprised how many people have homosexual sex but proudly proclaim they're not gay. Repression is like a massive denial of the truth—a refusal to allow the truth to enter our consciousness—a refusal to connect the dots right in front of us in our thoughts, our dreams, our fantasies, sometimes even in our actions. But it doesn't sound like this particular truth is there to be denied in your case."

"How can you be so sure?" he persisted.

"I can't be sure. I can only work with what you give me. That's why I say: *If you're being honest with me,* it doesn't sound like you have homosexual tendencies."

"I *am* being honest with you. But what if I'm not being honest with myself? What if I'm one of those who *has* been able to repress the attraction?"

"You want to know what I think you've been repressing?" she challenged him.

He didn't dare even nod.

"Okay. I think you *have* been repressing homosexuality."

He held his breath.

"Your father's," she said.

She gave him a look which challenged him again to say something. He was still holding his breath.

"Do you know why I say this?"

He shook his head.

"Because you're so sure of the meaning of those magazines. You found no other evidence. None. Anywhere."

He acknowledged this with a brief nod.

"There are several other possible—plausible—explanations for the presence of those magazines in the drawer of your father's desk. Do you know— one time?" she said musingly, suddenly changing tone. "I came across a stack of *Playboy* magazines in my husband's bedside table? I was furious with him. His explanation?"

How would I know? he thought irritably.

"The magazines were being delivered by mistake, my husband said, and he was afraid if he threw them away, I'd see them in the trash. So he just stuck them in a drawer and forgot about them. Yeah, right, I thought. But when the next issue came in the mail? This time he saved the cellophane wrapper—that they use to hide the cover—and sure enough, we found it had our neighbor's name and address printed on it. It was smudged and hard to read, but it was the neighbor's name and address. We alerted the mailman, and I had to apologize to my husband."

She paused, but he had nothing to say.

"Without any other proof to support your conclusion about the magazines in your father's desk, you are absolutely certain of what they mean. You just *know*."

This was true.

"On some level then," she continued, "you must have known about your father for a long time. Based on your observations or perceptions or intuition or whatever. But you censored that information from your conscious mind. You put it under lock and key, so to speak, and thought you could simply escape from it, by putting all manner of distance between yourself and your father—what he is, what he does. In this way, I think perhaps it became confused in your mind with the family business. Or any business. Any adult work or employment. It may also have become confused in your mind with marriage as well. You've been running away from two things that could save you because you thought they would destroy you. And in the process of trying to save yourself by running away, you've been slowly destroying yourself."

She paused to give him a chance to respond. He didn't know what to say just yet.

"Usually," she went on, "the truth wreaks the worst havoc when we hide it away. But if we take the hidden knowledge out of the locked drawer, it's not a piece of radioactive material we're handling. Often it's something quite simple and banal."

"You think homosexuality is simple and banal?" he asked incredulously.

She gave a slight, casual shrug. "To me it is," she said. "It's quite literally a matter of fact. It exists; it happens. That's it. That's all. Move on. Next."

He shook his head.

"Perhaps my perspective is a little different," she conceded. "Because I see it A LOT in my practice. If you're right about your father, he isn't the only one in his predicament. Not by a long shot. As you well know."

He thought of Louis Lankford, and supposed she was alluding to him and Dooky St. John.

191

"But I think," she continued reflectively, "we would all be better off—those who are gay, those who are not gay—if we treated it like something that *is* simple and banal. Just a matter of fact. This simple fact of life doesn't pose a threat or a danger to anyone; it's the cover-up that does the damage."

He'd have to think about that one later.

"My point to you is this," she said. "So what if your dad is gay? The problem is not his sexual orientation, whatever that is; the problem is the way your home life was affected by your parents' relationship, which is probably unhappy and loveless. But it doesn't mean your dad's a villain. And it doesn't mean that you're gay."

He had just sat there, unsure if he could trust her diagnosis and therefore as yet un-liberated from his fears.

"What are you so afraid of?" she said, as if reading his thoughts. "So what if you *are* gay?"

An image of his mother's frowning face instantly crowded his mind like a nightmarish vision. He didn't mean to say anything, but he must have alluded in some way to his mother as he struggled to banish her scowling countenance from his imagination.

"What about your mother?"

He stared at Lauren blankly. The answer was so obvious and terrible that it defied language or his ability to use it. But his therapist waited expectantly for the words to come out of his mouth. There were no words to express the horror of the emotional annihilation he would suffer if his mother deemed her only son to be something less than a proper son. He tried unsuccessfully to speak, but he could only manage to close his eyes and stammer a few syllables.

"What more could your mother possibly do to you that she hasn't done already?" said his therapist softly. "The contempt, the disapproval, the rejection, the loathing—whatever it is you fear—you've suffered all of that already. As if your mother assumes 'the worst' about you and treats you accordingly. Frankly, I don't see how her treatment of you could be any worse. If she'd washed her hands of you, turned her back on you and disowned you, she might have done you a favor. You might have been better off. But as it is, you can probably congratulate yourself for having survived the attack on your true inner self, whatever that may be. Now you need to move on."

"Move on?" he croaked. His throat was dry and his lips were chapped, as if all the moisture had been sucked from there and was draining out of his palms, which were now slick with sweat.

"Let me ask you this," she sighed. "I realize this is an uncomfortable topic for you. I know you don't want to talk about it, because I've tried before. But it will help us both if you address it."

His grip had tightened again around the seat of his chair.

"It's been a year and a half since you parted from your last girlfriend. What thoughts have you had about sex during that time? Who have you been attracted to? Have you had any erotic dreams?"

At first he had wearily tried to convince her yet again that he hadn't had any thoughts about sex, hadn't been attracted to anybody, and didn't have erotic dreams. It was clear she didn't believe him. She crossed her arms against her chest and waited for him to tell the truth. Grudgingly, he had finally told her about that stupid dream involving Erica Cooley he'd had several months ago. True to her calling, his therapist had been disproportionately intrigued by the sexual climax he had achieved while he slept through it. She wanted to know all about Erica Cooley. He tried to tell her the dream had nothing to do with Erica; she just happened to be in it.

At first he couldn't remember a thing about the actual content of the dream. But as she pressed him for details, bits and pieces came back to him, though there was nothing sexual about any of it. All he could really remember was—in the dream—bringing Erica a cup of tea while she sat on his sofa. She reached out her arms to take the cup, and he, in his infinite incompetence, had done exactly what he feared he would do and had tried not to do, which was to spill scalding tea in her lap. Except it was his own lap that got wet from the dream. And now he was getting red from the embarrassment of telling his therapist all this. But as far as he could see, the dream had nothing to do with either Erica or sex. Rather, it was a simple re-play of a simple scene that had recently occurred in his apartment after he had gone to see one of the French films. As for any interpretation, he thought this had to do with his own fear of failure and his essential incompetence, his fundamental inability to successfully perform even the simplest and most basic tasks, like bringing someone a cup of tea.

But instead of following this lead or tracing this line of thought to its ultimate conclusion, his therapist had reverted to the topic of Erica. She asked question after question, wanted to know all he could tell her, and sat there patiently but persistently until she was certain he'd done so. As a result, he had found his own mind dwelling on the subject of Erica for days and even weeks after this session. He hadn't had time since to return for another appointment. So the topic of his last session had lingered with him. Erica Cooley had been much in his thoughts, and so, when he was next alone with her: BAM! But now he needed to extricate himself.

At that moment, the problem became a literal one, as Erica turned over in her sleep and created a tangle of bed sheets that tightened around him and left him trapped. The sheets were binding him like rope. He became desperate to get out of bed, make his coffee, clear his head, and think what to do. Carefully he tried to disentangle himself by peeling back the covers ever so slowly. To his shock, he discovered that he was naked and so was she. Somehow he had forgotten that of course they both would be. He couldn't help but stare at her body, since he really had not had a good look at it last night. He was surprised by the grace of her physical form, since she looked so graceless and awkward in her clothes, like a child's home-made stick doll with a few mismatched scraps of leftover fabric for clothes. In the repose of sleep, with her muscles relaxed and free of tension—and without the stupid clothes—her body looked quite different from the bundle of twigs yoked together by rubber bands she usually resembled. She even looked—well, what was the word? He continued to stare at her body as he tried to figure out how to characterize it. Beautiful? Was that the word? She stirred unexpectedly, moving her arms and laying bare her small, firm breasts, now pointed right at him like two beautiful eyes gazing on his own nakedness. Beautiful. Yes, that was the word for it. And naked. And right next to him. She had not been unresponsive to his body either.

She stirred again and a frown travelled fleetingly across her face as she slept on. Obviously the chill was disturbing her body and disrupting her sleep. Gently he tried to replace the covers without waking her up, carefully pulling the sheet up and placing it underneath her chin. At first he thought he'd succeeded in his efforts, but then suddenly she was wide awake, staring at him with terror and horror. She looked as if she were just seeing a monster. Which would be him. He couldn't help but laugh.

"What's wrong?" he said. "I'm not planning to eat you for breakfast."

In reply she sat bolt upright, clutching the sheets to her body to cloak not just her nakedness, but something more, like embarrassment and shame. Her look of fear and dismay only seemed to increase as she became more and more conscious of where she was.

"Ham, I'm so sorry," she said, almost tearfully. "I can't believe I've done this to you. Please forgive me."

"What have you done to me?" he said, amused. According to his memory, *he* had done something to *her*.

"Imposed on you like this. Breaking down, falling apart, pouring out my silly sob story. I hope you don't think it was. . . ." She paused and her eyes nervously swept the room, as if literally looking for the word she wanted. "Intentional," she said.

"Intentional?"

"You know what I mean. Like one of my mother's heavy-handed tricks."

"Tricks?"

"You know," she said impatiently. "To make you feel sorry for me. So you would . . ." The words choked in her throat.

"So I would what? Take your beautiful body into my arms?"

She shrank back as if slapped, and to his astonishment, tears pooled in her eyes. He had no doubt he was romantically maladroit; still, he had not expected she would cry when told she was beautiful.

"Don't, Ham," she pleaded. "Please don't make fun of me. Just let me leave here and pretend this never happened."

He felt the dismay spreading across his own face as he realized she could only assume he was mocking her in a most cruel way.

"But I don't want you to leave," he assured her. "Please don't take your beautiful body and go. Stay with me. Please."

It was clear she didn't know what to think now. Her face was a battle-ground where confusion and disbelief were at war with hope and the possibility of happiness. Confusion and disbelief had the upper hand, were gaining ground and threatening to crush hope and the possibility of happiness.

All in all, he thought the best thing to do was to take her beautiful body into his arms and demonstrate to her in no uncertain terms how much he wanted her to stay.

It was necessary to immediately implement Jill's prescriptive program for ministering to the female "pleasure points" before it was too late. And once again, it seemed to work. Kudos to Jill and her Ph.D. in gender studies, which had focused less on any literary texts than on the inscrutable, mysterious and enigmatic text of the female body. At the time they were in graduate school together, he had endured a mild but constant state of outrage that she could obtain a Ph.D. in English by focusing more on the clitoris than on the literary canon or even on one truly great writer. Now he was grateful. She had taught him well.

Afterwards Erica became shy, staring rigidly and quietly at the ceiling, as if to distance herself from the unrestrained impulses she had just revealed. When he reached over to take her hand, she did not withdraw it, but she was clearly relying on him to lead the way out of bed, on into the day and the rest of their lives.

What was this to be?

He knew he wanted to repeat the experience he had just enjoyed many times. Also he wanted to talk to her for hours and hours and find out everything he could about her. He wanted to sit across the table from her and share meals with her. But not here, in his apartment. He wished he were in surroundings that matched the loveliness of her body, the loveliness of what was happening. For the first time, he realized that his apartment was a dump: a beat-up student flat with a threadbare carpet, peeling wallpaper, and moldy grout between the bathroom tiles. Every piece of furniture was from a rental store, including the bed where they now lay. The ratty blanket that covered her body was the same one from the Army/Navy store he had used in college. So the first thing he wanted was to take her away, to some place as beautiful and dear as she was to him now. But how to say all this?

"Would you like some coffee?" was what he actually said.

Her face clouded over. Perhaps he should have said something more romantic. With relief he learned that the problem was simply she didn't want coffee; she preferred herbal tea. This was fascinating, this preference for herbal tea. No doubt there were hundreds and hundreds of other fascinations to her personality that he had yet to discover. The prospect of all the discoveries that awaited him was almost as exciting as the sight of her body.

When he came back from the kitchen bearing the steaming cup of tea, she was sitting on the edge of the bed wearing his nephew's tee shirt. She reached for the cup and he hoped he could manage not to spill the hot liquid in her lap like he'd done in that ridiculous dream he'd been forced to describe to the therapist. The memory of the dream jolted him into realizing what he had already spilled—in a way—in her lap. Just as suddenly, the meaning of the dream became clear to him, and he almost *did* spill the tea in her lap. For the first time he recognized some of the possible ramifications of his earlier deeds. He felt faintly sick as he groped for a seat beside her on the edge of the bed. As she sipped her tea, he stared at the carpet. She looked over at him.

"Is anything the matter?" she said softly.

He continued to stare at the carpet. "I guess . . ." he began, afraid to look up. "There were things we should have discussed earlier, I guess."

"What things?" she said, anxiety creeping into her voice.

He didn't know how to bring up the subject. The women in his past had taken care of this matter. He had never been involved in these discussions or precautions. He didn't know what to say. She set her teacup down on the bedside table and took his hand.

"I understand, Ham," she said gently. "This was all a mistake. I'll get my things and go."

"No, no," he protested.

"Yes, yes," she said firmly in her paradoxically flutey voice. "This was just something that happened. We don't need to pretend it means anything."

"No," he protested again, more firmly. "This was not just something that happened. This happened because. . . ." He paused to find the right words. "I wanted it to happen," he concluded, before pausing again. "I just—" he broke off. Finally he blurted out: "Are you on birth control?"

"No," she said, abashed. "I'm sorry. I should have told you."

"Don't be silly. I should have asked."

"Is that what was bothering you?"

He nodded, abashed at himself.

"Well," she said nervously. "I'm afraid it's not something you need to worry about."

"Why not? You just told me—"

Interrupting, she stammered something unintelligible, then blushed and fell silent. He waited.

"I don't really have regular . . . periods." She spoke with shame in a barely audible voice, as if her failure to have regular periods was a deliberate failure of femininity. No doubt her mother had told her as much. "Sometimes I'll go six months. . . ."

"I don't understand," he said. He just barely knew the female body, and didn't at all understand female anatomy.

"The doctor says it's because I'm too thin. I don't have enough body fat or something. I've been told it will be very difficult for me to *get* pregnant. It's the opposite of most women. I'll have to take pills if I want to get pregnant."

He only nodded, not feeling qualified to comment. Just then the telephone rang.

"Drink your tea," he said as he rose from the bed.

It was his mother on the other end of the line with the news that Erica Cooley had gone missing. Virginia was distraught. She and her daughter had "exchanged words" yesterday, and Erica had dashed out into the pouring rain. Her car had been discovered at Ginger's house, but neither Ginger nor anyone else had seen her. She was not answering her cell phone. Did she get run over by a car in the rain? Did she do something to herself? Should they go to the police? Did *he* know anything about where Erica could be?

He didn't. Promising to call if he heard anything, he hung up the phone and went back to where Erica sat on the bed.

"Your parents are frantic," he said.

Slowly she rose, putting her hand over her mouth in horror. "I completely forgot," she said. "What should I do?"

"Well," he considered, "I rather like the idea of your mother having to go down to the station and explain to the police why she believes her daughter may have been driven to suicide. On the other hand . . ."

"On the other hand . . ." she echoed, with the beginnings of a smile.

"On the other hand," he continued, "I'm not sure I want the police barging in at an inopportune moment when neither of us has any clothes on."

Now she giggled outright.

"And I'd like to take you somewhere."

"Take me somewhere?"

"Yes. For the weekend. Did you have plans?"

She pondered briefly and shook her head. "Just the usual Easter brunch at the country club."

"Yeah. Me too. Would you like to go somewhere else? Together? Out of town?"

"Where?"

"Anywhere. It doesn't matter. I never wished we had a vacation home before, but now I do. Only we don't."

"We have one," she said. "Do you like Florida?"

"Of course I like Florida. The best part about growing up in Alabama was the two weeks we spent in Florida every summer."

She giggled again. "Me too," she said.

"Where's your place?"

"Seaside."

"Will anyone be there this weekend?"

She shook her head. "Ginger and Hugh took their children there in March, for Spring Break."

"So the place is free?"

"It's free. It's kind of a long drive, though."

"Not necessarily," he mused. "Why don't you call your parents, tell them you're fine, you're safe, not to worry, you just need some time and you think you'll spend the weekend alone—at Seaside. If they want to reach you, they can call on your cell phone. Does that sound right?"

She nodded in agreement, but bit her lip. Clearly something was bothering her.

"What is it?" he said.

Abruptly she sat back down on the edge of the bed. He sat down beside her.

"What is it?" he repeated.

"A minute ago," she began, turning to look at him. "When you said we should have talked about something earlier, I thought you were going to bring up. . . ."

"Bring up what?"

"Dooky St. John," she almost whispered.

"Dooky?" he said, surprised. "Why would I bring up Dooky?"

"Isn't there something going on between you?"

"Not at all," he said.

"I keep hearing that you're always with her. That you're practically engaged."

"Who told you that? Your mother?"

She nodded, biting her lip again.

"It sounds like something your mother would say. But she's wrong. Like she usually is. There is nothing between Dooky and me. We're just very good friends."

"I know there's more to it than that."

"Well, of course I've always loved Dooky," he said.

From the look of pain that seared her face, he knew it was the wrong thing to say.

"I knew it," she said sadly.

"No, no," he protested. "It's not what you think. It's not the same. . . ."

"What's not the same?"

"I don't love Dooky . . ." his voice trailed off.

"I thought you just told me you did."

"I did. I do. But I don't love Dooky like. . . ."

"Like what?"

"Like I love you," he said.

He was as stunned as she was by the words that came out of his mouth. She put her face in her hands, and before long, tears were dripping through her fingers and words were hiccupping out of her mouth to the effect that she had always loved him, had fought against it, refused to accept it, could not believe that what her mother wanted and plotted to obtain could possibly be the right thing, but finally she had come to the realization on her own, in spite of everything. Somehow he knew all this already too, felt like he'd heard it all before. He put his arms around her and she sobbed on his chest just as she had the previous evening. It was clear he had a long way to go. She had almost broken down when he told her she was beautiful, and began weeping when he said "I love you." He had not planned on saying this anymore than he had planned on making love to her last night or this morning. It had all just happened. But at this midpoint in his life, he'd had enough therapy to realize that it had happened because he wanted it to happen, just as he'd assured her earlier. And he wanted it to happen again and again and again.

* * *

At the small private airport in Birmingham containing the hangars for corporate jets and twin engine airplanes, there was a log for the plane owned jointly by **Whitmire Realty** and **Cooley Construction**. When the plane was used for a business trip, as it usually was, the code name for the project, like "Memphis," was entered in the log and the expenses of the fuel and the pilot's services were shared by both companies. For the occasional recreational use, the code was "Personal," and either the name "Whitmire" or "Cooley" was entered in the log so that this party would bear the total cost. In the log, Ham wrote "Personal/Whitmire" and boarded the plane with Erica.

Later, after they had walked abroad on the spring evening, admired the white sands and emerald waters of their Southern coast and eaten its oysters, they settled into the loft bedroom of the Cooley's Seaside cottage looking out toward the Gulf of Mexico. Erica told him she had just had the best day of her life. He didn't have to think too hard to realize that it had been the best day of his own life as well, (with the possible exception, he admitted, of the day in fifth grade when he hit the game-winning grand slam). But at age thirty-seven, with almost no other truly great days behind him, he knew this was not the culmination, but only the beginning of many other great days ahead.

~ 18 ~

When Dooky St. John had called to see if he could take a poor girl to dinner on the night of her birthday, he had thought he might as well go and use the opportunity to get it over with. He wasn't sure about the etiquette of the situation—he was never sure of any point of etiquette—but he had a general understanding that a girl's birthday was not the time to deliver unpleasant news. However, he and Dooky had never been—involved—and he hoped his news was not unpleasant to her and didn't mean their special friendship had to come to an end. But when he entered an empty house with her upon their return, he became clammy with unease. He'd expected to find her mother there with the boys, as they had been when he'd picked Dooky up earlier in the evening. Usually her mother was at the door to greet them—drink in hand—and lead them back to the sunroom, where she would want to hear "all about it." What they ate, who they saw, how was his father? and so on. The boys should be bouncing around past their bedtime, while Mrs. St. John waved her hand in cavalier disregard, saying, "I thought just this once, I'd let them stay up," as Dooky rolled her eyes fondly at the grandmother's laissez-faire. In his imagination, he had foreseen a casual "Oh, by the way, I've got something to tell you" moment soon after the departure of Mrs. St. John and the boys, right before he himself was to head out the door. What a fool he was. What had he been thinking?

"Where is everybody?" he said, in what he hoped was a natural voice, not full of the panicking nerves he felt inside.

"I banished them for the evening," said Dooky gaily. "After all, it *is* my birthday, and school's almost out for the year. So they're spending the night with my parents."

When they reached the sunroom, she went over to the mini refrigerator as she always did to get her diet Dr. Pepper. He sat down carefully in his accustomed armchair, trying not to wipe his hands on either his pants or the arms of the chair.

"Don't you want a drink, Ham?" she said, sinking into her usual place on the parrot sofa and kicking off her shoes.

"Not tonight, thanks," he said. Although his therapist had recently pointed out—in defense of the anti-depressants she wanted him to keep on taking—that he hadn't been clearing his throat like he used to, he now cleared his throat.

"I know it's hard for you now to go out during the week—you've become so unbelievably busy and all—but I wanted to see you alone tonight. I have a favor to ask you."

He wiped his palms on the legs of his pants. "Favor?"

"Yes," she said, sitting up suddenly and placing the Dr. Pepper on the coffee table. She leaned forward to face him closely and look earnestly into his eyes. "If I'm asking too much, I want you to tell me. I don't want you doing this just to be sweet. And you are so sweet. Just about the sweetest man I know."

Sweet? Him? Sweet? Dooky was always projecting her own sweetness on everybody else. He'd never felt the least bit sweet in his life. On the contrary, up until recently he mostly harbored a seething boil of anger, outrage and bitterness. If he came across as sweet, it was only because he made no effort to bring his interior life up to the surface for others to pick at.

"Promise me you'll be honest?"

"Sure," he said, hoping this might not be so bad after all. He would simply tell her his news, and that would be that.

"Okay, then," she said. "Excuse me for just a minute."

Before he knew what was happening, she'd risen from the sofa and left the room. Then he was terrified. Why had she left the room? What was she doing? When she came back, would she be—undressed? Naked? Clad in a filmy piece of lingerie? Would she come sit on his lap before he could stop her? It wasn't that he thought himself worthy of Dooky or likely to attract her interest; among his many faults and problems, an overblown sense of his looks or appeal had never been among them. Still, the shocks of recent months had been so earth-shattering and life-changing, he was constantly expecting to be confounded or flabbergasted yet again. He knew he should have told her the simple truth quickly and clearly over dinner and not planned to put it off till afterwards. That was his old habit of procrastination, and it had caused trouble yet again. Now it had landed him in a situation where he had not one single social skill he could draw on to avoid causing pain or embarrassment to someone he cared for deeply. And he felt sorry for Dooky, more so even than when he'd first heard about Louis. Since then, he himself had miraculously managed to crack the code that set himself free; Dooky St. John had not.

Fortunately, when she returned to the room, she was dressed exactly the same as when she'd left. However, she was holding a videotape that seemed to make her hands tremble as she carried it over to the television. Already he dreaded this thing—whatever it was—that he was apparently meant to watch with her. As Dooky arrived at the entertainment center housing the television and related equipment, she seemed to lose her natural poise and turned back around toward him. She became hesitant and shy.

"I think I'm asking too much of you," she said nervously.

He was definitely beginning to think the same thing.

But then she appeared to gather resolve, turned back around, and thrust the tape into the machine with a low moan of indeterminate meaning. Instinctively he braced himself for the worst sort of sex tape featuring he knew not what to imagine—orgies of nude men and women, he supposed. Normally, of course, it would be the last thing he'd expect of Dooky St. John. But then again, he had never expected what he'd learned of his father, or Louis Lankford. He would never have expected himself to be doing what he currently was in his own personal and professional life.

It was actually even worse than he had imagined. There was indeed a group of men and women, but they were not nude. Instead, they were dressed in flowing diaphanous robes of gauzy white material which sprouted gold filigreed wings from the back. Haloes with similar gold filigree were attached to their heads. Dooky was the lead singer for most of the choral numbers, and was the solo vocalist for "You Light Up My Life" and "Just You and I,"—a grammatical mistake he abhorred whether committed in the service of a pop song's rhyme scheme or out of the misguided attempt at proper usage. He didn't know what to think, even less what to say. Dooky's voice could go around the world and back, but the music itself was of course execrable. Then it hit him.

Dooky St. John was a true Christian. Perhaps the only one he'd ever known. He'd long since concluded there was no such thing, for lack of evidence to the contrary, even in his native Bible-belt state, which was full of so many self-professed "true Christians." Of course they weren't the real thing. Show them a black person; they'd call him a damn nigger. Show them a homosexual; they'd treat him like a leper. Show them a homeless person; they'd say get him off the street. Put them in the situation Dooky was in; they'd be filled with loathing and rage. In one way or another they would fail to live up to their principles and ideals, yet they would continue to call themselves true Christians. These "true Christians" weren't as prevalent in Mountain Brook, where religion was supposed to take place within a few prescribed hours on one particular day of the week, if at all. But there were still plenty in the city—as in her mega-church—as well as in the state at large. Dooky was the only real one he'd ever met. And he had just now recognized her for what she was, because unlike the false ones, she didn't proclaim herself from every street corner.

"What do you think, Ham?"

She sat anxiously on the sofa a few feet away, nervously twisting her hands in her lap.

"You don't need to ask me. Look at all those people in the congregation standing up and clapping. Cheering for you. There's your answer right there."

"Do you think I have talent?" she asked.

"I'm no judge of music," he said. "But it strikes me that your greatest talent is for being a true Christian soul. You shouldn't just be leading the choral group, or whatever it is. You should be leading the whole church."

Joy spread swiftly across her face. "Ham!" she cried. "How did you know? It's what I've wanted to do for the last five years!"

"Do they let women?"

"In this church, as lay ministers, they do. But I'd have to go through this program. I could do it in two summers. The boys would have to be with their dad, and my parents think I'm crazy."

"Why?" he said, although of course, he knew. People in Mountain Brook did not join mega-churches, and certainly didn't serve in them as lay ministers.

"Oh, you know my parents," she said, taking a sip of her Dr. Pepper. "They think I should just get married again, the sooner the better. That's the only thing they can think of for a girl to do. I don't blame them, but I wish I'd had someone in my life like you had, to show me the way out, like that fat man in your school. What's his name?"

"Mr. Laney?"

"That's right," she nodded. "Mr. Laney. I appreciate what he's doing for my boys. But no one did that for me. Do you know what my major was in college?"

He shook his head.

"Dietetics," she said. "Because somebody told me it was easy and a lot of Kappas did it. Now I ask you: Do I look like a dietician?"

He thought of the colorless, shapeless women in hair nets and white uniforms who'd been in charge of his college cafeteria. He could only laugh and shake his head again. Dooky didn't look like that. And no doubt, her diet Dr. Pepper wasn't exactly in accord with the nutritional guidelines.

"See what I mean?" she said. "I never gave any thought to what I was really going to *do* with myself, my time on earth—except get married—and you see how that turned out. For some reason I thought that was all I really wanted to do. But it's not. Do you think I'm crazy? Is it too late?"

"No, no," he said. "It's exactly what you should do."

"Really?"

"Really."

She looked at him intently as if trying to determine whether he was telling the truth. She seemed satisfied, took a deep breath, and said, "Okay, here's the favor." She paused to see if he was going to flinch. He tried not to. "Do you think," she began, then paused again. She had to fortify herself with another sip of Dr. Pepper. "Do you think you could find a way to help me convince my parents—or at least my mother—that I'm doing the right thing?"

Ham thought for a minute and wished he had poured that Scotch for himself earlier. This was really not a job for him, for someone of his limited social, political and interpersonal skills. This was a job for. . . . "You need Mr. Laney," he told her.

"Mr. Laney? From the school? The fat man?"

"Yes. Make an appointment. Lay it all before him. Then invite him to dinner with your parents. Highlands Bar and Grill is his favorite. He'll have them eating out of his hands in no time flat. Believe me. If he can do it with my mother, he can do it with anyone."

"Are you sure?"

He nodded. "I'm not sure my sister's wedding would have happened if Mr. Laney hadn't—intervened."

"What happened?"

"Oh, my mother's usual stuff and nonsense. She really didn't want my sister getting married to Mark. So she made a fuss about the rehearsal dinner, which his parents wanted to have at the Petsinger Hotel, downtown, where they were planning to stay for the wedding. Only my mother was threatening there would be no wedding at all because she wasn't about to suffer the humiliation of having her daughter's rehearsal dinner in downtown Birmingham, of all places. By the end of the conversation with Mr. Laney, she was quite pleased that she was going to be a trend-setter with this wedding and show Mountain Brook how it was done in other major capitals. Like New York, for example. Somehow the thought of 'Adelaide Whitmire/trend-setter of the Birmingham social scene' made her forget about 'Mark Ellis/future son-in-law.'"

Dooky giggled appreciatively. "But this is a little more complicated," she said, "with Louis and all. . . . I'm getting full custody, you know."

"Trust me. Mr. Laney will have them thinking they can do nothing else but let a grown woman pursue her life while her sons spend some time with their father. This will be easy for him. I'll call him and let him know he should expect to hear from you." He paused. "How do you feel about Louis having the boys in the summer?"

She shrugged. "No different than I did when he had them here. Before he—before we—She paused. "He's a good father. The boys should spend time with him, even if I have full custody."

"Your parents disagree?"

"Yes, of course. But Louis is a good father and even was a good husband. When we were young, he didn't know what to do with himself anymore than I did, so we got married like we thought we were supposed to do. He had no way out, until he was found out. I'm not mad at him; I still love him. If it weren't for the public disgrace, I'd probably still be married to him. So many of my friends' marriages have turned out so much worse, and their husbands aren't even. . . ."

Suddenly she reached across the coffee table and grabbed his hands with her beautifully manicured fingers. "Listen at me," she said, "rambling on about myself. I also wanted to talk about you. You're the one who needs to get married now. My parents think I would only be too lucky to have the chance to help you do that, but I've had my marriage and I've got my three boys. There are other things I want to do now. Did I tell you I finally got together with that voice coach? She's agreed to give me private lessons, and we start next week. I've got so much lost time to make up for! It could be I'm better off divorced than married. So it's not fair of me to monopolize your precious free time like I've been doing. I need to get a life, and you need to get a wife. We did things opposite, didn't we?"

"Are you implying that I have a life?" he said. "I'm flattered."

"Ham," she said. "Don't always be putting yourself down. Though I love that about you. But you seem happy with what you're doing now. I can't say I know what that is—I've never known exactly what your family's business was all about, though I know it's very successful."

"I never did know either," he admitted, "and I'm still on a learning curve." He cleared his throat. "And I—actually I—have met someone." He cleared his throat again.

She clapped her hands in delight. "Oh, Ham! Who is she? Do I know her?"

"Well," he began, "remember that night we first went to Highlands Bar and Grill?"

She nodded eagerly.

"Do you remember meeting Ginger Cooley's—Ginger McNamara—her sister?"

Of course Dooky St. John—with her sorority president's memory for names and faces, remembered meeting Ginger Cooley McNamara's sister. Dooky clapped her hands again and whooped with glee. "That adorable girl with those fabulous turquoise earrings? How perfect!"

"Yes," he agreed. "Though I'm not sure why, exactly. . . ."

"It's so obvious, silly. She's every bit as much an—individual—as you are. It's the perfect match."

"I guess we're the perfect pair of funny valentines," he said.

"She couldn't be as funny as you are, Ham."

Dooky had no trace of irony in her Christian soul and no doubt had never heard the song. So he knew what she meant. He suddenly realized that he had done what he came there to do, and just as suddenly realized how tired he was. He rose to leave. Dooky hopped up with her boundless energy and moved to accompany him to the front door.

"How can I get to know her better? I know! Can we have you over here? For dinner! With the boys and my parents! Mama will be dying to meet the girl who did what no other girl has ever done, and captured your heart."

Driving back to his apartment, he reflected that it never paid to underestimate Dooky St. John. She too, had cracked the code.

"Nobody gets married in August," his mother said. "Nobody. It's fine if you don't want a long engagement. Fine. But nobody gets married in August. It just isn't done. I know about these things."

"We've made our decision, Mother, and it's final."

"But why? Why must you be so stubborn? Even September would be better. Plenty of people get married in September. I wouldn't want it for myself, but I've gone to many weddings in September. That would be so much better than August."

"Actually, what would be better than August is July. Next week would be even better. But as you know, her parents are in Europe till the end of July."

"Yes, and how you expect them to pull a wedding together in a few short weeks. . . . Can you just tell me why?"

He sighed and decided the time had come.

"Erica is pregnant, Mother," he said.

"Oh, I'm so sorry," she said, sinking abruptly down into "her" chair in the den.

"I'm not sorry."

"You don't have to marry her, you know. It's *her* problem. You don't have to be the one to rescue her."

He sat down on the loveseat beside her chair. "I want to marry her," he said.

"Who is the father?"

"What do you mean?"

"Who is the father of the baby?"

"The father of the baby?" he echoed, wondering if the stress of the last six months had really been "too much" for his mother, as she kept telling everyone. "I am, Mother. I am the father of the baby."

"You?!" she exclaimed in disbelief. "She told you that?! That *you're* the father of the baby?"

Obviously she didn't think he was capable of being the father of a baby. He didn't know what to say.

"I told you that girl would do *anything!* I warned you!"

"Well, she's been—ah—doing it with me, Mother."

His mother shook her head and muttered. "It's the oldest trick in the book, son. With all your education, you fall for the oldest trick in the book. I'll bet her mother put her up to this."

He didn't dare give his mother the satisfaction of knowing how greatly Erica had feared he would have the exact same reaction when she told him the news. Eventually he had been obliged to put her fears to rest in no uncertain terms. Afterwards, he had not planned on proposing marriage, but that's what happened. Because, he knew, he wanted it to happen. In fact, he went so far as to suggest, the pregnancy itself had happened because that's what they wanted to happen.

"I did want it to happen," she acknowledged. "Only not quite like this."

"You wanted to be married first?"

She had nodded in her timid way, nervously gauging his reaction.

"Well, that's what we'll do."

"Haven't we already missed that boat?"

"No one but us has to know."

"We'll have to do it soon, then."

Hence August. Even then, Erica's wedding dress would have to be like a Southern belle's ball gown, with a generous hoop skirt effect and an empire waist. It wouldn't be any more ill-fitting or look any worse than any of her other clothes.

"Hamilton," said his mother sternly, straightening her back and drawing herself up. "I'm afraid it's my duty to point out certain unpleasant possibilities that have not occurred to you. As a woman of the world, I know things about life you may not. And as your mother, I am obligated to speak out even if it hurts you and damages a lifelong family friendship and business partnership." She sat ramrod straight like a woman preparing to perform her hard and terrible duty.

At that inopportune moment, Lois came in to clean the room. As neither the mother nor the son turned to greet her or showed any signs of leaving the room, she quickly deduced they were having a most serious discussion. Accordingly, she parked the vacuum cleaner in the middle of the rug and left the room quickly as well as wordlessly. Lois, thought Ham, was no fool. She knew his mother liked this visual symbol—the vacuum cleaner in the middle of the rug—that her orders were being carried out and her house was getting cleaned even when none of this was happening because Lois was in the kitchen having a cup of coffee with Harry. His mother kept her counsel till Lois was well out of earshot.

"What is it, Mother?" he said.

She gave him a withering look of either pity or scorn, or possibly her own special mixture of both. "I know you will find this shocking, son, but often in situations like this . . . a 'miscarriage' will occur soon after the wedding."

He shrugged. Was that all? "I suppose that's possible," he said.

"No, Hamilton. You are even more innocent than I supposed. I am trying to point out that there's every reason to suspect that this so-called baby doesn't even exist."

In response, he took out his wallet from his back pocket and produced a rumpled sonogram of the so-called baby. As he held it out to his mother, she fumbled for the glasses she always wore around her neck, as if she spent most of her day tending to bills, correspondence and household accounts. From the way she studied the little piece of paper at such great length, it was clear that the clinical X-ray with "Cooley, Erica" printed on the side had made an impact. Nevertheless, she handed it back with a "Humpf. How do you know it's yours?"

"It could hardly be anyone else's."

"Hamilton, Hamilton." She put a hand to her brow and shook her head. "Don't be so naïve, son. I fear you are headed for major trouble. It's not too late to avoid it. There are plenty of other ways to help Erica out of a difficult situation, if that's what you want. There are places she can go—in other states—where she can stay till she has the baby and puts it up for adoption—if she doesn't want to do the other. No one will ever know. You'd be surprised how many young girls I've heard about in this very town who have done this exact thing."

He sighed. The conversation was becoming tedious, and he did not want to descend to the level of explaining that his unborn child would be neither aborted nor adopted by someone else.

"What is your evidence?" she demanded, suddenly looking back up at him. "How are you so sure the child is yours?"

Surely he did not need to go into the mechanics or the ramifications of sexual intercourse.

"Well, for one thing, Mother," he said, "she's been living in my apartment."

"Living in your apartment?!" She put a hand to her mouth in horror. If anything, his mother was more scandalized by this than by the news of the pregnancy. "What do you mean, *living in your apartment?* Her parents know nothing of this, I assure you."

"No," he agreed. "They don't."

"That little . . . If she'll lie to them, she'll lie to you too, son."

"She told her parents she was moving into an apartment. That was no lie, even if the apartment is mine. So you see. . . . We're together every night, and, as you know, up until the end of the school year, she was substituting at Brook-Haven School for Mme Boyer, who had the premature baby. So I hardly think there's been the opportunity for . . . another candidate . . . to be the father of the baby."

"Living with you!" repeated his mother, mainly to herself in a dazed fashion as she gazed at some undetermined spot in the middle of the room. She looked as if she had literally been struck in the head with this additional piece of information. Her eyes lost their focus and she appeared lost in thoughts that she could neither process nor assemble into a coherent whole. "At least the girl must really love you then," she said, mostly to herself, "to take such a huge risk, one that could ruin her for life."

Then he understood. In his mother's generation, a girl might make the mistake of having sex "too soon," or getting pregnant as a result, but these were private matters that could be kept private without destroying a girl's "chances" for marriage. But no girl would choose to live openly and publicly with a man before marriage; not if she ever wanted to get married and have a life. While the rest of the world might have progressed to a more enlightened point of view regarding cohabitation, his mother had not. He had forgotten the myriad ways in which his native state held on to the skewed values of bygone ages.

When his mother's eyes focused on him again, he thought he noticed a smidgeon of respect she'd never shown him before. Her son was someone on whom a girl had staked her claim for happiness without benefit of a marriage license. Her son was desired not for his money or his family name, but for himself alone. He must be something, then. At any rate, he was a man. A man who was giving this girl enough . . . happiness . . . that she was risking everything for him.

His mother rose heavily and with great effort from her chair. "Now let me go tell that fool of a maid she needs to clean this room before your father wants to watch his programs. I hope this girl makes you happy, son." She moved stiffly out of the room with no other sound but the swish of her pantyhose against the silk of her dress. Normally she left a wake of anger and indignation, but this time she left behind a lump in his throat.

211

This was as close as she'd ever come to telling him she loved him. But it was enough. She who had most probably never known real happiness in her own marriage, or anything like joy and passion, was wishing for him to have happiness in his. She wanted her son to have that which she'd never had. And that was love. She had not herself known how to give it, or show it, perhaps because it had never been given or shown to her. But she had harbored it in her own heart for him, in her own perverse way, nonetheless. Of course it was totally in keeping with his mother's sense of timing that she offered it only when he no longer really needed it anymore.

* * *

The wedding of Wilmer Hamilton Whitmire III and Erica Olivia Cooley took place at 5:30 P.M. on Saturday, August 23rd at St. Luke's Episcopal Church, to which both the Cooley and the Whitmire families belonged, primarily for the purpose of having a place that could perform a wedding, christening or funeral service, as needed. Adelaide Whitmire had insisted that the rehearsal dinner the previous evening take place at the Mountain Brook Club. This had placed Mrs. Cooley in a common Mountain Brook quandary about where to have the wedding reception, since the two mothers agreed that it could not be held at the same venue as the rehearsal dinner. The wishes of the bride and groom were considered irrelevant and were not consulted. When Ham had ventured to offer an opinion, the two mothers had exchanged looks of exasperation and consternation. Ham could be so . . . obtuse . . . and any ideas he might formulate were more likely to create a problem than solve one. But when he suggested the Birmingham Country Club as the place he'd like to have his wedding reception, the two mothers had then exchanged looks of wonderment. But of course—it was the obvious, perfect solution. Why hadn't they thought of it themselves? Virginia Cooley's sister and her husband belonged to the Birmingham Country Club, so it could easily be reserved under their membership. And as the less exclusive, much larger country club, it would more easily and graciously accommodate the number of guests—at least a thousand—who were expected to attend. After all, it would be a much larger wedding than Ginger's, because her husband, Hugh—poor man—had grown up in Greenwich, Connecticut, of all places, so only a mere hundred or so of his family and friends had come to that wedding.

"That is what happens," said Adelaide, "when a girl goes *away* to college. She marries a man from *away.*"

But Ham and Erica would have the ultimate Mountain Brook wedding, uniting two prominent Mountain Brook families. According to their mothers, it was the first truly sensible thing either one of them had ever done in their lives.

"Hamilton has come such a long way since he moved back to Birmingham," observed Adelaide. "If only he had come back sooner, he would have come to his senses long ago. I tried for years, as you know."

"And Erica, bless her heart," said Virginia Cooley, "is finally beginning to look like a grown woman. Even her figure has finally filled out a little after all this time."

Adelaide nodded and pursed her lips. She really thought Virginia ought to *know.* In case there was trouble later, everyone would understand where it came from, and it would not be the Whitmire side of the marriage. But then, as her son pointed out, everyone else might find out, and that was really unthinkable.

"Why do you think they insisted on August?" asked Virginia. "When I was their age, June was the cut-off. It was either June or after Labor Day. You never heard of weddings in July or August."

Again Adelaide pursed her lips. "Well, young people nowadays . . ." she said.

Virginia nodded in agreement. "At least these two found each other," she said. "Though we know who they have to thank for that." She gave Adelaide a look of complicity. "If left to themselves, I don't think they ever would have figured it out. But they really are perfect for each other. I've always said so. We did a good deed there, and little do they know, this wedding will be *our* celebration."

"In a way," noted Adelaide, "even the timing is working out for the best. The weekend before school starts. Everybody's back in town. Everybody will be there."

"Yes," concurred Virginia. "Norman Laney says it will be the social event of the year."

"Of course it will be," said Adelaide. "So we better get on with it." Thus she concluded the conversation abruptly with her usual tact and diplomacy.

* * *

Everyone agreed that the food, the flowers, the music and the decorations were the most exquisite and spectacular of any Mountain Brook wedding they'd ever attended, though the florists, the musicians and the chef at the country club were the same ones who supplied most wedding receptions in Mountain Brook. However, there *was* something to be said for having the very best of everything, and lots of it. There were even two different bands playing in two different reception rooms—one for the young people, like the bride and groom, and a more Lawrence Welk-type group for the older couples. Dooky St. John had offered to sing either "You Light Up My Life" or "Just You and I" at either the wedding ceremony or the reception. The wedding was out of the question, both mothers agreed. Mrs. Cooley didn't like the idea *at all.*

"You know," she told Adelaide, "that woman would have married Ham if she could have."

Adelaide had shrugged. "Lots of girls would have married Wilmer if they could have," she pointed out. "But he married *me.*"

Thus Mrs. Cooley learned the wisdom in allowing her daughter's defeated rival to sing at the reception—in the room with the young people's band. At Ham's request, however, she sang "My Funny Valentine," as he and Erica moved stiffly on the ballroom floor and the photographer snapped pictures of the couple's first dance.

When the cake was sliced, Mr. Laney was the first to present his plate for a piece.

"You know," he observed to Erica, with his mouth full of cake. "I thought I was going to get myself two new teachers, not lose them," he swallowed. "That day I asked you to come tutor at the school when I had the appointment with Ham? Remember?"

Erica nodded and blushed, hoping Ham had not overheard. She also hoped that he wouldn't think that *she* had been in on any plot of Mr. Laney's. . . .

"Are you *certain* about not teaching?" Mr. Laney asked her, mouth full again. "Ham is so busy at his father's office, I hear. You might enjoy it, and I sure could use you. Even for just a year or two."

But Erica was sure, especially after substituting for Mme Boyer while she herself was pregnant. She and Ham had discussed the matter at length. Although the last thing she had ever wanted to be was a stay-at-home mother like those in her own mother's generation, that's what she was now opting to become.

"Only it won't be like my mother," she explained to Ham.

"There's no way it could be," he assured her. "You're so totally different from her."

"Well, what I mean is," began Erica. "My mother—and your mother—they were called stay-at-home mothers. But somehow, I don't ever remember my mother staying at home with me. Did yours?"

He shook his head. "Not more than she could help it."

"I know she must have some time, but I don't have one single memory of my mother playing games with me, or taking me to the zoo, or even the movies. Most of the time, I stayed at home with the maid, and my dad's old maid sister was the one who took me to the zoo or the movies. I don't know what my mother was doing, but she wasn't at home with me."

"Mine was usually at meetings," he said. "The Junior League, or the Garden Club, or her book group. Then she was on the board at the Museum, and the Brook-Haven School board, too, for a while. She *did* come to all my practices and games, though."

"I'm not criticizing them," said Erica. "They were just doing what all the other women were doing. But it wasn't exactly staying at home with the kids."

"No, it wasn't," he agreed, thinking of all the lonely summers of deadly boredom he'd endured as a child. In many ways, his adult life up to this point had been only an extension of the existential ennui of a long hot Alabama summer with nothing to do.

"Maybe if there were something I really wanted to do, that I was really good at," said Erica. "Like your sister. But she always seems so stressed out to me. For now this seems like the right thing for me to do." Her hands instinctively moved to her belly. "If it's okay with you," she said nervously.

"Of course it's okay with me. Why wouldn't it be?"

"All your ex-girlfriends," she said shyly. "They're so accomplished. One's a lawyer in New York; the other is a professor of English. . . ."

"That's just who they are," he said. "I think the whole idea of 'accomplishment' is overrated. It would be different if we needed the money, but since we don't, why does it matter if this is who you are? I think being a parent is probably one of the hardest things of all to get right. And if you get it right, you will be more accomplished than most people."

"I'm not saying I'm going to get it right," she said dubiously. "But I'd like to try."

"Good for you," he'd said.

Mr. Laney had finished his cake and was leaning over toward Erica in a confidential manner.

"If the baby's a girl now," he said in an undertone, "I want you and Ham at least to *think* about naming her after Ham's grandmother. This city could use another Bella Whitmire."

Meanwhile, Erica's sister Ginger was busy congratulating her new brother-in-law.

"Oh, Ham!" she said. "Did I tell you? My roommate from Yale? The one who's now a literary agent in New York? She said for me to let you know that so far she's received nothing but rejections on your novel! She's not sure it's publishable, but she's going to keep trying! As a favor to me! I've been meaning to tell you for ages."

"Well, I'm so glad you picked this moment to let me know," said Ham, smiling, before turning toward Mr. Laney, who was approaching him after snatching one last uneaten gobble from Erica's plate.

"Congratulations, dear boy," said Mr. Laney. "This is a happy day. You're looking particularly well."

"Not bad," Ham acknowledged, shaking Mr. Laney's substantial hand. "Not bad at all for a failed novelist and an ex-suicide."

"I think finally you have really arrived," said Mr. Laney, in the authoritative manner of one making an official announcement. "You can actually call yourself an ex-suicide now."

Indeed, he could. He was, in fact, the happiest he had ever been in his life. It was only an ordinary happiness he had achieved, based on work he enjoyed well enough and a woman he loved more than any other person in the world. But he had worked extraordinarily hard to achieve this ordinary happiness. It had not been given him, although some had tried to thrust it on him, and the work he was doing and the woman he was marrying were none other than what others had attempted to foist upon him. It was true that much had been given him, and he was now in a position to be grateful for it: the money that his grandmother had bequeathed him; the sane and sensible family business that his father was handing over to him; and above all, this other person named Erica Cooley (Whitmire) whom the world seemed to have intended to be his kindred spirit. And he was more keenly aware than ever of the debt he owed to those who had been given nothing, or less than nothing—a debt that needed to be paid out of all that had been given to him. There were many whose lives would never know the happy ending such as he now felt was his own blessed fate. He vowed that his would not be a happiness maintained at the expense of others, and that it would not be blind to the unhappiness of others, especially those who had been enslaved and subjected so that he could inherit a privileged birthright. He thought of his friend and colleague Ivy Greer, who was not among the guests at his wedding reception, because black people still could not enter the Birmingham Country Club except as hired help. This was another battle among the many he wanted to fight with the power that came with his birthright.

But out of all that had been given to him, none of the happiness he now enjoyed had been included along with these other stupendous gifts from the universe. Happiness could not be given, or bestowed, or bequeathed like money and power and status, nor could these advantages automatically engender happiness, although they could certainly help create all the conditions for it. Still, each individual had to earn, and achieve, his own kind of happiness on his own terms. He had arrived at it through a long, slow, arduous and circuitous journey. Harvard, Heidelberg, his degrees in literature, his master's in philosophy, his years of depression and therapy—even the aborted law degree, the unpublished novel and the dismal teaching career—it was all a necessary part of being able to arrive back where he started, in the provincial and ignominious city of Birmingham, Alabama, where he had joined the family business and married the daughter of his father's partner. It was exactly the kind of fate he had fought and struggled against for most of his life. But he was exactly where he wanted to be. In fact, he and his bride were at the top of the wedding cake now, and they were not going to fall off. At that moment his father approached him, walking more steadily than ever with his cane, and gave his son a wink.

AUTHOR'S NOTE
AND ACKNOWLEDGMENTS

The house in Mountain Brook where the author Walker Percy spent his early childhood is still there, across the street from the Birmingham Country Club. However, I have never been inside this house, nor have I ever met any of its owners. The family described as living there in my novel is a product of my imagination, as is my description of the interior of the house itself.

There is a historically black college in the part of Birmingham known as Fairfield, and I have visited its campus once. Otherwise, I have no knowledge or experience of Miles College, so the Cahaba College of my novel should not be interpreted as its fictional equivalent. On the other hand, I taught for six years at a historically black college in New Orleans, so I am not lacking in direct knowledge and experience of at least one such institution. While teaching there, I made it my business to educate myself about historically black colleges, and I did a good deal of reading and research on the subject. My portrait of the fictional Cahaba College is best understood as a product both of what I learned from my own observation as well as from my reading. While the college in my novel is designed to provoke productive discussion and debate, it is not intended to be representative of all historically black colleges.

As always, I am indebted to my first readers, Tom Uskali and Sean Smith, for the feedback and encouragement that help my work progress from rough draft to completed novel. Peer reviewers John Sledge and Lanier Scott Isom provide invaluable commentary which helps me revise and refine. Former publisher Jonathan Haupt of Story River Books took an enormous risk and showed tremendous faith in my work by publishing in such rapid succession my series of Mountain Brook novels, which contain little sex, few dead bodies, and no vampires or paranormal beings. Story River Books' former editor at large Pat Conroy had no equal. A famous, best-selling author who could have legitimately been spending all his time on his own next novel, he generously spent an inordinate amount of that time mentoring and championing emerging writers like me. I will mourn his loss for the rest of my life.

Thanks also to Kathe Telingator, for loyal and longstanding representation.

And my love and gratitude go to Brandon Dorion, who makes my writing life possible in every conceivable way.

ABOUT THE AUTHOR

KATHERINE CLARK holds an A.B. degree in English from Harvard and a Ph.D. in English from Emory. She is the coauthor of the oral biographies *Motherwit: An Alabama Midwife's Story*, with Onnie Lee Logan, and *Milking the Moon: A Southerner's Story of Life on This Planet*, a finalist for a National Book Critics Circle award, coauthored with Eugene Walter. *The Ex-Suicide* is the fourth in her series of novels featuring Laney and his students and is preceded by *The Headmaster's Darlings* (winner of the 2015 Willie Morris Award for Southern Fiction), *All the Governor's Men*, and *The Harvard Bride*, all part of the University of South Carolina Press's Story River Books series. Clark is working on Pat Conroy's oral biography, also forthcoming from the University of South Carolina Press. She lives on the Gulf Coast.